ELIZABETH FAIR
THE MARBLE STAIRCASE

ELIZABETH Mary Fair was born in 1908 and brought
up in Haigh, a small village in Lancashire, England.
There her father was the land agent for Haigh Hall,
then occupied by the Earl of Crawford and Balcorres,
and there she and her sister were educated by a
governess. After her father's death, in 1934, Miss Fair
and her mother and sister removed to a small house
with a large garden in the New Forest in Hampshire.
From 1939 to 1944, she was an ambulance driver in the
Civil Defence Corps, serving at Southampton, England;
in 1944 she joined the British Red Cross and went
overseas as a Welfare Officer, during which time she
served in Belgium, India, and Ceylon.

Miss Fair's first novel, *Bramton Wick*, was published
in 1952 and received with enthusiastic acclaim as
'perfect light reading with a dash of lemon in it . . .'
by *Time and Tide*. Between the years 1953 and 1960,
five further novels followed: *Landscape in Sunlight*,
The Native Heath, *Seaview House*, *A Winter Away*,
and *The Mingham Air*. All are characterized by their
English countryside settings and their shrewd and
witty study of human nature. In 2022, Dean Street
brought out a seventh, hitherto unpublished, novel by
the author, *The Marble Staircase*, written c.1960.

Elizabeth Fair died in 1997.

NOVELS BY ELIZABETH FAIR
And published by Dean Street Press

ELIZABETH FAIR

THE MARBLE STAIRCASE

With an introduction
by Elizabeth Crawford

DEAN STREET PRESS

A Furrowed Middlebrow Book
FM84

Published by Dean Street Press 2022

Cover by DSP

ISBN 978 1 915393 06 7

www.deanstreetpress.co.uk

INTRODUCTION

UNDER the heading, *The Italian Legacy*, on 24 April 1959 Elizabeth Fair (1908-1997) wrote in her diary, 'Still no clear view of this book, though it haunts me. The beginning was as clear as could be – it wrote itself – but what does it lead to? Life itself, full of promise and turning to common day – but I see the Italian journey as a liberation of the mind and Charlotte as forever profiting by it; perhaps not always aware of what it brought her, but aware of it at the end. If the Italian journey isn't that, it is nothing.' A seasoned novelist, Elizabeth Fair had sufficient faith and skill to bring to life this ghost of an idea, transmuting *The Italian Legacy* into *The Marble Staircase*, published now for the first time.

Represented by Innes Rose, one of London's leading literary agents, Elizabeth Fair had published her first novel, *Bramton Wick*, in 1952. Others followed at regular intervals, with her sixth, *The Mingham Air*, appearing in 1960, its delightful dust wrapper designed, like that for *The Native Heath* (1954), by Shirley Hughes. Her novels of 'polite provincial society' were praised by the middlebrow reviewers of the day, such as John Betjeman, Nancy Spain, and Compton Mackenzie, who variously compared her to Trollope, Thirkell, and Jane Austen. However, by 1960 a literary epoch was drawing to a close; publishers no longer had an appetite for works later categorized by Marghanita Laski in a *Country Life* review (19 April 1984) as 'admirable novels by intelligent Englishwomen'. If Barbara Pym is perhaps the most famous casualty of this publishing *volte face*, Elizabeth Fair was another. At the time of the publication of *Bramton Wick*, she had noted in her diary that it 'was pretty certain of a sale to lending libraries and devotees of light novels', but by 1960 sales of such books were dwindling. Her novels were to all intents and purposes 'library books', but the two most popular circulating libraries, those operated by W.H. Smith and by Boots, were on the verge of closure, and sales to public libraries could not account on their own for the numbers necessary to ensure a publisher a profit.

That the typescript of *The Marble Staircase* was submitted by Elizabeth to her agent is evident, as the blue paper covers of the typescript bear the rubber stamp of the John Farquharson Literary Agency, of which Innes Rose was a director, and we can only imagine the despondency she felt when the work was returned to her, presumably accompanied by a letter explaining it had proved impossible to place this new novel with a publisher. The typescript was then destined to lie undisturbed in a black tin trunk for another 60 years until Elizabeth's heir, intrigued by the interest generated by the reissue of her six published novels by Dean Street Press, thought to take it out and read the story of Mrs Charlotte Moley, her Italian holidays, taken in the 1930s, and the house at Nything that she had, as a result, 25 years later inherited.

This story of rediscovery is entirely fitting, adding another stratum to the evolution of *The Marble Staircase*, because the novel itself is a palimpsest, in which elements of Charlotte Moley's life, past and present, are layered with that of the author. For, as Charlotte, on her first evening in Nything, stands on the seaside esplanade looking back across The Green towards the house she has inherited from Mrs Gamalion, so, in the 21st century, the Furrowed Middlebrow reader need only look on Street View for 16 West Beach, Lytham, Lancashire, to see the house as described by Elizabeth Fair, the right-hand of a pair that 'from the distance . . . still looked like one villa'. For Charlotte's house is the one-time home of Elizabeth's paternal grandfather, located in the seaside town that the Fair family had for several generations been responsible for developing, as land agents for the Clifton family. Although Elizabeth had grown up at Haigh, 40 miles or so away, where her father pursued the family business of land agency for another great landowner, the Earl of Crawford and Balcarres, the importance of Lytham to Fairs, and Fairs to Lytham, would have run as a thread through her life, an outline of which is set out in the introduction to the Dean Street Press reissues of her six previously published novels.

In that April 1959 diary entry Elizabeth stated that the novel was to be fashioned out of a series of contrasts, one of which was 'Lytham and the Lung' Arno'. The latter holds no mystery, for it was in a pensione in Florence that Charlotte Moley encountered a Galahad who then constructed around her a cult of 'La Fioren-tina', posing her against a *seicento* painting of a girl standing on a marble staircase, but it is Lytham that holds the key to unravel-ling the topography of Nything, where, a quarter of a century after her last view of the Lung' Arno, she meets her destiny. Later in 1959 Elizabeth noted that her current intention was for the novel (now tentatively renamed *The Beautiful View*) to provide 'A view of the beautiful present, but seen, as it were, through the past. Layers and layers, superimposed.' But, while skilfully interleav-ing Charlotte Moley's past and present through the medium of Mrs Gamalion's Nything house and its artefacts, loaded as they are with memories of Lake Como, Florence, and the band of Old Faithfuls, Elizabeth was also drawing deep on her own and her family's association with Lytham. It may be, if one but knew it, that not only the geography of Lytham but also some of its personalities are reflected in the people Charlotte encounters in Nything. Certainly, there is one off-stage character in *The Marble Staircase*, blind Canon Cowper, who had his real-life equiva-lent in blind Canon Hawkins, some-time vicar of St Cuthbert's, Lytham. It is in the churchyard of St Cuthbert's that members of the Fair family, including Elizabeth's grandfather, are buried, and it is in the Nything churchyard that, sometime in the 1950s, in the aftermath of Mrs Gamalion's funeral, we first encounter Charlotte Moley.

Very young when she entered a loveless marriage and soon then widowed, Charlotte had in the 1930s felt enclosed 'in a glass shell', caught between her mother and her daughter, who shared 'the same rigidity of mind'. However, during the course of a recu-perative holiday at Lake Como she met eccentric Mrs Gamalion, from whom emanated 'waves of enjoyment of life, enthusiasm, absurd but endearing skittishness [which] beat on the glass shell and splintered it to fragments'. Elizabeth Fair's early idea of setting Charlotte on an Italian journey that would allow 'a liberation of the mind' played with a theme that had proved attractive to many other authors, including E.M. Forster and Elizabeth von Arnim. That this journey should eventually lead Charlotte to the fictional equivalent of Lytham was a development that only Elizabeth Fair could have fabricated.

In her review of *Bramton Wick*, Nancy Spain had perceptively remarked, 'Miss Fair is refreshingly more interested in English landscape and architecture and its subsequent richening effect on English character than she is in social difference of rank, politics, and intellect', an observation borne out by a reading of Elizabeth's subsequent novels in which she lovingly portrays a variety of cottages, houses, villas, rectories, manors, and mansions. This characteristic is certainly a feature of *The Marble Staircase*, with Mrs Gamalion's crumbling house taking centre stage, but with bit parts played by the gadget-dominated, overwarm, new-build bungalow, doubtless a common phenomenon in Lytham, in which the Wakelins hope to stave off death, and Harley Coker's solid villa, where his late mother's taste still prevailed upstairs, but where downstairs the housekeeper had decreed 'contemporary' decoration with 'orange-yellow wicker chairs and shiny orna-ments in the hall', there to greet the paying guests now deemed necessary if bills were to be paid.

For the theme of ageing and decay runs through the novel, made manifest in other buildings – from Warley Hall, in the countryside close to Nything, once ancestral home of Mrs Gama-lion's family, now standing empty, its grounds unkempt (probably based on Warton Hall outside Lytham, formerly owned by the Cliftons, on the estate of which an earlier generation of Fairs had lived), through the crumbling Florentine palazzo on whose wall hung the painting of the marble staircase, to La Residenza, Mrs Gamalion's vision of a permanent home for the impoverished gentlefolk she gathered around her in Florence, the reality prov-ing if not exactly a chimera, certainly a ruin. That house had been set at the top of a marble staircase, although, unlike the one in the Florentine painting, its steps had collapsed, as, now, did Mrs Gamalion's dream.

But the marble staircase that had remained in Charlotte's mind was that of the painting, seeing herself as the girl standing on its lower step, but horribly conscious that with 'umpteen steps still ahead of her . . . she had already become a person who preferred to look back at the past'. However, as Elizabeth Fair had planned in the early mapping of the novel, Charlotte had, indeed, profited from the 'Italian journey', both literal and metaphorical, that had taken her from Lake Como to Nything, by way of Florence. She had developed the 'liberation of mind' that allowed her to break away from her former life and, while doing so, find love. She realises finally that she is able to look to the future, happy that even 'Mrs Gamalion's legacy would soon slide into the past and become a memory . . . would be demolished or unrecognisably transformed into flats'. For she could hear Mrs Gamalion admonishing her, 'I meant you to enjoy yourself! I meant you to live!'.

Elizabeth Crawford

CHAPTER I

ON A very wet day at the end of summer Charlotte Moley came to Nything to say goodbye to a friend and to look at a legacy which she had not expected to receive.

She hadn't expected anything. Sometime in the years since the war – or perhaps during the war itself which was still less than a decade away – she had given up expecting things. The nineteen-forties became nineteen-fifties, Alison grew up, her own fortieth birthday came and went; looking back she could not remember when she had settled down to mere existence, no longer expecting any changes in the pattern – let alone something as extraordinary as Mrs. Gamalion's legacy.

The goodbye was a formal leave-taking, though not a mere empty gesture; it was formal because it had to be. The real fare-well, with all her heart behind it, had been said six months ago, when she had last seen Mrs. Gamalion and guessed she would not see her again.

The churchyard where she took her formal leave was deep in rank grass and crowded with tilting, time-worn gravestones. It was, they had told her, no longer used for burials, except where there was a family vault. Mrs. Gamalion, of course, had been heir to a family vault, not for her the bleak new cemetery beyond the gas-works, she would have disliked it as much as she disliked the idea of cremation. Knowing her views Charlotte felt glad she had been given a place in the vault, with her parents, her grand-parents, and the brother who had died in childhood seventy years ago. But how desolate the churchyard looked, so sad and uncared for, as if there was no one left alive to tend these graves and remember the dead.

She thought how different it was in Italy; the dead affection-ately commemorated by life-size flattering effigies, or by framed photographs of themselves affixed to their marble tombs; the graves so lavishly decked out with immortelles under glass domes, with poems on black-edged paper to show the loved ones they were not forgotten; the Campo Santo a place to be visited by whole families as they would have visited grandmother in her lifetime, a place of sunshine and gaiety and ghastly bad taste, but better – more bearable – than this place where the dead were left to lie alone.

But of course it's the weather, she told herself; for she was a sensible creature, not given to extravagant complaints, and she knew that no churchyard looks its best on a wet day. And what did it matter, anyway? – to a Christian, St. Innocent's churchyard and the sands of Egypt were all one. The sands of Egypt, the hills of Tuscany . . . as she turned away she was thinking of Italy again, not as a final resting-place but as the place where it all began, and, so thinking, she came out into the street, and crossed it, and walked through some singularly uninteresting municipal gardens and across another street to the Green and the sea front.

Or rather, the mouth of the estuary. For Nything was not quite on the sea, although it proclaimed itself to be. Mrs. Gamalion, too, had insisted that she lived at the seaside and had often told Charlotte how splendid it was to be able to look out from the windows of her house across the Green to the sea. She had also enthused about the gulf stream which made this north-west coast so mild, and about the unspoilt charm of the Green itself with the dear old houses on the landward side; and latterly she had written a great many illegible postcards about the iniquities of the town council, which had not only permitted the pier to fall down but was minded to permit Development at the northern end of the Green and so destroy everything. "They are all Bolshies," she had written, "but we will never let them lay hands on the Green! I have been all along the front and half the people have promised already that they simply *won't* agree to it. It would be the thin end of the wedge and quite spoil my little houses."

Her little houses, a semi-detached pair that had once been an early-Victorian villa, were in the centre group on West Beach. In front of them stretched the Green, and on the other side of the Green was the narrow esplanade (for pedestrians only), with seats and glass-sided shelters at intervals, all facing the wide estuary which at high tide could justifiably be called the sea.

Charlotte Moley walked along the esplanade until she reached the steps which led down to the shore. Then she turned and stood with her back to the sea and looked across the Green at the house that was now hers, the right-hand one of the pair, the house Mrs. Gamalion had lived in for all those years, the extraordinary little ruin which was her legacy to Charlotte.

From the distance the two houses still looked like one villa, but the right-hand half was entirely covered with ivy. Ivy climbed over the gutters and across the steep roof, and hung down in festoons in front of the windows. The ground floor of both houses was hidden by the privet hedge, which had grown fifteen feet high and correspondingly thick, and only the two little iron gates, side by side, showed that there were two front doors somewhere behind. As Charlotte walked across the Green the marks of decay became more visible; she could see the broken slates on the roof, the peeling paint and the crumbling brickwork. The house on the left was little better when one looked at it closely. But it had been tenanted, and the tenants had kept the ivy within bounds and trimmed the front of the hedge, so that at a casual glance it looked like a habitation and not like a ruin.

Charlotte felt rather sorry for the tenants, who must have had a great deal to bear in the way of leaking roofs and windows before they gave in and fled. The house on the left had a board on the gate saying it was To Let; but the right-hand house waited for her to decide its future.

Inside, as she knew, it was crammed with the hoarding of a lifetime, with furniture and carpets and pictures, all worm-eaten or moth-eaten or spotted with damp, with innumerable souvenirs of Italy, all worthless and broken, with cupboardfuls of clothes going right back to the nineties, all unwearable. These things were hers too. Feeling quite dizzy at the thought of it, she advanced down the side-street which led to the back-door, fished out the large key from her handbag, entered the house, and walked through the tumbledown scullery and the stone-flagged kitchen to the dusty little drawing-room where she meant to begin. She had been over the house that morning with the solicitor who was empowered to give her possession, but there had not been time then to do more than blink and stare. She had stared as little as possible, saving it all for the moment when she would have the ruin to herself.

"I shall be here for a month," she thought now, looking round at the crowded chaos. And she wondered what Alison would say if she wrote that she was staying for a month. Then, as if in a dream, she heard the voice of Mrs. Gamalion crying, "Does it matter what Alison says?", and she laughed and – in the dream – agreed that it did not.

But in reality of course it did. Alison was her daughter, and one's daughter's views counted. Alison was sensible and capable, but she would resent it if her mother stayed away for a month, without any warning and for no good reason. "Giving way to sentiment," Alison would say – and she would be right. The only practical thing to do with the legacy was to sell it, the broken, useless furniture and the derelict house, for what it would fetch. "What is the good," asked Alison's emphatic voice, "of going through all that stuff in search of a past that doesn't exist any more? It isn't even as if it really *was* your past. I mean, you didn't see anything of Mrs. G., except all those donkey's years ago in Italy before the war. I know you wrote to each other and all that, but her possessions can't have any sentimental associations for you. No, not even for *you*, Mother."

Sentimental associations were abhorrent to Alison and she was always very stern when she suspected her mother of enjoying them. But she suspected it too often. Charlotte sometimes thought that the Mother whom her daughter saw and conscientiously tried to reform had never existed outside Alison's rather conventional imagination; that she was derived from novels and accepted theories about the older generation.

But perhaps she had existed once, the Mother whom Alison still frowned at. Perhaps she was derived from the impression the young Charlotte had made on her infant child – from the inexperienced, docile girl who had tried so hard to be what circumstances required. It had not been wrong in those days to acknowledge sentimental associations, so naturally Charlotte had acknowledged them. As a young widow it had positively been expected of her that she should cherish the past; her own mother would have thought her very heartless if she had thrown away the things that had belonged to Gabriel. "It was my own fault," she said, forgiving Alison for her occasional obtuseness. And she looked back at the young Charlotte, so blinkered and obedient and timid, and thought that but for Mrs. Gamalion she would be like that today, only more so. She would be encased in a shell harder than any glass, and by now she wouldn't even know it was there.

"All those donkey's years ago," she thought placidly, conceding Alison's right to ridicule the whole affair. But that was the beauty of the past, of this particular aspect of it that it had been absurd as well as enlightening, and could be remembered without regret.

Apart from the tangled churchyard and her own inheritance Nything looked extremely neat. The Green was mown, the seats along the esplanade were smartly painted, the side streets leading off the front disclosed views of modest brisk terraces which reminded Charlotte of aquatints in an early-nineteenth century album. At the far end of the Green she could see the pier, which according to Mrs. Gamalion had been allowed to fall into decay; but at a distance the decay was not visible and the horizontal outline of the pier, silhouetted against the leaden water, looked as trim and sturdy as the brick and stucco villas on the landward side of the Green.

They matched one another, and the autumn evening light completed the harmony. Fading daylight, with a pale gleam of gold in the west where the estuary merged into the sea; time gone by, and the neatness of the place masking its failure as a seaside resort. For it was the neatness of genteel poverty.

Charlotte walked along the esplanade with the wind at her back blowing off the sea. She thought she would walk as far as the pier. The tide was ebbing and she could make out where the deep channel of the river ran, a line of posts marking its navigable course. The channel came quite close inshore, and beyond it, far away across the wide expanse of the estuary, she could see a few faint lights on the other shore. It would soon be night.

Halfway to the pier there was a shelter, a small pavilion with the seats divided by an interior glass screen. You could sit on one side or the other according to the prevailing wind. She went to the lee side to light a cigarette, then, looking back at the last shreds of the sunset, she changed her mind about walking to the pier and returned to the side that faced west. The wind blew in her face now, smelling of the sea. The tattered clouds, burnished red and gold, were dimly reflected in the water, and as their colour faded the reflection faded too, until sea and sky became one in the dusk.

"Not a bad sunset," said a voice from the other end of the seat.

Charlotte looked round. The other woman, whom she had not noticed till now, was simply a shapeless figure muffled in a coat and scarf.

"Not bad at all," she agreed. "But I missed most of it, walking towards the pier."

"You should always walk the other way at sunset. Though I sometimes think – it's an illusion of course – that they aren't as good as they used to be."

"Not so spectacular?" Charlotte hazarded.

"Yes, and not so long lasting. But as I said, that's an illusion. When you're my age you must always remind yourself that it's your fault, not theirs."

"You mean that one doesn't respond so much?"

"Old people don't. And they mope for the time when they were young and active, so that everything that happened in the past seems better than what's happening now. It's silly to mope, especially for a healthy old woman like me. But I catch myself doing it all the same."

The voice was pleasantly vigorous but the sentences came jerk-ily, as if the speaker was not accustomed to putting her feelings into words. She would not have confided in me if it were daylight, Charlotte thought; and in the freedom of darkness she replied,

"You must have had a very happy life. Not many people can look back on a past where everything was better than the present."

"Oh, but it's because it *is* the past. You remember the sunlight, the good times, and forget the worries and the rain. Surely we all do that? But you're still young, so there hasn't been time yet for you to – to blot out the sadness."

"I'm not 'still young'. I have a grown-up daughter."

"What's that, compared with grown-up grandchildren!"

"Only halfway, I suppose," Charlotte said laughingly. "But you must admit I'm not *young*."

The word rang out in the darkness and the wind blew it away, while Charlotte congratulated herself on its going. No longer was she young Mrs. Moley, who had married and borne a child and been left a widow before she was twenty, and who had been forced to live for so many years in the shadow of her youthful bereavement.

"You sound young to me," said her companion. "But that's because I'm older, of course – or because I'm feeling particularly old this evening. It's being a widow," she burst out suddenly, "absurd of course but there it is. I never felt old – or thought of myself as getting old – until my husband died. It's not a question of missing him, though of course I do, it's widowhood itself. It puts one in a different pigeon-hole."

"Yes," Charlotte said with sympathy. "Oh yes, it does."

"Then you too –"

"My husband died a long time ago," she said. "So it isn't quite the same thing. But I understand what you mean about widowhood putting one in a different pigeon-hole. And I suppose, if your children are grown-up when it happens –"

"Oh yes, it's the children who make one feel it! They start being protective, and fussy, and they worry about whether I ought to go on living by myself and about being too far away to keep an eye on me. My daughter is married and my son is a clergyman," said the voice out of darkness, as if these facts explained their absence from the scene.

Charlotte murmured something about mistaken kindness.

"Oh yes, they're dear, kind children. One couldn't wish for better. . . . And it's something – it's everything, isn't it? – to be loved."

Staring into the night, Charlotte wondered whether her capable daughter, who organized their life and made all the decisions, was in her own way demonstrating a protective love. She supposed it was so, though she had sometimes suspected that a widowed mother was simply one of the responsibilities Alison shouldered, like her secretaryship of the junior Conservatives or her Duty Night in the Community Centre canteen. Still –

"I couldn't wish for better either," she said.

It was true. The failure, if it was one, was hers and not Alison's. Alison was like her grandmother, Charlotte's own mother, and Charlotte could be likened to grit in their smooth-running lives. Not a good simile, she thought, because grit had the quality of grittiness which she conspicuously lacked. Not grit, then, but some undefined substance that clogged or hampered the machine.

"Why aren't the lights on?" the other woman demanded abruptly.

And not a machine either, Charlotte told herself reprovingly. Such efficiency as machines possessed had been implanted in them by human beings, and to use them as a standard of comparison was ridiculous. Besides, Alison was dear to her.

"What lights?" she asked politely.

"They ought to have been on long before now."

As she spoke, and like an answer to criticism, the lights sprang into being. The lamp posts along the esplanade were set rather far apart and the lights themselves were rather dim, so that the effect was not so much to illuminate the sea front as to define it. For a moment Charlotte gazed with pleasure at the long line of lamps pricking the darkness, shaping the land's edge against the blackness and emptiness of the sea. Then she turned to look across the shelter at the other woman, who was staring unashamedly at her. There was a lamp quite close to their retreat and the wan, yellow light fell on their faces, revealing – so Charlotte thought – two people who might never have exchanged a word if they had met before sunset.

For she wasn't a beginner of conversations herself, and the big, robust woman at the other end of the seat looked much too self-reliant to confide in strangers. The clergyman son, the married daughter and grown-up grandchildren, were hardly credible at first sight; but then she moved and Charlotte perceived the shadows of age round her mouth and eyes, contradicting the first impression of undiminished vigour.

She understood why this woman resented growing old.

"Another power failure, I suppose," the woman said chattily. "Or else they simply forgot to switch them on."

"Do they often do that in Nything?"

"You don't live here, then?"

These were steps back to normality, a joint agreement to begin as strangers.

"No," said Charlotte. "I'm only here for – for a visit."

They were standing up now, a little self-conscious but still aware of the current of sympathy they had felt in the darkness. It would have seemed absurd to part as casually as they had met. They turned in the same direction, facing the wind, and walked along the esplanade side by side.

"I wondered whether I knew you," Charlotte's companion remarked. "Nything is a small place, one knows people by sight if not by name. I thought you might be someone I saw quite often, out shopping or at church."

"No. I arrived only yesterday. But I think I may be here for some time."

The idea, which had come to her in the darkness, stood the test of being spoken aloud, in lamplight, to the women who had unwittingly inspired it. It wasn't till she put the idea into words that Charlotte began to take it seriously. She knew she must enlarge on it, expand it into a definite plan, before it became blurred by doubts and second thoughts and fears of what Alison would say. She stood still and looked across the Green to the row of houses on the farther side. Lights shone out from most of them, but nearly opposite there was a dark, humped outline which was her own house and its twin. The crumbling, ivy-covered chimney stack formed the hump, and in the light of the street lamps she could just see the upper windows, also covered with ivy, above the rampant privet hedge.

"I am going to live there," she said pointing.

"You've taken a house? But which one – I don't quite see –"

"That one without any lights. The rather overgrown one. That one on the right of those two," Charlotte said incoherently, forcing her idea to take shape.

"But that's where Mrs. Gamalion lived," her companion cried in astonishment.

"Yes, I know, you see, she left it to me."

CHAPTER II

"BUT you can't live here!"

"Not for ever, of course. Just for – well, perhaps a few months. I'm staying at an hotel just now," Charlotte added reassuringly.

"Not even for a night, until you've aired it very thoroughly," Mrs. Bateman insisted.

Mrs. Bateman was her companion of the sunset, who by daylight looked even larger and solider, and brimming over with kindness and common-sense. She had arrived at the front door ten minutes after Charlotte had entered the house, and since it was impossible to open the front door (which was sealed with wads of newspaper and strips of carpet and hadn't been opened for years) Charlotte had shouted to her to go round to the back and had then felt compelled to admit her.

It had hardly needed a glimpse of the scullery and kitchen to tell Mrs. Bateman that Charlotte could not live here; even if she had approached it by the front door, the drawing-room reeked of damp, and of all that good housewives find abhorrent. Dust and soot and decay; and more pungent than any of them, the smell of the past.

"Oh yes, I'll air it," Charlotte assured her. "I shall start upstairs, in the bedroom I'm going to use. This can wait a bit" – she waved her hand at the chaos around them – "until I've settled in."

She hoped she sounded practical and efficient.

"But it's so *damp*," Mrs. Bateman protested.

"The house has been empty for a long time."

It wasn't in this house that Charlotte had said goodbye to Mrs. Gamalion. The cheapish, bleakish nursing-home, to which old age had brought her in the end, had smelt of soap and anti-septics and condescension, not of damp.

It was not in Nything, because the Nything nursing-home had refused to keep her after she had rebelliously attempted to set it on fire; but the other one, five miles up the coast, had taken her in and kept her till the end. And glad to have her, Charlotte thought resentfully, remembering the lack of comfort and the ill-mannered nurses and the hard, avaricious mouth of the matron-proprietress. But she had seen the place only once and would have hated it anyway, for being the background to that last, sad meeting.

"And even before that, the house was neglected," she went on. "Mrs. Gamalion was too old, she couldn't look after it properly. . . ."

"Yes, of course," Mrs. Bateman agreed. She paused. "It was the same at Warley, before the Wakelins bought it. I remember going to the sale. It must –" And her glance strayed over the room, as if dazed by the sheer accumulation of objects, "– it must run in the family."

"What family?"

"Why, the Ellans. Mrs. Gamalion was an Ellan before she married, though I believe only a cousin of the ones at Warley Hall. They were a big family, but I think they're all dead now. It was a bit before my time – I only came to Nything in 1922, and there were some Ellans at Warley Hall then, but –"

"Warley Hall," Charlotte exclaimed. She could see in her mind's eye the faded photograph Mrs. Gamalion used to show her, with the big rambling house in the background and a varied assortment of Ellans grouped in front of it. The girls had worn bell-shaped skirts and high-necked blouses, the young men wore Norfolk jackets and one of them held a fox-terrier on a leash. How in the world could she have forgotten Warley Hall!

"And you went to the sale?" she asked with interest. "It's quite near Nything, isn't it? Who is living there now?"

Mrs. Bateman dealt with the last question first.

"It's empty at present, since the Wakelins left. They sold it."

"I thought you said they bought it."

"So they did. But that was – dear me, nearly thirty years ago. *That* was when I went to the sale – not this time. They sold it to a man from Manchester who thought of retiring there but then he changed his mind because of the threat of the aerodrome being re-opened. It's empty at present and I really don't know what will happen to it now."

"I must go and look at it," said Charlotte.

"The Wakelins would love to take you. They've built a new house in Nything, quite near mine – that's in Church Street, beyond the church – but they often drive over to look at Warley. They chose comfort, because like me they're getting on. But I believe they both have secret regrets about leaving Warley."

"Was it so uncomfortable?"

"It was too large for them," said Mrs. Bateman. "And their standards of comfort are much higher than mine, or perhaps yours. My dear, I'm afraid you will be far from comfortable if you stay here."

"I shall be all right."

Mrs. Bateman gave a great throaty laugh, like a good-natured lioness. "I can see you mean to stay," she said. "You have just the expression that I must have when I'm standing up to my Robert and Mary. When they're trying to persuade me to do something I don't want to do. You're insisting on moving in, and I'm refusing to move out – but children always think their mothers can't look after themselves. You made me feel just like Mary, then."

"I'm sorry –"

"Don't be sorry. I'm obstinate and so are you. It's good for us to experience the effect it has on our children. But I won't go on arguing, I'll leave you to act as you please. Do you go to church?"

"Yes," said Charlotte.

"Then come and have lunch with me on Sunday after morning service. I shall be at church. I'll look out for you."

"Thank you very much."

There was a fire to be lit, bedding to be aired, shopping to be done, but Charlotte wasted ten minutes wondering whether Alison was going to feel just like Mary and what those feelings would entail. It had been a surprise to hear herself described as obstinate; and looking back she couldn't believe she had ever shown much obstinacy in the past where Alison was concerned. But she was undoubtedly prepared to be obstinate in the future. She felt strangely bold and determined, and she wondered whether this was because she was in Mrs. Gamalion's house, where something of Mrs. Gamalion's enlivening spirit still remained. But probably it was because she was far away from Alison. It was much easier, she thought ruefully, to be bold and determined in a letter.

And she must write at once, to let Alison know she wasn't going home at the end of the week. (Three full days would be quite enough time, Alison had said, to choose the souvenirs and arrange for the sale of the rest.) A postcard at once, to give Alison this vital information, and a letter to follow; a firm, well-expressed letter which would show her that her mother could fend for herself.

There was a packet of postcards on the dresser in the kitchen, where Mrs. Gamalion had latterly spent her days until she was removed to the nursing-home. Sitting at the kitchen table Charlotte felt the past closing in on her; she could have been Mrs. Gamalion writing the familiar address for the last time, scrawling her illegible message, keeping open as well as she could – far-sighted, old, and rather crazy – the channels of communication with youth and Italy.

So few of them left, by that time. Mrs. Gamalion had outlived her contemporaries and alienated her neighbours; there was no one to listen to her chatter or to remember the lost world of her youth. No one but Charlotte, who by being so much younger had crept into Mrs. Gamalion's world at the very end of its existence and was linked to a past remotely more distant than her own.

It was at Menaggio, nearly twenty-five years ago, that Charlotte Moley first met Mrs. Gamalion.

The pensione had balconies and a view, the chambermaid spoke a little English, the food was Italian and delicious, the holiday was in fact just what young Mrs. Moley had dreamed of – and yet it wasn't. Alone, shy, unhappy, overwrought, she felt herself as much a failure in Italy as she was in England. She sat in corners, or went for sad walks by herself, down to the lake or up the hill, and everywhere she went she seemed to be enclosed in an impenetrable glass shell, outside which there were people, noise, laughter, life surging past in kaleidoscopic patterns, and the bright Italian landscape. She could see and hear everything but she could not be part of it. The glass walls imprisoned her.

Young Mrs. Moley was accustomed to this isolation, but she had hoped to escape in Italy. A holiday, they had said, was what she needed, and she had supposed they must be right. They always were right, her wise and experienced advisers, her mother, Dr. Beckett, her uncle who was also her lawyer; even her infant daughter Alison, too young to give verbal advice, had an air of knowing more than she did. They had advised a holiday and combined to make it possible. Dr. Beckett had planned it, the lawyer-uncle had calculated the cost and told her she could afford it, her mother had undertaken to look after Alison. And Alison, perhaps aware that she would be looked after more efficiently than at home, had settled down, without the slightest fuss.

If they had not been unanimous, her advisers, she would have cut her holiday short and gone back to England. But she dared not face them. A month at least, they had said, and she could imagine – though she preferred not to – what they would say if she came back after a week, as thin and nervous and list-less as when she had left them. So she conscientiously sat in the sun, and ate as much as she could stomach, and went for a walk every day and very early to bed every night. Alone in her glass shell, which appeared to other people a barrier of icy reserve, she moved among the pensione's visitors, who pitied her for being so young and a widow. Those thin arms, that cloud of very dark hair so quaintly long in an age of shingles, the pale skin that unfairly never got red and sunburnt like other people's skins . . . "Not really at all pretty," the other women said triumphantly, as if it were an argument they might easily have lost.

They had learned of her widowhood from Francesca the chambermaid, who said the lady had confided in her. This was not true, but Francesca was an inspired guesser and in this instance she hardly needed to puzzle out the letters Mrs. Moley left about in her bedroom. The photographs of the baby and of the baby's begetter made it all clear to Francesca; Mrs. Moley's wedding-ring, and even more her air of respectable bereavement, were a guarantee that she mourned a husband and not a lover.

So her grief and reserve were accounted for and she was left alone and soon forgotten. It was easy to forget about her, she was so quiet and unassuming, she had the small table by the door and she retired to her bedroom as soon as dinner was over. The other visitors in fact were quite glad to forget about her, for bereavement and misfortune were tacitly recognised to be out of place in the Pensione Bellavista, where people came year after year to escape the English spring and all the troubles of their own lives at home.

On the day of Mrs. Gamalion's arrival Mrs. Moley had walked down to the lake, where she had sat in the sun for an hour, on a marble bench in a small public garden, reading an old newspaper in snatches and sometimes looking at the lake and always thinking about herself and Gabriel and their daughter Alison, who was now sixteen months old and had been just ten weeks when her father died. It worked out that Gabriel had been dead for more than a year; and indeed she remembered the anniversary of his death vividly, because she had been staying with her mother whose views on anniversaries were rigorous.

"Of course you'll wear your black coat," her mother had said, as she lifted Alison into her pram.

Of course, of course. A daily outing for Alison was obligatory, but Charlotte had worn her black coat and had kept to quiet side streets. Later in the day her mother had accompanied her to the church where she and Gabriel had been married, and they had attended a mid-week Lent evensong and sat quietly in the pew until everyone else had gone and then walked home in silence. But after supper they had talked about Gabriel in voices that were steady and unhushed (Charlotte taking her cue from her mother), and had even managed to smile in recalling one of his pet jokes. Charlotte had obediently copied the smile, just as she had copied the tone of voice.

Her mother, unlike herself, always knew what to do. She had known that Charlotte must wear black, and go to Evensong, and afterwards pull herself together before bedtime.

The marble seat grew harder and the view less dazzling. When she looked at it again all the colours had faded and grey clouds filled the sky. A wind whipped up lively waves, it began to rain, and famous Como assumed the blurred outline of any lake on a wet day, the mountains invisible, the garden mere dripping vegetation. She thought of Windermere where she had stayed as a child and Loch Tay where she had spent her honeymoon. Out of the driving rain a steamer appeared, chugging towards the landing-pier as steamers had chugged on Windermere and Loch Tay, and as she hurried to shelter she remembered that the arrival of the steamer had been a recurrent excitement of the Windermere holiday long ago. The game had been to choose one of the disembarking passengers and invent reasons for his journey. At Loch Tay she had timidly tried to teach Gabriel the game; but he had not understood it.

The rain was heavier, lightning flashed, and thunder echoed between the mountains. She waited under an arcade close to the pier, where she could see the passengers disembarking. It was a long time since she had played the steamer-game or cared to invent a history for anyone, but with Rome merged into Windermere she found herself merging into the vanished inquisitive child. She looked at the passengers and chose Mrs. Gamalion.

A moment ago Mrs. Gamalion had not been visible. But no sooner was the gangway in place than she appeared at the top of it, bursting through the little crowd as if she herself were made of a harder, more penetrating substance or propelled with great force. There were protests, some loud, but she ignored them and scurried ashore ahead of everyone, clutching at her hat with one hand and waving a furled umbrella in the other. Prodding the nearest porter into action she addressed him loudly in Italian and commanded him to make haste.

"Vivace, molto vivace!" There was much more, about the bagaglio and the due signorine and the giorno cattivo, but Mrs. Moley could not understand it. An excitable foreigner, she thought, watching the bizarre figure whose vivid colouring and brightly striped dress made her think of a parakeet that had escaped from an aviary to flatter and screech in an alien countryside. Then she got a shock, for the parakeet turned to face the steamer and its speech became abruptly intelligible.

"Alice! Muriel! Oh you stupid girls, why didn't you follow me? Come along quickly, we shall all get soaked!"

No foreigner would speak English like that, Mrs. Moley decided; the excitable creature must be her fellow-countrywoman. But how different from the English at the pensione – how different from the other prudent travellers now shuffling down the gangway with their mackintoshes and their resigned expressions. There was no trace of resignation in the woman who waited for Alice and Muriel. Declaring that it never rained when she was at Lake Como she stood angrily enduring it, disdaining to open her umbrella. Mrs. Moley waited too, quite eager to see what Alice and Muriel would be like.

They were young, pink-faced, English from their strap shoes to their sensible travelling hats, and nearly the last to leave the steamer. Descending the gangway they held their heads high, looking into the distance and trying to dissociate themselves from the flamboyant screeeching figure on the pier; it was evident that they disliked being shouted at.

"Nieces?" Charlotte Moley thought tentatively. But somehow they hadn't quite the air of nieces. Protégées, certainly, and doomed to be shouted at again as soon as they came ashore.

"Have you got the dressing-case? And the rug? Come along, you girls, don't stand there dreaming. Oh my beautiful Como, how stupid of it to rain! But it's only a thunderstorm. Come along quickly! Look, it's beginning to clear already!"

"Then let's wait till it does," said the one Mrs. Moley had labelled Muriel. She was the stronger character of the pair and carried nothing, while Alice was bowed down under traveller's accessories.

"Don't be silly – why, it will be over before we're up the hill. The porter will bring the luggage up and we shall be there in no time!"

But as Mrs. Gamalion spoke the lightning flickered again and a new deluge descended. Small torrents of water rushed down the street and the dejected palm trees rattled their leaves in a sudden gust. Mrs. Moley felt strangely excited, as if the thunderstorm were the prelude to some dramatic event. Mrs. Gamalion, defeated by the elements, fled under the nearest arcade – which was also Mrs. Moley's shelter. For a moment they stood side by side without speaking, still strangers, without a single thread of common knowledge or interest to tie them together. Then, the thread was spun.

"Pensione Bellavista," Mrs. Gamalion cried to the porter, who with Alice and Muriel had retreated to the arcade opposite. She pointed behind her, indicating that the pensione lay beyond several walls and up the hill, high up, over there.

"Subito," said the porter, indicating comprehension and an instant willingness to start as soon as the rain abated.

"Oh . . . that's where I'm staying," said Mrs. Moley, in a little, breathless voice which was perhaps an indication of her surprise at finding herself addressing a total stranger.

Mrs. Gamalion turned quickly to face her. Amid a flurry of first impressions – she *was* like a bird, an exotic, rather comic one, beaky-nosed, bright-eyed, her gay plumage all ruffled and bedraggled by rain – Mrs. Moley stood her ground, waiting with tingling excitement for more to happen. The thunderstorm had not lied; the steamer-game had at long last surpassed invention. A benefactress had arrived, who could demolish the walls of glass and set her free.

"You couldn't do better," Mrs. Gamalion screeched loudly. She turned again, to direct a few encouraging squawks at Alice and Muriel, then she pointed to the sky and showed Mrs. Moley a gap in the clouds. "All over in ten minutes – rain never lasts in Italy – we shall see all the mountains this evening." She shook out the folds of her wet skirt, tweaked at the feather boa which so improbably accompanied the striped cotton dress, settled her big straw hat more firmly, all with the air of a bird preening its plumage. "The *best* view of beautiful Como," she cried. "That's what I always tell the Signora. Bellavista, bellavista!"

Bellavista, bellavista!

Across the years the weird parrot-cry came back, but changed now, changed and mellowed, just as the far-off spring sunlight had mellowed, with time, to a golden radiance. Claude might have painted the landscape Charlotte saw in her mind's eye, so luminous and perfect; the view she would never see again, the view she had perceived when she was twenty and her sight was restored to her.

"Yes," she said to the dusty room. "Yes, it was beautiful."

CHAPTER III

THE Wakelins were called Lily and Bart. Mrs. Bateman had known them for years, for her husband and Bart had been at school together and had always kept up, even when Bart was in the army and the late Hugh Bateman a solicitor tied to his home town, which wasn't Nything but a big industrial town further inland. It was really the Batemans' move to Nything which had brought the Wakelins to the neighbourhood.

"They came to stay with us," Mrs. Bateman explained, "and they were house-hunting at the time, and saw Warley and fell in love with it. Of course Bart had retired quite young, because – well, he could afford to. They could afford to buy Warley and do it up – which it sadly needed – and now they've been able to afford to build this new house for their old age, which you're going to see. It's full of wonderful labour-saving devices and ingenious contraptions. They planned it for absolute comfort."

She spoke kindly, but with an undertone of mockery. Charlotte guessed that comfort wasn't very important to Mrs. Bateman and that planning for it ranked dangerously close to self-indulgence.

"It looked a very nice house from the outside," she said. Mrs. Bateman had pointed it out to her as they walked back together after morning service.

"But no garden," said Mrs. Bateman. "Nothing but gravel in front, and at the back they've built a big paved terrace, and then a minute lawn and a border full of flowering shrubs. Labour-saving again, you see. They're forever considering their old age and arranging for it in advance."

She looked at her guest and laughed.

"Not so much in advance, you're thinking? Yes, the Wakelins are about as old as I am. But I'm perfectly hale and hearty – and so are they. It's a mistake, all this planning for your dotage. Still, they're great dears, the pair of them. I'm sure you'll like them."

"It's kind of them to drive me out to Warley," Charlotte said.

"They'll enjoy it as much as you will. Perhaps more," Mrs. Bateman predicted. "There's nothing much to see at Warley, just an old house and all those flat fields. We'd better give them another half hour, I think. They rest after lunch, put their feet up and have a nap. Practising for their old age!"

Her affectionate snort made Charlotte laugh. Mrs. Bateman in daylight, as she had guessed at the start, was very different from Mrs. Bateman in darkness. Robust, kind, matter-of-fact, she admitted no fears or regrets; there was simply no time for them in the crowded hours of daylight.

The visit to Warley Hall had of course been her idea, and it was typical of her to arrange this expedition to please Charlotte and the Wakelins, without any understanding of why they wanted to go. 'An old house and all those flat fields . . .'

They had lunched, they had washed up, and now there was still half an hour before they could disturb the Wakelins. Being allowed to help with the washing-up was a mark of closer acquaintance, Charlotte thought, and it led on, quite naturally, to more personal talk than they had had earlier. She was neither surprised nor disconcerted when Mrs. Bateman asked how Alison was 'managing'.

"I haven't heard from her," she replied, "but I'm sure she's managing perfectly. She's a much better manager than I am."

"And she doesn't mind being alone?"

"She isn't alone. We have a flat, and a girl called Evvie – Alison's closest friend – lives with us. Our lodger," said Charlotte, making a joke of it and remembering too late that Evvie had now grown up into Evelyn.

"Oh, that's all right, then. Two of them together. I dare say they'll quite enjoy being on their own – for a short time anyway."

"For a long time, I think," Charlotte said calmly.

"But . . ."

"It's quite a small flat and they can afford to keep themselves. They've both got good jobs. Of course I can help if they need help; it's my flat, really. But I shall stay here."

"But you're their mother," Mrs. Bateman exclaimed.

"Alison's, not Evvie's. Evelyn's. – I've known her since she was a child and I can never remember not to call her Evvie. But that isn't the point, is it?" (Mrs. Bateman shook her head in bewilderment, seeking for a point she could grasp.) "It's really *too* small," Charlotte continued. "Or else I'm beginning to suffer from claustrophobia, though that isn't, I think, the right word for it."

"What is too small?" Mrs. Bateman asked anxiously.

"The flat."

"Couldn't you find a larger one?"

"Oh, it suits us all right. At least, it suits them. Alison likes it very much, because it's part of my mother's old home. Alison was very fond of her grandmother, and we all lived together in the end – until her death, then it was turned into flats."

Mrs. Field's house, The Laurels. Halfway down the street, with a double entrance and a towering stone porch. You can't miss it.

"Yes, that's different – if you're attached to a place," Mrs. Bateman conceded.

Nothing to do with sentiment, Alison had said. This is a well-built house in the best part of the town and it can be converted into very good flats. So why leave it?

"We sold the house – Alison thought it better – but we arranged to buy a flat after it was converted. Of course that was before Evvie came to live with us."

"And now it's a bit too small." Mrs. Bateman had seen the point this time; she was prepared to offer sympathy. But Charlotte waved it aside.

"We could manage if we all thought alike. But as it is, I'm decidedly in their way. I've known it for some time, without quite admitting it. Refusing to face facts, my daughter would call it," she added with a smile. "But what's the good of worrying about a problem to which there isn't a solution? It was only when I came to Nything that I saw what to do."

"Simply to stay here?"

Charlotte nodded. The simplicity of her plan was perhaps its greatest attraction; but there were plenty of others. The legacy hung before her like a child's Christmas stocking, bulging with presents she was impatient to unwrap.

Mrs. Bateman's glance shifted to the mantelpiece, where a brass carriage clock was flanked by two photographs in matching leather frames. It was at these photographs she looked, their originals clearly in her mind as she said briskly,

"Of course, one doesn't want to be a burden."

It wasn't being a burden but bearing one, Charlotte thought rebelliously. The burden on her own shoulders, the oppressive weight of failures and stupidities, had eased remarkably since her arrival in Nything. But she could agree with the general principle.

"Yes," she said, "independence is the thing."

"Those photos were taken a long time ago," Mrs. Bateman remarked, with a seeming irrelevance which did not deceive her hearer. They had talked about Alison and now it was time for Robert and Mary.

"Your children? They're very good-looking."

Charlotte stood up to examine the photographs more closely, glad that the offspring they portrayed could justly be described as good-looking. The young clergyman with his thick dark hair and regular features was like the hero of a Victorian novel, and although his sister's face was less distinguished she was pretty enough to be praised.

"Oh well, they were younger then," Mrs. Bateman said deprecatingly. "It was when Mary was engaged; I had her photographed and I made Robert come too, though he didn't want to."

Charlotte mentally acquitted Robert of a tendency to conceit; it was not by his own wish that he had visited the photographer. "He must have been a very popular curate," she said laughingly.

"All curates are popular," Mrs. Bateman retorted. "Well, nearly all – we had a thoroughly disagreeable one here last year but thank goodness he's left. Look – these are my grandchildren."

The snapshots of the grandchildren, a boy and a girl, were small and indistinct, but Charlotte dutifully admired them.

"Are they your son's children?" she asked.

"Oh no, Robert's not married. I wish he were. These two are Mary's."

The grandchildren had names, ages, and ambitions, which remained as indistinct as their faces to Charlotte because she was wondering why Mrs. Bateman wished Robert was married. Did she disapprove of celibacy, or was she lamenting an unrequited passion . . . or the death of a fiancée and a life saddened by loss? The hero-of-a-Victorian-novel deserved some romantic story to match his romantic face; and the note of regret in Mrs. Bateman's voice was quite enough to stimulate Charlotte to invent one.

It was no more than a way of passing the time, a game; for her own experience had taught her that tragic-romantic endings were not true to life. All the more reason then for enjoying them in fantasy, as one enjoyed a change of air or scenery. It was in this spirit – consciously at one remove from reality – that she set herself to invent a history for Robert.

"We could start now, I think," Mrs. Bateman said presently.

There was a short delay while she put the grandchildren's snapshots back in the drawer and set the fireguard in front of the fire. Charlotte, already on her feet, took another look at Robert. It was the last time she was to see him as a romantic hero, unrelated to everyday life. For her companion, perceiving her game, broke off the humdrum conversation about coal fires, their advantages and drawbacks, and abruptly became confidential.

"He's coming to stay with me quite soon, while he makes up his mind what to do," she began. "He's been ill, you see, and had to give up his living, and he doesn't know whether to take another he's been offered or not."

The image now presented, of a clergyman both delicate and indecisive, clashed badly with Charlotte's invention, but she managed to utter sounds of sympathy,

" . . . very worrying for you," she ended.

"Oh yes, it was. It is. This illness . . . but it may be all right. We must hope for the best. The danger is –"

Mrs. Bateman paused as if some cautious hand had checked her plunge into intimacy, and left the sentence unfinished.

"I expect you'll enjoy his visit anyway," Charlotte offered consolingly.

"I'm looking forward to it, yes. Only I'm rather dreading it as well, in a way, because it will be so difficult to keep him amused."

What could one possibly say? A delicate and indecisive son who was also liable to boredom aroused little sympathy, except for his mother. Making a conventional response, Charlotte felt quite vexed with her companion for revealing what she would have preferred not to know; though a second later she was laughing at herself for begrudging the loss to fiction. He was gone for good, the Robert whose face had inspired her, but facts less daunting than these would have been equally destructive. And since he *was* gone she could even manage to feel a little sorry for the real Robert, when she remembered that he had been ill. But for some reason she retained the impression that this illness was the least of Mrs. Bateman's worries, much less important than the problem of keeping him amused during his convalescence.

In spite of descriptions the Wakelins came quite as a surprise. Great dears, the pair of them, and Charlotte could recognize their dearness, but she had not expected them to look so fragile. They looked both fragile and well-preserved, they reminded her of a careful arrangement of dried flowers and foliage which would fall to bits if you tried to alter it. But 'everlasting' in favourable circumstances.

Lily Wakelin was small and fair-skinned, her grey hair still giving the impression of fluffy yellowness, her pale blue eyes matching her light, childish voice. Bart was taller and thinner, with a jerky walk like a puppet toy soldier. They greeted Mrs. Bateman affectionately and Charlotte with enthusiasm. They were looking forward, oh, tremendously, to showing her Warley Hall.

First, Bart must get the car out of the garage. While he did this they waited in the house, Lily standing at a window to watch his manoeuvres – the garage, she explained was narrow and so was the drive, and he wasn't yet accustomed to them. Mrs. Bateman said he had had plenty of time to learn. Lily shook her head, smiling at her friend's ignorance and said it was more difficult than she thought. With a big car like theirs there was no room to spare, and only a good driver like Bart could have done it at all.

It was indeed a big car. Boomy, high-bodied, deeply uphol-stered, like a cross between a first-class railway compartment and an unusually luxurious hearse. It was perhaps the funereal pace that suggested a hearse to Charlotte. She sat in the back with Mrs. Bateman, watching the flat fields move slowly past, the distant belt of trees grow gradually taller, listening to the mellow horn Bart sounded at each bend and to Lily Wakelin's voice telling her about Warley. They were approaching it, it was over there behind those trees – far too many trees and too close to the house but Bart had had a lot cut down when they made the new rose garden, including a big beech tree which they had afterwards regretted – although it had made that side of the house rather damp.

Charlotte ceased to attend. It was not the Wakelins' improve-ments that she had come to see. Under the trees the road seemed narrower and darker, a tunnel leading back to the past, strewn with autumnal leaves that had once been green.

The car turned left between stone gate posts, the gate itself standing open as if they were expected. (No caretaker, no one to keep an eye on things, Lily piped disconsolately.) At the end of a short drive, against a background of dark woods and clouded sky, stood Warley Hall.

The wrong time of year, Charlotte thought. For she had seen it only in a faded photograph and the pale sepia of a lost summer. But the house itself was unchanged, the same house in a different season, its façade as familiar as if she had been Mrs. Gamalion returning to her ancestral home. The strangeness was not in the house but in the silence and emptiness, in the chill wind and drifting leaves. They had come at the wrong time of year.

She was taken round the garden. The wind blew from the west across the flat fields, the paths were slippery with moss and the lawn squelched damply underfoot. Late roses and chrysan-themums bloomed among the weeds but the effect was rather melancholy. It was a beautiful garden sinking into decay.

"Colder than I thought. You should have worn your boots," Bart told Lily.

"How early the leaves are falling! We used to sweep them up every day," Lily said to Charlotte. "We made a big stack to rot down for compost, and we had bonfires as well. We worked like slaves."

"You had a gardener, too," said Mrs. Bateman.

"Yes, but it was far too much for one man," said Lily. "It was when he died and we couldn't get another that we decided to leave. Bart said we ought to start planning for our old age."

She laughed, as if their old age was a time still in the future. The designing of a new house, with every provision for the comfort of an enfeebled old couple, had begun as a kind of joke.

"But I miss the scent of the bonfire smoke," she said. It was autumn for Lily and Bart – autumn, not winter. The scent of wreathing bonfire smoke and newly stored apples, the tawny blaze of chrysanthemums and wood fires, marked their memories of Warley. But for Charlotte it was high summer, with the young Ellans arranging themselves on the lawn to be photographed and the beech tree in full leaf.

"Can we go into the house?" she asked.

But the house was locked up, shuttered and barred. And that was as it should be, she thought afterwards, for behind the façade lay a past she could not enter, unknown territory where there were no memories to guide her. She wasn't sorry, either, that her first glimpse of Mrs. Gamalion (for the photograph, now given depth and clarity, must count as the start) should reveal her in an exterior setting, among her friends, in summer weather. It was appropriate and endearing.

The first-class hearse deposited Charlotte outside her house on the Green. The Wakelins had insisted on giving her and Mrs. Bateman tea at Nything's best hotel – which was called The Pier Hotel and stood opposite its namesake – and then on driving her right to her own front door, to save her the walk from Church Street. A short walk still awaited her, round the block to the back door which was her only means of entry, but she did not want them to know this and hoped Mrs. Bateman would not tell them. They were so kind, they might insist on driving her to the back door, or alternatively feel that their good deed had been wasted.

She stood on the pavement, waiting for the car to move off before she moved off herself.

"Glad you enjoyed seeing Warley," Lily said in farewell. "Of course it was really too late in the year – to give you any idea of the garden, I mean."

"Garden's ruined," said Bart. "Quite gone to pieces. Heart-breaking, after all our hard work."

"But that was why you left, wasn't it?" Mrs. Bateman reminded them. "To save yourself all that hard work. You can't have your cake and eat it."

The Wakelins looked very small and frail, sitting side by side in their enormous car and swathed in enveloping scarves and bulky coats. Charlotte found it hard to believe that a year ago they had still been at Warley, sweeping up leaves, coping with a house which must always have been much too big for them. She thought it unkind of Mrs. Bateman to laugh at them for choosing an easier life.

"Good night," she said. "Good night, and thank you again. It was lovely."

The interior light was extinguished, extinguishing Mrs. Bateman and the Wakelins and the deep blue upholstery and richly gleaming fittings. Darkness swallowed them up, the car moved ponderously forward and Charlotte watched its rear lights dwindling into pinpoints, before she turned away.

She walked back along the Green, down Beach Street to the cul-de-sac which ran parallel with the road in front, and along this to her own back garden. The back gardens had high walls and hers was extremely narrow because it had been divided when the villa was turned into two houses with another high wall separating it from the strip next door. Both halves of the garden contained a number of trees, sycamores and horse chestnuts – tall, thrusting trees which had shot up above roof-height in their bid for air and sunshine. The solicitor had told her that the neighbours had often complained about these trees, whose branches and roots trespassed on their property, but that Mrs. Gamalion had absolutely refused to have anything done about them.

"A very strong-minded old lady," he had said. "The neighbours couldn't stand up to her. Very strong-minded indeed. Defied the town council, you know, about that front hedge of hers – wouldn't let their men touch it, though it was right out over the pavement. Surprising, really, how she got away with it."

Charlotte didn't find it surprising; but she had known Mrs. Gamalion much longer than he had. She was pleased to learn that extreme old age had not reduced Mrs. Gamalion to dull docility. A garden full of outsize trees, a front hedge that was the Waterloo of the town council, showed that she had kept her fighting spirit to the last.

"But I shall have to have the trees cut down, and the hedge trimmed," she thought. She knew she was incapable of defying town councils and grumbling neighbours; nor in fact did she want to.

Meanwhile the trees remained, and the rampant hedge, and the bulging Christmas-stocking of a house. It was almost as if Mrs. Gamalion were jogging Charlotte's elbow, urging her to be firm, reminding her of how firmness paid. Her voice underlined words as her pen underlined them on the postcards.

"Of course you can't go home next week," she cried gaily. "Why, you haven't seen *anything*! Warley was only the beginning – and you went there, anyway, *much* too late in the year!"

Yes, I did, thought Charlotte, but I had to go when I could. Tomorrow there may be a letter from Alison . . .

"Why, you *silly* girl – surely you're not afraid of Alison! Tomorrow you're going to start sorting out all this stuff. The precious souvenirs – and my Book – and all the letters! Why, it will be like being back in Italy, Charlotte – back in Menaggio which did you so much good although of course it was *much* too early in the year and I wouldn't have been there myself except for thinking I'd meet Poppy Castleton who had that villa by the lake. And then she wasn't there – but I met you and that was splendid, wasn't it? I can't *think* why your people sent you to Menaggio as early in the year as that!"

Too early or too late. So often it seemed to be one or the other, and people complained of it and felt a grievance against Time for being so contrary. But Charlotte could only rejoice at the good fortune that had brought her to Menaggio at that season, to the Pensione Bellavista where her benefactress always stayed.

CHAPTER IV

"OF COURSE the Signora knows me! I stay here every year and bring all my friends. I can't tell you how many people I've sent to this pensione," Mrs. Gamalion declared. "It's a wonderful position – the best in Menaggio – but don't forget you have to be *firm* with them!"

Her firmness had transferred Alice and Muriel to a bedroom they did not like, and Mrs. Moley to one with a balcony and a view. The bedroom of Alice and Muriel was on the second floor and smelt, they complained, of something funny, not quite drains or mice but – well, funny. Mrs. Moley's new bedroom looked much more expensive than the one she had left and she was surprised to find it cost no more. Much later, she wondered whether Mrs. Gamalion had made some private arrangement with the Signora whereby Alice and Muriel paid the price of her room, and she of theirs. It was the kind of arrangement Mrs. Gamalion excelled at making, though generally to benefit herself.

But in the beginning Mrs. Moley put it all down to Mrs. Gamalion's fluent Italian and her kind heart. She did not quite understand why Alice and Muriel should be relegated to the second floor but she was sure there must be a good reason for it.

"The Villa Carlotta – Bellagio – the trip round the lake!" Mrs. Gamalion exclaimed. "Do you mean to say you've been here a fortnight and not done any of them? Oh, you lazy girl!"

Waves of energy radiated from her, waves of enjoyment of life, enthusiasm, absurd but endearing skittishness. They beat on the glass shell and it splintered into fragments. Mrs. Moley felt the sunlight, saw the blueness of beautiful Como in all its dazzling reality, and was suddenly presented with a world full of people alive.

For the Villa Carlotta Mrs. Gamalion wore a purple linen dress, a shady hat trimmed with feathers, and carried a parasol. Her thick black hair was coiled on the top of her head in a then archaic style and the feathered hat perched on top of it looked dreadfully insecure in spite of two large hatpins. She wore white lisle stockings and pointed shoes ornamented with steel buckles. She was heavily made-up with rouge and lipstick and a creamy-white powder much too light for her skin, but the general effect was rather dashing. She had fine dark eyes and she must have been handsome in her youth. A popular, confident girl, Mrs. Moley thought enviously.

Alice and Muriel accompanied them. Indeed it was for their sake that the excursions took place. "I know every *inch* of this place," Mrs. Gamalion declared, as she was to declare everywhere. "I could take you round blindfold!"

Her protégées did not put her to the test. They were clearly ashamed of Mrs. Gamalion in her conspicuous finery and they soon contrived to attach themselves to some acquaintances from the pensione and to drift away down the first alley that offered cover. Deploring their stupidity – there was no view down there, nothing at all to see – Mrs. Gamalion led Charlotte to the upper terrace, where there was a view and also a seat from which to admire it. "Just like a summer's day," she cried happily, opening her parasol.

Like a summer's day it seemed to Charlotte, but a better one than she had ever known. She felt the full force of her companion's lively interest dissolving her reserve as the hot sun had dissolved the morning mist. In no time at all she was telling Mrs. Gamalion the history of her brief married life.

"Gabriel was eighteen years older than I," she said. "He was a civil servant like my father . . . but my father died when I was six. Of course I'd known Gabriel for ages. He was – I was very fond of him."

It was the first time she had told the story to anyone, but not the first time she had heard it told. Listening to her own voice speaking so fluently she realized she was repeating a tale learnt by heart, a trite, sad little tale about a girl called Charlotte who did not seem to be herself.

She knew the tale by heart because they had told it so often, her mother and her good, solicitous friends; they had told it to her and she had believed it. An ideally happy marriage – a tragic bereavement. She had adored Gabriel with all her heart. Yes, but she had the baby. A shy, reserved girl, she felt it even more than we guessed. His child, his baby daughter, all she has left to live for.

In a calm voice Charlotte Moley continued to relate the story, with no more than minor revisions and omissions. It was the version she had been taught and she did not feel quite bold enough to repudiate it in public. But inwardly she was repudiating it all the time, with a wonderful feeling of new-found strength and freedom. The facts and dates were right, of course, the duration of her marriage, Gabriel's death from pneumonia, but almost everything else was wrong. The emotions they had given her, the inferences they had drawn, the heart-broken widowhood they had assigned her, even the maternal devotion that was to be her only outlet. They were wrong about everything; and she would never believe them again.

"You *poor* thing," Mrs. Gamalion interrupted. "I do feel for you most awfully. No wonder you looked so peaked! But Italy will do you all the good in the world – there's nothing like it! I've been through the same thing and I know what it means. . . ."

". . . He was so kind," finished Mrs. Moley, paying her last tribute to the dead. Kind Gabriel; well-meaning Gabriel; but I never adored him and my heart isn't broken after all.

"And it's all the worse when you're so young, just a girl – it seems like the end of everything! I know, I know, it happened to me too," Mrs. Gamalion assured her.

Not the end of everything, Mrs. Moley thought, because there had never been a beginning. But gratitude compelled her to postpone her rethinking and give her attention to her benefactress.

"I'm a war widow, you see," Mrs. Gamalion was saying. "Of course I married very young – no older than you – and it was all over in less than a year. He was in the army and I was a V.A.D. He was killed in eighteen-eighteen, just a year after our wedding!"

Charlotte Moley made sounds of sympathy.

"Of course everyone said I was *much* too young to get married – my parents were dead against it! All my friends too! But as I told them, I wasn't a *schoolgirl* – I was old enough to do my bit, old enough to be nursing in France and seeing all those awful sights. People say all those war weddings were a mistake but I've never regretted mine. I thought when Hubert was killed it seemed like the end of the world. That's how I know what you've been through, losing your husband when you're still just a girl!"

Again Charlotte made noises of sympathy. They were vague and non-committal yet in an odd way they were genuine. But she knew without a shadow of doubt that the story could not be true.

If Mrs. Gamalion had been 'just a girl' when she married in 1917 then she would be still under forty now. Yet in spite of her dashing clothes and her make-up – or perhaps because of them – it was immediately obvious that she was a good deal older than that.

How old, Charlotte could not guess. She hadn't till that moment given a thought to Mrs. Gamalion's age, and even now it did not seem important. She felt sorry for Mrs. Gamalion if she minded being – say – something over fifty, and at the same time she admired her for refusing to let this tiresome fact cramp her style. The fantasy of having been a girl-bride in the Great War was, she recognized, a necessary prelude to being abundantly alive today.

"And my story isn't true either," she thought. Though that wasn't quite the same thing, because she had dutifully accepted it as true until that moment, and in any case it was her own feelings, not the facts, that were in question. But somehow it strengthened the bond between her and her companion; that both of them should be holding themselves out as heartbroken girl-widows.

"There are Alice and Muriel coming back," Mrs. Gamalion exclaimed. "Now there will just be time to look round inside the villa before lunch. It's only the ground floor and not very interesting but we might as well see it while we're here."

While Alice and Muriel dawdled towards them Mrs. Gamalion had time to tell Charlotte that they were the daughters of very old friends, people she had known for years, otherwise she would not have brought them to Italy. She had known they would not care for Italy, they weren't a bit interested in that sort of thing, only in dogs and hunting, but their parents had persuaded her to take them in the hope that it would broaden their mind. They were awfully nice girls of course, but not half as much fun as the two she'd brought last year, Aileen Manners and Joan Carter-Browning, who had simply adored everything and longed to come with her again.

Charlotte guessed that Mrs. Gamalion did not bring girls to Italy for nothing. Perhaps she got expenses, or a fee for being a sort of chaperon. She hadn't the tactful manner of one who earned her living by these means, on the contrary she was independent and sometimes hot-tempered. It was an informal arrangement between friends whereby she 'kept an eye' on her sulky protégées – whose minds were so resistant to broadening that they might just as well have stayed at home.

Not that they attempted any open rebellion. They lacked the spirit, for one thing. But whenever possible they ignored her, as they had done coming off the steamer, and the apathy they showed towards the Italian scene was also a rejection of her enthusiasm. Perhaps it was a similar reaction to her abundant energy that made them so listless, so easily tired.

Charlotte was to remember them as forever complaining of some physical woe: the burning sun, the fatiguing stairs, the cricks in their necks brought on by too much sight-seeing.

But that was later, when they had reached Florence and apathy had really set in.

"Am going to Florence with some other people from this pensione," Charlotte wrote. "Shall not be home till the 15th. Hope you won't mind having Alison till then."

Brevity was permissible on a postcard, but as a sop to tradition she added, "Writing soon". It was her mother, not her conscience, that needed placating but at this distance the matter did not seem urgent. It was a distance not to be measured in miles.

Travelling with Mrs. Gamalion was both exhausting and exhilarating, something like a cavalry charge led by the Red Queen. Naturally there must have been hours of sitting in trains, but in retrospect it was all spirited action – rushing down the hill to the steamer, pushing through crowds to get good seats, racing up and down railway platforms in search of coffee and ladies' lavatories, counting and transporting and re-counting the luggage, leaping out of trains before they had quite stopped. "Faster, faster!" was Mrs. Gamalion's watchword when travelling, for she had learned that it paid to be fast and first. Porters, corner seats, an unfairly large share of the luggage-rack, were for those who could get there first and grab them. Hard on her heels came Charlotte, rushing, pushing, leaping in a manner not unworthy of her mentor, but Alice and Muriel lagged behind and had to be waited for.

The blazing afternoon changed imperceptibly into golden evening, long shadows crept across the hills and the olive trees turned grey. "I told Mrs. Mollison to meet us," said Mrs. Gamalion, and Muriel whispered to Alice, "More fool she if she comes." Over their drooping heads Charlotte stared out at the beginnings of Florence, the anonymous approaches to a city, the view-from-a-train-window that is the curtain hiding the stage.

There on the platform at Florence had waited the first of Mrs. Gamalion's Old Faithfuls – or rather, the first of them whom Charlotte was to meet. There must have been others long before her time; and she could recognize herself, twenty years later, as probably the last. An odd collection, she thought, as odd as Mrs. Gamalion herself, of people who had been fascinated, mesmerised, bullied, or perhaps like the young Charlotte liberated and consequently evermore grateful; an odd collection of people whose function it was to be useful. More fools they, but they came.

With parrot shrieks Mrs. Gamalion identified Mrs. Mollison as the train drew in, and Mrs. Mollison, hearing the shrieks above the babel of other reunions, forced her way along the crowded platform and was in time to receive the luggage, which was handed out to her piece by piece through the corridor window.

"No need for a porter, Margery," Mrs. Gamalion screamed. "We can manage it ourselves now you're here."

Mrs. Mollison, middle-aged but sinewy, accepted her role of substitute porter without argument, and the arguments of Alice and Muriel were drowned in the flood of talk; for by now Mrs.

Gamalion was fully roused from the torpor of the afternoon and eager to hear all the news of her world's capital.

The world of English ladies abroad; of English ladies escaping from dull winter loneliness and hurrying south to the sun; the world of English ladies living in pensiones, meeting one another annually in Bordighera or Alassio, discussing the rate of exchange and the churchmanship of the new British chaplain, frequenting the tea-rooms run by other, more adroit English ladies and the library run by a genial but uncommendable lady who had taken to drink.

The world in which English ladies were allowed, and even expected, to be cultured, to have at least a smattering of know-ledge about the Guelphs and Ghibellines and to know the great names of the Renaissance and where the masterpieces were to be seen. Baedakers were unnecessary when one had been abroad so often but little books about painting and architecture were carried and consulted; the more talented ladies also carried sketching materials, and the richer ones cameras.

But the really rich did not belong to this world but to another one, of luxury hotels and first-class travel, to which few English ladies abroad could aspire.

It was a world that stretched from Nice to the Adriatic, but for Mrs. Gamalion and her friends Florence was the capital. Rome was considered too big, Venice too damp and smelly, and only the gamblers, the unrepresentative desperadoes, looked on Monte Carlo as the centre. No, it was to Florence they returned, year after year; to walk beside the Arno and drive out to Fiesole; to gaze at Giotto's tower and Brunelleschi's dome; and to recollect, in late and worsening seasons, the season of first wonder and delight.

Menaggio had been but a break in the journey, a slow intro-duction, one might say, to the great theme. In Menaggio Charlotte had been rescued from bondage; here in Florence she was made free of the world. The world of English ladies abroad, cultured and untrammelled, with no overbearing elders to dragoon them into broken-hearted widowhood, the world of beauty, sunshine, and happiness.

*

Sunshine. How could Mrs. Gamalion have borne to live in a house that never got any sun, Charlotte wondered.

Even if it had been a fine day the trails of ivy, the cobwebs and dirt on the windows, would have kept out the light, and on this wet afternoon the drawing-room was as dark as a cave — a miser's cave of treasures hoarded and hidden for years.

She switched on the standard lamp by the fireplace, the only lamp in the room and a very dim one. The poor little treasures could not have stood anything brighter, for even in this pale glow they were revealed as shabby and worthless and quite incredibly dirty. But here among the relics of an unknown life (how little she had been told, how little, really, she had discovered!) was the past they had shared, pressed flat like faded flowers between the pages of a book. The book was written in a language she could not read, but the flowers were still recognisable.

Here were the dreadful watercolours painted by old Colonel Hetherington – no fewer than six of them framed in passe-partout and hanging in a crooked row about the desk.

Views in Tuscany, but unidentifiable; for Colonel Hetherington had painted very badly. A hillside and some cypresses, blue sky and perhaps a campanile, and there was his picture, ready to be framed and sold to some weak-willed fellow-guest. He did not charge much but they would have been expensive at any price.

"She must have been sorry for him," Charlotte decided, since no one could suppose that Mrs. Gamalion had been weak-willed.

And indeed he had needed the money, everyone knew that and forgave him for touting his pictures. But not everyone felt sorry enough to buy them.

And here was the bulky album, known baldly as "My Book", which had accompanied Mrs. Gamalion everywhere. It was tattered and broken-backed, stuffed with photographs and cuttings and autographs and family crests, with captions and comments scrawled where there was space, interleaved with loose photographs which had never been pasted in and now never would be. Here at the beginning, among a welter of unknown names and faces, Charlotte recognised one or two Old Faithfuls in an earlier stage of their existence. Margery Mollison looking unexpectedly frivolous in V.A.D. uniform, Sister Wainsford looking coy in a very modest bathing-dress. "It's cold in Blighty," Sister Wainsford had scribbled beneath her photograph, thus dating it almost as clearly as if she had put the year, and underneath Margery Mollison's, Mrs. Gamalion had written: "Rouen."

All that, Blighty and Rouen and the hospital groups and antique ambulances, belonged to the unknown life. Charlotte turned the pages rapidly, until the groups stopped being in uniform and the background changed to Italy.

Why, here was Harley Coker, poised on the edge of a precipice and turning back for a last fastidious glance at the world he seemed about to leave. Behind him, empty space and distance; in the foreground, a small footstool. How did that get there, she wondered, before wondering why the footstool should now seem more interesting, more mysterious and melancholy, than Harley Coker who had once been all those things and more. She sighed for the sighs she had once expended on Sir Galahad; then, turning the page, she frowned.

For here was Miss Glyn-Gibson, that snake in the grass, tucked into the corner of a picnic group and rather out of focus.

She could be identified however by her boots and her brave smile.

Charlotte recognized the scene of the picnic, and the snake's presence in that scene surprised her. Surely Miss Glyn-Gibson had never accompanied them to San Mamette, she belonged to a different summer and a different place. She belonged to Florence. Yet memory recalled that her materialization in Florence had not been unforeseen, that her coming had been expected and had cast a faint shadow in advance.

Yes, of course. But it hadn't been at a picnic. It was not in Italy but in London, at Mrs. Gamalion's club, that Charlotte had first met Miss Glyn-Gibson. She thought it must have been during the winter after her first visit to Italy. That miserable winter when she had almost slipped back into being the heart-broken young widow of the Marston legend, the daughter of splendid Mrs. Field and the mother of bonny little Alison.

In Marston, where she had lived all her life, legends of that kind, touching and edifying, had a power it was hard to resist. Particularly when they were legends sponsored by Mrs. Field. Even now the legend persisted, kept alive by Alison who had inherited all her grandmother's strength of character and also her liking for conventional categories.

In Marston, Charlotte thought ruefully, she had never quite managed to disentangle herself from the lay-figure in widow's weeds.

CHAPTER V

ALISON's letter arrived the next morning. It lay on the mat looking innocently thin and brief, and for a moment Charlotte allowed herself to hope that this meant acquiescence.

She should have known better. It wasn't in Alison's nature, any more than it had been in her grandmother's, to agree without argument, without a careful balancing of all the pros and cons. 'Discussing the whole thing sensibly' had been Mrs. Field's term for it; and the phrase stood out of the letter now, written in ink no blacker than the rest but immediately catching the eye.

Charlotte sighed. All at once she was back in the past among her advisers, being guided in the way she should go. She hadn't after all avoided the sensible discussion and the lengthy arguments, the only difference was that she would have to face them here in Nything instead of on the home ground. Alison's letter was short because Alison herself was coming north as soon as she could manage it; and this in itself held an ominous hint of determined opposition. It wouldn't be to agree, to settle a few minor details, that Alison was coming to Nything.

". . . the first weekend I can manage. A pity it's such a long journey, but I'll wait until I can get a Monday off, to give us more time for discussing the whole thing sensibly.

"We're very busy at the Ministry at present but I'll let you know when Mr. Goldsmith can spare me."

And Evelyn sent her love.

"Oh dear," said Charlotte, looking round with Alison's eyes at the disgraceful kitchen. For that weekend, she thought, it might be better to return to the hotel where she had spent the first two nights before she moved into her inheritance. But of course Alison would want to see the house, and she would have an argument ready to hand if it wasn't, by any standards, inhabitable.

How lucky that Alison was so conscientious about the Ministry, and so indispensable to its functioning. Charlotte could never believe that civil servants were overworked but she was thankful that Mr. Goldsmith and his subordinates were at present busier than usual, otherwise Alison might have been in Nything tomorrow. As it was there would be time to do some cleaning up and clearing out; which wouldn't bring the house up to Alison's standards but would stop her from utterly condemning it.

"Scullery waste-pipe," she wrote, listing the priorities on the envelope of her daughter's letter. "Anti-moth powder. Front door. Bathroom. Bedroom for A. Air more blankets. Clean the oven."

Then she stopped, feeling there were more priorities than she could deal with even if she had seven maids with seven mops to assist her. But her panic had lessened; the prospect of facing Alison in these surroundings no longer appalled her, because the surroundings themselves gave her an assurance she had never known in Marston. Whatever Alison might say about the inheritance it would support and sustain its possessor.

"My House," she said, as proudly as Mrs. Gamalion used to say, "My Book."

The house in Marston had belonged to Charlotte's mother. Charlotte had lived in it until she married and then gone back to it in 1939, when Mrs. Field had had her nearly-fatal illness and needed a daughter's care. Alison had been almost ten years old and had welcomed the move; for even in those days she and her grandmother had much in common, and the big house with its solid, gleaming furniture had been Alison's ideal of a home.

But then, she was privileged, she was Mrs. Field's only grandchild and had inherited her looks and her character, she was treated as the rightful heir – while Charlotte remained a mere dependent, a not very efficient nurse and housekeeper.

The house no longer belonged to them yet in a sense it was still Alison's. It was she who had settled its future after Mrs. Field's death, negotiated with the purchaser and seen to it that they got a suitable flat. She had been only twenty at the time; the builder who had bought the house had been greatly impressed by her good sense – and also perhaps by her youth and good looks – and many people had congratulated Charlotte on having so capable a daughter.

"I was too tired to bother," Charlotte thought now. "I let my chance go by. I was glad to have her settle everything."

If she had not been so tired, worn out by the strain of nursing her bedridden mother through the difficult years of the war and its aftermath, she would have tried to get Alison to leave the neighbourhood. It would have been a tussle, but she might have succeeded. They could have moved to a new little house in the new part of the town, well away from Chamberlain Avenue and its painful, oppressive memories.

But of course they were not painful or oppressive for Alison. She had greatly admired her grandmother, and in her grandmother's eyes she could do no wrong.

"Anyway she doesn't like the new part of the town," Charlotte reflected. "She'd never have gone there. It would have been like going back to Rivermead."

She thought about Rivermead. Gabriel had bought the house when they were engaged, without consulting her. More significantly, he had not consulted her mother either, and only Mrs. Field's genuine affection for him had kept her from taking offence. Or at least from showing it openly. Her criticisms, which were chiefly concerned with the situation of Rivermead and its distance from Chamberlain Avenue, were an oblique indication of what she was feeling.

"It's convenient for the station," Gabriel had explained.

He went up to London daily, as Alison did nowadays.

But even then there was a good bus-service to convey him to the station from the select heights where Mrs. Field lived, where Gabriel had lived in his own mother's lifetime, and where it had been taken for granted he and Charlotte would continue to live when they were married.

Mrs. Field was never reconciled to Rivermead, though after Gabriel's early death it acquired for a while the hallowed status of a memorial chapel. But in the ten years Charlotte remained there its sanctity had time to fade, and its inconveniences, as a residence for a widowed daughter, to become steadily more apparent. By and by Mrs. Field grew convinced that the dampness of the low-lying district near the river had given poor Gabriel his pneumonia.

But it was Mrs. Field's own illness – that grappling-iron for dutiful daughters – that brought Charlotte back to Chamberlain Avenue.

"Gabriel was wise," she thought. "He was fond of Mother but he knew better than to live in her pocket. He bought Rivermead because it was the other side of the town."

When she looked back Gabriel and his house seemed perfectly to match each other. Rivermead hadn't been a house to fall in love with, but it had been modestly prosperous and comfortable . . . with nothing to distinguish it from its neighbours but the flagpole on the small front lawn. The flagpole gave it a touch of pomposity even when the flag wasn't flying, but it had come from Gabriel's parental home and was a symbol of family piety.

Poor Gabriel. She had never been in love with him but she remembered him now with affection. He had been pompous but well-meaning, fussy but kind. Their marriage had not been put to the test, it had ended while it still resembled the new house, all fresh paint and clean wallpaper, unmarked by the scars of time. And Rivermead had sheltered her from the storms, even after it grew shabby.

Alison had known almost from babyhood that Granny could not come to see them as often as she would have liked because Rivermead was such an awkward journey from Chamberlain Avenue. Charlotte had known it too. It was in a Rivermead frame of mind – gently secure and relaxed – that she read through her list of priorities and decided to start with the front door. It wasn't the most urgent item, but never mind . . . if Rivermead was an awkward journey from Chamberlain Avenue, Nything was even more so. And she wanted to see what the Green looked like, standing at her own front door.

She prized off the strips of old carpet and newspaper tacked round the door's edges, and with some difficulty drew back the lower bolt. But the top bolt defeated her, nor could she turn the key in the old-fashioned lock. Mrs. Gamalion had fastened up the door fifteen years ago and the lock was probably solid with rust.

The yellow strips of newspaper were dated November 1939. The first winter of the war, Charlotte thought, the winter we struggled with the blackout, the winter when Mother's illness began. All that dark winter seemed to have been spent hurrying from Rivermead to Chamberlain Avenue and back again, until she gave in and sold her own house and went to live with her mother. So sensible, the only thing to do.

She remembered Mrs. Gamalion's postcards, a steady flow of patriotic war-cries interspersed with complaints that the Red Cross would not send her, a trained V.A.D., to France. That was in the war's beginning and Mrs. Gamalion was sixty-nine, but no one knew it. She had always kept her age a secret, even from close friends like Margery Mollison.

"I don't know how old she is," Margery Mollison had said, long ago on a summer evening in Florence. "She's older than me, but you must never say I told you. It seems silly, but she minds dreadfully. And she doesn't *look* older than me, does she?"

"No, I suppose not," Charlotte had replied, not knowing how to answer the question politely. "Neither of you looks old," she had added, shivering a little in spite of the warm evening. Margery Mollison had laughed, saying that everyone felt cold after a visit to the Hudsons but after seeing them no one else looked *old*, and had taken her arm and walked her along by the Arno, along the southern bank to the Ponte alle Grazie, not the shortest way back to their lodging but a walk in the sun was what they needed after visiting the crumbling palazzo where the Hudsons lived with their ghosts.

"No colder than this house," Charlotte thought now, feeling the draught blowing in through the cracks she had just unsealed.

The draught seemed to grow stronger, and a minute later she realized that the back door must be open as well and that some-one was knocking to attract her attention. She had been far away, watching the swallows and the evening sky with Margery Molli-son at her elbow.

"I just looked in to see how you were getting on," Mrs. Bateman remarked. She had come through the kitchen and was standing in the hall, so it was hardly necessary for Charlotte to explain that she was trying to unlock the front door.

"I heard from Alison this morning," she said. "She wants to come for a weekend, to see the house. So I thought I'd better make a start."

"Next weekend? There won't be much time –"

"No, not next weekend. But quite soon, I think."

"Not next weekend," Mrs. Bateman echoed on a note of relief, though she carefully refrained from glancing at the dusty chaos around her.

"It's hard to know where to begin, isn't it? But I thought if I could get the front door open it would seem more welcoming."

"First impressions are important. I dare say your daughter might object – well, she might think it odd, if the front door didn't work."

"I've been trying to make it work. But I can't turn the key."

"You'll probably need a locksmith. Or perhaps Robert could do it, if it's only stiff. Men are stronger than women."

Charlotte wasn't listening, she had turned back to face the door and was trying the top bolt again, Mrs. Bateman was a nice woman, kind and sensible, but at the moment she was a nuis-ance. "Perhaps if I stood on a chair," she said, half to herself and half to Mrs. Bateman.

There was no response. Charlotte looked round and her visitor had disappeared. She must have gone back to the kitchen to get a chair; her practical eye would have seen at once that the chair in the hall was unsafe. One of its legs was missing and only the wall kept it upright.

"There's a strong chair by the window," Charlotte called after her.

Again there was no response. No sound of chair-shifting either; and when Charlotte went to the kitchen, no Mrs. Bateman. Could she have taken offence, felt herself to be unwanted and simply departed? It did not seem likely, she was not a hyper-sensitive woman, or quick-tempered, and she surely would not have left without saying goodbye. Besides, her shopping-basket was still on the kitchen table and the back door was wide open.

While she stood wondering Charlotte heard the click of the backyard gate, and when she looked out Mrs. Bateman was coming up the path towards her, as if she had only just arrived. But she was not alone. She was accompanied by a clergyman, bespectacled and middle-aged, who walked rather slowly as though he were reluctant to advance.

"He was waiting for me outside but I fetched him in," Mrs. Bateman said briskly. "This is my son Robert, whom you know about. Robert – Mrs. Moley."

Charlotte could hardly believe it. Though her appreciation of his good looks had been lessened by hearing that he was delicate, indecisive, and easily bored, she had retained the impression that Robert was quite young. It was stupid, she realized now; for hadn't Mrs. Bateman distinctly said that the photograph was taken a long time ago? But in spite of being told so she had somehow not grasped that he must be – well, at least as old as herself.

She held out her hand and then withdrew it, for it was black with cobwebs and dust. Robert looked at her and smiled. So for a fleeting moment he resembled the boy of the photograph, but as a dry leaf resembles a green one.

"I didn't know you'd arrived," she said.

"He got here two days ago," said Mrs. Bateman, "but yesterday he was resting."

Charlotte could see herself annoying Alison in exactly the same way, drawing attention to something she did not want discussed. But Robert's annoyance barely betrayed itself.

"Shall I try to turn that key for you?" he asked.

They went into the hall. Charlotte was still confused by her error, which seemed all the more absurd when she remembered the other photographs, those blurred snapshots of the almost grown-up grandchildren who were Robert's nephew and niece.

"Oil," said Robert. "That's what it needs. Have you got an oil can?"

These were not the first words spoken since they entered the house. A part of her had been hearing and responding to Mrs. Bateman's neighbourly talk, which had flowed on a little faster than usual since Robert joined them. To cover his quietness, perhaps, but it had covered Charlotte's confusion as well. Or so she hoped now, when she at last managed to wrench her mind away from her absurd mistake and attend to the real Robert, who was battling with the rusty lock and calling for oil.

Mrs. Bateman's glance was expressive. "He wants an oil can," she said.

A cherished son, Charlotte thought. She felt that future good relations with Mrs. Bateman might be imperilled if she did not produce an oil can instantly, but luckily she remembered seeing one in the shed outside the back door. She fetched it, and subsequently fetched a skewer to clear the blocked spout, and a bit of rag to catch the drips, and a pair of pliers to help Robert get a grip on the knob of the bolt. It was Mrs. Bateman who demanded these latter items but Charlotte could see she was speaking on Robert's behalf, anticipating his wants and saving him the trouble of asking for them. Mrs. Bateman stood beside him holding the things he was going to need, while Charlotte sped to and fro fetching them. It was diverting to find herself back in a domestic situation she had almost forgotten, one of the female entourage attending a man engaged on household repairs.

Squeaking, the bolt slid back. Mrs. Bateman voiced her appreciation, gleefully echoed by Charlotte. Robert transferred his attention to the lock, which he had already dosed with oil. While he wrestled with it Charlotte found herself thinking about Harley Coker.

She couldn't imagine Sir Galahad being handy about the house but he had certainly had an adoring mother in the background. In the background, for Charlotte, she had remained, because owing to some physical weakness she had not accompanied him to Italy. (How odd, Charlotte thought, that memory so obstinately refused to record the exact nature of Mrs. Coker's weakness, which Harley had certainly discussed with her.) Nevertheless she had been immanently present, watching over her beloved son as Mrs. Bateman was watching over Robert now.

Yes; it was Robert's mother rather than Robert himself that had prompted those thoughts about Harley Coker. Observing her as she stood beside her son Charlotte was carried straight back to a distant afternoon at Fiesole, where the disembodied spirit of Mrs. Coker had stood beside Harley and saved him from making a fatal mistake. Poor Harley – Charlotte could still see the change that came over him as he listened to that inaudible voice, and in retrospect she could smile at his swerve back into safety. The speed of their departure from the sundrenched amphitheatre, the cultured hour that had followed, talking to the archaeologists and studying the new excavations, were episodes which could now be viewed as comedy. But how painful they had been at the time.

Harley Coker and his Mama, she knew, had once lived in Nything; that was how he came to be in Mrs. Gamalion's Italian party that summer. But Mrs. Coker must be dead by now and her son gone elsewhere, for it was years since Mrs. Gamalion had mentioned either of them.

Perhaps they had left Nything in Mrs. Coker's lifetime, for it wasn't like Mrs. Gamalion to omit to mention a death or a funeral – a funeral which she would certainly have attended.

In her latter years she had much enjoyed attending the funerals of her contemporaries, though her triumph at having survived them could never be openly admitted because it would have meant revealing her own age.

"I must ask Mrs. Bateman about them," Charlotte thought; which reminded her that she hadn't for the past five minutes asked Mrs. Bateman anything, or shown any interest in Robert's good-neighbourly struggles.

"Please don't bother," she began, feeling that he had bothered enough. Or that his mother might be thinking so.

Mrs. Bateman's reply rather confirmed it. "You'll have to get a locksmith," she said.

"Yes, I will. It's very kind of you to have tried, but I think the lock must be broken."

"Very likely it is. You'd better give up, Robert. The lock is probably broken. I shall have to get a new one. Thank you so much for trying, but I'm afraid it isn't any good going on."

"Just a minute," said Robert.

It was typical of the handy man, the man about the house, to insist on continuing the struggle long after his female entourage had seen that the thing could not be done.

If Mrs. Bateman recalled Mrs. Coker, Robert at that moment recalled poor Gabriel; Charlotte could see herself and Cook steadying Gabriel on a stepladder and could remember feeling Cook nearer than a sister in their shared longing for him to stop trying to fix a plug in the crumbling plaster wall, which both of them knew would be inadequate for the picture he wanted to hang there. And so it had proved. She looked with amusement at Robert's unresponsive back, his head so obstinately turned away from them. We shall be here all the morning, she thought, and in the end he will explain to us, as if we had never suggested it, that the lock is broken.

And he was a clergyman, she thought. There was no reason why the clergy should be less handy than other men but somehow one thought of them as rather unpractical. Though that was probably out of date, because nowadays the clergy could not afford to employ skilled artisans, they must have to learn how to do minor repairs themselves – especially inhabiting, as so many of them did, dilapidated vicarages where repairs were often needed. All the same, this particular clergyman struck her as being one of the old, unpractical kind, undoubtedly good-hearted but incapable of mending anything.

At that instant, to confound her mocking thoughts, the key yielded to Robert's persistence. Almost before she realised what had happened Charlotte saw him seize the handle and tug the door open. A shower of dust and fragments of newspaper fluttered round him as he stepped forward over the threshold. It was a moment of dramatic triumph when he stood there in the sunlight with his entourage confessing itself mistaken.

"I didn't think you'd manage it, Robert! I felt sure the lock was broken."

In his moment of triumph Robert remained modest.

"Oil was all it needed," he said. "Oil and a little coaxing. Nothing to what you're going to need for the next obstacle."

Beyond him lay a mass of ground-ivy, and the towering hedge. Through a sort of peephole in the hedge, where the gate was, Charlotte could glimpse the road and the Green, but she could not have reached them without wading through the ivy, which had obliterated the path as well as festooning itself over objects that might once have been rose bushes and a sundial.

She thought of Alison wading through ivy to the front door . . .

"I'll come round tomorrow and clear the path," Robert was saying.

Mrs. Bateman's intervention was prompt. "Oh Robert, I don't think you'd better. It's too hard work for you."

"Of course he mustn't. I'll find someone else to do it. I expect there are jobbing gardeners –"

"Just the path," Robert said mildly. "I'm not sure whether I can deal with the hedge, but that doesn't matter so much if we can get to the gate."

He was speaking to both of them, but more particularly to his mother. Charlotte was about to protest again when it occurred to her that the mild voice concealed a degree of exasperation. She changed her mind; for she too had been ruled by a mother who always knew what was best for her.

"Well, just the path," she said. "If you're sure it won't be a bother."

To placate Mrs. Bateman she added that he was not to come if it was a wet morning, or a very cold one, or if something more important turned up.

CHAPTER VI

"I MUST get going," Charlotte said to herself at intervals. "I really must make a start."

But capricious Time was favouring her now, giving her the feeling that clocks and days had a more leisurely pace in Nything. This was literally true of the clocks in the house; the only two that went at all were always slow, sometimes stopping altogether and needing a tap or shake to set them off again. Neither of them, moreover, was an alarm clock, which after years of being ruled by a shrilling bell was a great relief. Charlotte was not a late sleeper but she liked to lie awake in bed in the early morning, knowing that no clamorous alarm clock would order her to get up.

Not one alarm clock but three had rent the morning air in Marston. Alison's clock was just the other side of a thin dividing wall and Charlotte could hear Evvie's extra loud one in the bedroom across the passage. Evvie wasn't deaf but she was a heavy sleeper and needed a really loud bell to rouse her.

The three alarm clocks were synchronized and they had to be instantly obeyed or the careful routine would be disorganized. Breakfast must not be a minute late or Alison and Evvie would miss the bus that took them to the station and the train that took them to London. Alison had worked out the routine, allowing sufficient time – but no more – for every phase. As she said, it was just as inefficient to get up too early as to get up too late.

Lying in bed at Nything, with a mute tin clock ticking erratically on the mantelpiece and the sea breeze stirring the curtains, Charlotte wondered what was happening at Marston now. Who was getting breakfast? Who would wash it up? There were her other tasks too, the sweeping and dusting, the silver to be cleaned on Tuesdays, the floors to be polished on Thursdays; a timetable of domestic duties thoughtfully planned by Alison so that things shouldn't pile up. "If you follow the chart, Mother, you'll get through it much more easily. Housework isn't a problem in a flat this size if you do it methodically – one special job every day and just the ordinary dusting. Of course Evelyn and I will give a hand with the spring-cleaning, but I honestly think you could cope with the rest if you don't let it pile up."

And if I'd been more efficient, Charlotte thought.

She knew the allotted tasks always took longer than the allotted time, partly because of interruptions and partly because of inefficiency. She dawdled, stopped to look out of windows, forgot her shopping list and had to make a hasty second journey to the shops; or someone came, a neighbour or the woman with tracts or the man with sweepclean brushes, and whoever it was could never be briskly dismissed because it was not in her power to be ruthless with talkative callers.

Alison and Evvie would be much quicker than she was. They would suffer no interruptions, they would never forget their shopping lists. Still, they would have to do the housework between them (neither would be content to let it go and live in squalor) and they would find it took time, even if they were efficient and quick. And the morning routine, the synchronized clocks and planned action, would have to be re-arranged to include the cooking of breakfast and probably the washing-up.

"Oh well, they'll learn to manage," Charlotte thought tranquilly. "And Evvie is quite a good cook."

"Evelyn," she said aloud. It always irritated Alison when she failed to remember that Evelyn had grown out of being Evvie.

It was a sunny morning. The tide was high and from Mrs. Gamalion's bedroom window she could see four ships coming up the channel one after the other, looking near enough to be touched from the esplanade railing. They were quite small, paint-scarred and weatherbeaten (tramp-steamers, she thought vaguely), but it was enchanting to watch them sail past in the morning sunshine with only the width of the Green between her and the procession, and beyond them the gleaming water stretching to the horizon. When the mudflats were covered the estuary looked much bigger and Charlotte quite understood why Nything proclaimed itself to be 'on sea'. She understood why Mrs. Gamalion's postcards enthused about the charms of Nything – our dear old Green, the mild and healthy air, the splendid view from my bedroom window – and why, even in feeble old age, she had tried to escape from the nursing-home and return to her much-loved ruin. Standing at the window, watching the ships disappear into the haze, she began to wonder whether Mrs. Gamalion had bequeathed the house to her precisely because it was not a ruin but a stronghold, a place one would not readily abandon and from which one could not easily be dislodged.

From the front windows downstairs there was of course no view at all; trailing ivy obscured the glass, and the high privet hedge hid the Green. After breakfast Charlotte opened the front door and gazed at the ivy-covered garden. She wondered whether Robert Bateman would come to clear the path, or whether his mother would dissuade him. Like Harley Coker's mother.

But the comparison was far-fetched. To begin with, Charlotte could not imagine Harley Coker offering to undertake such a task . . . those long-fingered, artistic hands were eloquent in gesture but quite unsuited to manual toil and Sir Galahad could justifiably have claimed that knight-errantry was a different vocation from jobbing gardening. And his mother – Charlotte had never met her but she felt certain that Mrs. Coker wasn't really like Mrs. Bateman. A subtler character altogether, who kept watch and ward over Harley without seeming to and never, ever, argued with him in public. Or perhaps in private either.

She was delicate, she had known much unhappiness (Harley's silence about his father led Charlotte to suppose it had been matrimonial unhappiness); and of course she was wonderfully brave and uncomplaining. A shining angel of a mother. "I should like you to meet her," Harley had once said, and Charlotte had felt both tremulous and elated at the suggestion. But that was in Italy, and Mrs. Coker was far away in Nything. The meeting had never taken place.

"It's a disgrace," a loud voice protested. Footsteps sounded on the pavement and through the peephole above the gate Charlotte glimpsed two women, who stared at her in astonishment and then hurried on. They must have meant the hedge, she thought, and their astonishment was very natural; for until yesterday that door had not stood open since the winter of 1939. She laughed and turned to go in search of a pruning knife or secateurs – there might be some tools in the shed at the back where she had found the oil can. If Robert Bateman wasn't coming she would tackle the path herself.

But before she had begun the search he arrived, entering by the back gate and bringing with him a powerful pair of shears and a sharp, curved knife. These belonged to Mrs. Bateman and she had wanted him to bring a lot more, a saw and her parrot-beaked cutters and a fork and a rake, "And I should have needed the wheelbarrow as well, to transport them," he said cheerfully. "So I thought I'd see how I got on with these. I can go back for the others if I want them."

Robert looked different this morning. Partly because he was not dressed as a clergyman and the old tweed jacket and flannels seemed the clothes of a younger man, and partly because he was no longer defending himself against maternal solicitude and fussiness. Charlotte supposed that was the reason. There had been a kind of weariness or melancholy overshadowing him yesterday, even when he stood on the chair and wrestled with the rusty bolt, and today it was gone.

It was easy now to see him as the young man in the photograph but not so easy to imagine him indecisive and easily bored.

Nor was he a man who required an entourage. He made it clear that he did not expect Charlotte to hover round holding whichever implement he wasn't using or to run and search for others. "You'd better shut the front door to keep the dust out," he said. "No, I don't think I need anything else. I'll just see if there's a rake in your garden shed." He found a rake and presently he was hard at work outside, only stopping once to open the door again and hang his coat on the ricketty chair. It was Charlotte who opened the door next time, to suggest a rest and a cup of coffee. Her cry of joyful surprise was a tribute Robert richly deserved.

In one corner of the little plot, heaped against the hedge, was a great pile of ivy. In front of her was now visible a paved path to the gate, and to the left a patch that had once been a lawn, and yes, a sundial in the middle. A few straggling rose bushes still remained in the bed under the wall of the house and Robert was replanting one that had been pulled up in the struggle. He was kneeling down, scooping out a hole with his hands and spreading out the rose's scanty roots. Charlotte instantly forgot that he was not a man who required female assistance.

"Wait, I'll go and look for a trowel. Or a spade. There's bound to be one somewhere."

"Don't bother," said Robert. "I'm afraid the rose is dead anyway."

"But your hands!"

"My hands were dirty before I started digging the hole – digging can't make them any dirtier than battling with that ivy."

He looked up and smiled. His hands and arms were black, there were streaks of dirt on his face, his hair was dishevelled and there were trails of ivy clinging to his head and wreathing themselves round his neck. Like Bacchus and his pards, Charlotte thought, before she remembered that a clergyman should not be likened to Bacchus. Anyway Bacchus wore a leopard skin, and vine leaves not ivy, and in pictures looked much cleaner than poor Robert. Though probably not really – one couldn't imagine Greek satyrs taking hot baths. She pulled herself together, banished the thought of Bacchus, and began to thank Robert for his wonderful achievement.

More light filtered into the drawing-room now that the ivy had been pulled away from the window. Charlotte hoped that when the privet hedge had been dealt with there might even be some sunshine. But in the meantime there was enough light to see by without switching on the lamp, and in this subdued daylight she and Robert sat drinking coffee. Robert had washed off the worst of the grime in the bathroom while Charlotte was washing cups at the kitchen sink. They were Mrs. Gamalion's best cups, snatched out of a cupboard when she noticed that all the everyday ones were cracked, and they obviously had not been used for years, if ever. "Best", for Mrs. Gamalion, meant sacrosanct, inviolable. The house had several little hoards of this kind – glass, china, linen sheets, immaculate new blankets – which even in dire need had been considered too good to use. Charlotte felt the breath of Mrs. Gamalion's disapproval and heard the echo of her strident objections, but another part of her mind was wondering how Robert had disposed of his wreaths of ivy, which he must have observed in the bathroom's cracked mirror. He was looking different again, not just tidier and cleaner. Suddenly she saw why.

"You weren't wearing your spectacles when you arrived," she said.

There was an awkward pause. She hoped he did not consider this too personal a remark from someone who was almost a stranger. Then he said quietly:

"Sometimes I think I see better without them. On this fine morning . . . and your garden wasn't in full sunlight. It's a form of wishful thinking really."

The spectacles, she noticed now, were lightly tinted.

But Robert's low voice and her own sense of having in some way upset him made her uncertain how to reply. Perhaps she had misheard him. It seemed strange that he should be wearing tinted spectacles in so dark a room if he thought he saw better without them in the open air. No, he couldn't have said that. Confused, anxious to atone for an unkindness she had not intended, she remarked sympathetically that spectacles one didn't wear all the time were a great nuisance, always getting lost when one wanted them. At which he laughed and took his spectacles off again, laying them on the table beside his coffee cup.

"They won't get lost if I put them there, but you must remind me not to leave them behind me."

"I will," said Charlotte. "Things get lost very easily in this room because it's so overcrowded. I suppose I shall have to discard some of the treasures – but it's hard to know where to begin."

"What kind of treasures?"

"Oh, not valuable ones. Treasured possessions bringing messages from the past. This room is full of them."

"But whose past? Surely it was Mrs. Gamalion's, not yours."

"It was partly mine. Not her earlier life. I can't decipher those messages – I came in much later. It's a long time ago in my life, when I was young. . . ."

"And happy?"

"Yes and no. I was very unhappy when I first met her. And she – oh, I can't explain it. But I was like a blind person and she gave me back my sight."

Robert took it gravely. "Then you must owe her a great deal."

"More than I can say." She had said too much already and a voice from Marston reminded her that exaggeration was her pet failing, especially when she got on the subject of Mrs. Gamalion. (All those donkey's years ago.)

"Yes, it's a long time ago," she repeated, apologising to Alison as well as to Robert. "But coming here, seeing Mrs. Gamalion's house at last, and all her treasures, makes it seem much nearer. As if the years between had shrunk to nothing."

"But Time is like that – one's own personal scale is independent of the calendar. But what do you mean about seeing it at last? Did you never visit her here?"

"I was always going to, but something always happened." (How difficult it had been to arrange the holidays in Italy! An extra holiday at Nything had never been possible.) "But I used to meet her in London; we lived just outside London and she used to stay a lot at her club. And I went to Italy with her every year, after that first meeting, until – well, until she stopped going."

"I suppose the war stopped her going."

"It was a year or two before the war. She lost a good deal of money." Charlotte suppressed a torrent of information about Miss Glyn-Gibson and the little gold mine. "And after the war, when she was old, she – she withdrew. No more visits to London. She never left anything."

"But why didn't you – ?"

"I proposed myself once or twice but she always made some excuse not to have me. She didn't want me to visit her then. I think she hated being too old to pretend she was still young, and that was why she shut herself away. We corresponded of course; she kept up with everybody but in the end I was the only one left. The last of the Old Faithfuls."

"Tell me about the Old Faithfuls."

Was it the room itself that had roused Robert's interest? Charlotte believed so. All Mrs. Gamalion's friends were commemorated here; the threadbare brocade cushions had come from the Hudsons' palazzo, Margery Mollison had made the Afghan rug that covered the sofa, Colonel Hetherington had painted the Tuscan landscapes . . . everything in the room spoke of the past and of the people who had filled it. They spoke to Charlotte, so why not to Robert? So many voices, such a mingling of good and bad, absurdity and pathos; no one sitting here could be unaware of the past.

But not everyone would find it interesting. Robert was beguiled, he listened and laughed and asked questions. Charlotte forgot about the Marston distaste for Italian reminiscences and talked freely, confident that she wasn't boring him. Both of them were surprised when at length a third voice was heard, calling faintly at a distance and accompanied by knocking. "There must be someone at the back door," Charlotte said, adding unnecessarily that the bell was broken. As she left the room Robert remarked: "I expect that's my mother."

Mrs. Bateman stood at the back door looking self-conscious, as if her arrival had to be explained. She had been shopping; she had just looked in to see how things were going; if Robert was still there they could walk home together. She looked surprised to learn that he was still there and Charlotte wondered if she had really come to see how much he had accomplished and whether he had been overworked. She hastened to explain that Robert was no longer toiling in the garden; he had finished some time ago and they had been having coffee.

"Oh, good," said Mrs. Bateman. "I mean, how kind of you." Her intervention had been unnecessary, Robert had not been toiling all morning, and she seemed uncertain whether to go or stay.

"But you must come and see," cried Charlotte. "He's done wonders. And it didn't take him very long," she added reassuringly.

She led Mrs. Bateman through the hall and opened the front door to allow her a brief glimpse of the garden – the cleared path but not the heap of ivy in the corner, in case it suggested prodigious toil – before ushering her into the drawing-room. Robert was standing with his back to them looking at a picture on the opposite wall, and as he turned round Charlotte noticed he was once more wearing his spectacles. He would not need to be reminded not to leave them behind him.

CHAPTER VII

NOT just yet, but as soon as she could manage it. Alison's second letter was briefer than her first and Charlotte began to wonder whether Alison and Evvie were enjoying her absence and perhaps deciding not to oppose her wish to live in Nything. She hoped so. She was useful to them only domestically and they would soon learn to run the flat without her, and be happier on their own. The flat was too small for three people, especially if one of them belonged to a different generation, and they must feel it as much as she did. The feeling of slight claustrophobia and wanting to escape.

But it was not a new feeling for Charlotte, nor was it connected with the smallness of the flat. The Laurels had not been over-crowded in her mother's day. Big rooms, high and airy, a nice big garden for Alison to play in, a much healthier position alto-gether than Rivermead. For years these advantages had been dangled before Charlotte and for years she had rejected them, thankful at the end of every visit to leave the house which Mrs. Field insisted on speaking of as 'home'. It was of course her own home, but she spoke as if it were Charlotte's and Alison's too. As if no other house deserved the epithet. Perhaps Gabriel's house would have qualified for it if Gabriel had lived longer, but after his death Mrs. Field never called it anything but 'Rivermead'. She was determined, even then, that Alison should think of The Laurels as her only real home.

"The name is so important. In Italian there is no word for home, but we must think of something that suggests it, so that people will feel they want to live there permanently."

Who had said that? Charlotte hardly needed to ask herself. It was typical of Miss Glyn-Gibson that she should insinuate her voice into one's memory when one was thinking of something quite different. Joining in, turning the conversation in the way she wanted it to go, looking so insignificant that few people noticed her quiet arrival on the scene. She came and went, it was not until later – much later – that they wondered who she was and how the business had begun. Too late altogether by that time. Miss Glyn-Gibson had glided into their lives and glided out again, and everyone remembered the beginning differently.

For Charlotte it was in London. She had thought it was the first winter after her meeting with Mrs. Gamalion but the associations of that intruded remark proved her wrong. It was the second winter when Rivermead's shrine-like status had somewhat diminished and Alison was being taught to think of The Laurels as her home.

In those years Mrs. Gamalion belonged to three different clubs, a grand one in Mayfair, a less expensive one off Oxford Street, and a very cheap one at the farther end of the Cromwell Road where she occupied a bedroom but to which none of her friends was invited. She came up to London twice a year, for the January sales and the summer season, and from her hideout in the Cromwell Road she paid daily visits to the other two clubs to collect her mail and meet her numerous acquaintance.

It wasn't until after the second holiday in Italy that Charlotte even knew of the existence of the Cromwell Road club, but by then they were close friends and she was told about it in confidence.

"One must have a *good* club," Mrs. Gamalion explained, "but I couldn't possibly afford to stay there."

"But why have two? I mean, two you don't stay at."

"I meet so many people. I can't be always entertaining them at the same place. Really, Charlotte, you ought to join a club yourself. It's far, far cheaper in the long run!"

"Not for just an occasional day in London," Charlotte argued.

"Oh, I suppose not. But you're a lucky girl, you know – you can pop up for the day whenever you want to! It's different for me living in the north. I always say it *pays* to belong to a London club."

Charlotte could never see that it paid to belong to three, but she came to understand that the grand club in Mayfair served a useful purpose. Its address impressed people, and its writing paper came in very handy. Mrs. Gamalion was a tremendous correspondent but she never spent a penny on writing paper: she collected it in sheaves from her clubs and from every foreign lodging, so that she always had an assortment of different grades suitable for her different acquaintances. The club in Mayfair was also used for her 'best' luncheon parties, and it was here that Charlotte first met Miss Glyn-Gibson.

"Such an interesting woman – I know you'll like her, Charlotte. She's absolutely mad about living abroad! She knows Italy so well – almost as well as I do!"

"Did you say you'd met her in Italy?"

"No, no! I told you – Nora Pearson wrote to me about her. Nora had had a letter of introduction from someone else and she knew I'd be interested – of course Miss Glyn-Gibson wants to meet as many people as possible while she's in London, because of getting the thing started. A pity I didn't know sooner – I could have written round to heaps of people and fixed up a big meeting for her. But it's too late, with the sales all finished and everyone leaving. I'm off myself on Thursday and I shan't be up again until we start for Florence."

The January sales, Charlotte had learned, were a social event for Mrs. Gamalion and her friends, a welcome break in the long winter hibernation before they all set off for Italy. But now the sales were over and the people who might have rallied to the meeting had all gone home, and only Charlotte and her benefactress waited, in the rather gloomy grandeur of the Mayfair club, for the tardy Miss Glyn-Gibson.

Charlotte thought about Florence, which she would see again this spring, and about Rapallo where she had spent a bare ten days last year, and then she thought about her mother, who had brought her back from Rapallo by threatening to have appendicitis. The threat had come to nothing, she had recovered almost before Charlotte got home, had subsequently reproached herself for spoiling her daughter's holiday, and had justified herself each time she uttered the reproach by reminding Charlotte that if she had been whisked off to hospital there would have been no one to look after Alison. Reliable old servants did not count, it seemed; a mother or grandmother was essential.

"She's awfully late," said Mrs. Gamalion, who was always late herself. But at that moment the swing door of the inner hall where they waited was pushed open, and a mild little face under a very dowdy hat came into view, Mrs. Gamalion sprang up with welcoming cries, Miss Glyn-Gibson edged the rest of herself round the door and diffidently entered the room.

Charlotte was relieved to see someone so plainly dressed and humble. She was conscious that her own clothes were not 'smart' enough for the occasion and she had expected Miss Glyn-Gibson to be rather grand and daunting, like the club, and to exude the air of efficiency which she found so hard to breathe at home. Thankfully abandoning this false image she felt all the more disposed to like the real Miss Glyn-Gibson, to whom she was now being introduced.

"Mrs. Moley is coming with me this year," said Mrs. Gamalion, when they had finished the soup and were awaiting the next course.

Till then Miss Glyn-Gibson had almost ignored Charlotte, not deliberately but because she was concentrating on Mrs. Gamalion. Now she turned her head and fixed on her fellow guest the meek but steady gaze which was to be Charlotte's most vivid memory of her. A pair of brown eyes which always looked straight at you; as if someone had once told Miss Glyn-Gibson that to look away was a sign of insincerity.

"How nice, Mrs. Moley. How very nice," she remarked. "Your first visit to Florence?"

"No, I went to Florence with Mrs. Gamalion the year before last, and last year to Rapallo."

"I can't tell you how many people I've taken abroad," Mrs. Gamalion cried. "And they all *loved* it! Well, nearly all. Of course I always have a girl with me and some girls are very silly these days. They don't appreciate it. But Charlotte does! She's simply longing to get back there."

"I dare say you'd like to live abroad, Mrs. Moley," Miss Glyn-Gibson suggested. She transferred her gaze to Mrs. Gamalion. "Of course, girls don't really count, do they? They wouldn't be permanent. They only go abroad to be finished."

"But they'd stay for months! A villa outside Florence, that's what you want to look for, somewhere high enough to be out of the heat. Not *too* high, of course, because of the winters. Some of those big old villas are going awfully cheap! I know exactly what you want and when I get to Florence I'll start looking round. A lovely old villa with a garden and cypresses about as high as San Domenico and with a hill behind to shelter it!"

Carried away by excitement Mrs. Gamalion delivered the last sentence in an unpunctuated shriek. Heads were raised at the surrounding tables, the air seemed to vibrate in sympathy, Charlotte thought of a train rushing shrieking out of a tunnel, rushing out of the darkness into Italian sunshine, taking her and Mrs. Gamalion and Miss Glyn-Gibson to the fantasy villa which would be so awfully cheap. She laughed aloud, loving Mrs. Gamalion for her enthusiasm, but when she glanced across the table Miss Glyn-Gibson was looking glum.

"My scheme is rather different from that." Miss Glyn-Gibson spoke meekly but firmly, and for the first time Charlotte suspected that her humility might be only a pose.

"It's to be residential, you see, and of course our funds wouldn't run to a place like that, not to start with, cheap though it may seem to you, Mrs. Gamalion."

For a moment she allowed herself to look round at the grand dining-room. She evidently supposed that her hostess was a woman of means.

"Security, that's what our watchword must be," she continued. "Everything on a sound financial footing – everyone knowing that their money is absolutely safe."

"Of course, of course! The way the lira goes up and down –"

"You never know where you are, do you?"

But they knew where they were now; the fluctuations of the lira was a subject that led them on along a familiar path, and Mrs. Gamalion was delighted to find that Miss Glyn-Gibson agreed with her about everything. When the luncheon party was over and Miss Glyn-Gibson had uttered her effusive thanks and edged herself through several doors and been waved good-bye to from the top of the steps Mrs. Gamalion turned eagerly to Charlotte and asked what she'd thought of her, and without waiting for an answer she declared that Miss Glyn-Gibson was an awfully clever woman, you'd know it at once just meeting her anywhere and of course coming from Nora Pearson made everything all right, she'd trust anyone who was recommended by Nora Pearson.

"But was she?" Charlotte asked. "I thought you said someone else had sent a letter of introduction –"

"Oh but Nora wouldn't pass her on unless she was quite sound," said Mrs. Gamalion, as if Miss Glyn-Gibson had been a bottle of wine. "Come in, dear Charlotte, it's a good room for a quiet talk because it says Silence."

She led the way into a small writing-room where two members were drowsing over the fire and a third was dealing with her correspondence. Silent it was, as directed by the notice on the door and duplicated above the chimney-piece, but it did not remain silent for long. Mrs. Gamalion began by marching across the room and flinging open the window, muttering as she did so that they kept these rooms far too hot. The drowsing members woke up, the corresponding member clutched at her fluttering letters; a chill wind rapidly dispersed the cosy fug.

"Come and sit here, Charlotte. No, not that chair, it doesn't look comfortable. This one and this one."

By the time Mrs. Gamalion had rearranged the chairs the drowsing members had abandoned any hope of going to sleep again and removed themselves from the scene. "So might as well have their seats," said Mrs. Gamalion, "then we can look after the fire. Poke it a little, Charlotte, to make it burn up. No, not like that. Give me the poker."

The poker made a lot of noise, so did the brush and shovel with which Mrs. Gamalion swept the hearth. Then she jumped up to fetch a cushion from a distant chair and two minutes later she crossed the room again in search of an ashtray. At this point the corresponding member gathered up her letters and departed, giving Mrs. Gamalion a long-suffering look as she went.

"That's better," said Mrs. Gamalion. "Now we can talk without those old women sitting listening. I always tell people to use this room if they want a quiet place for a talk, there's hardly ever anyone here and they never stay very long. Now tell me all about yourself, Charlotte. What have you been doing lately?"

"Nothing much, I'm afraid. Living at home and looking after Alison."

"But you ought to come up to town more often. If I lived as close as Marston I should be popping up every day! Did I tell you Muriel is engaged?"

"No, but I saw the announcement."

"He's not one of the Lincolnshire family," Mrs. Gamalion said obscurely. "I think you'll like the girl I'm taking with me this year, Veronica Crabtree, she was brought up in a convent but only because her people were in India. I'm trying to hear of another so that they can go about together. I suppose you don't know of anyone?"

"I'm afraid I don't. Marston girls aren't the kind that get sent abroad to be finished."

"Nonsense! All kinds of girls go nowadays and parents who haven't been themselves are always glad to find someone to take their daughters – someone like me who knows the ropes, and can take them for just a short time and really show them everything!"

"But how do you hear of them? Do you – have you ever thought of advertising?"

Mrs. Gamalion shook her head vigorously. "Margery Mollison suggested it once but she soon saw it wouldn't do. It's much better to get them through friends. I know heaps of people and there's always someone who has a friend who has a niece or something like that. It hasn't been quite so easy lately, though – girls seem to be so independent and some even go by themselves. So silly of their parents to let them!"

"Well," said Charlotte. She saw the situation through Mrs. Gamalion's eyes. "I suppose they might meet with adventurers?"

"Yes, it's terribly risky! But they're all right with me – I can spot an adventurer a mile away." Mrs. Gamalion spoke with great confidence, as if she had had a wealth of experience. "I know what to look out for, you see. They're always awfully plausible and start by pretending to think the world of you! And then they want you to buy shares in a gold mine or something. Something that isn't really *there*."

Listening to these words of wisdom Charlotte reflected that the adventurers who operated in the world of English ladies abroad could not make much of a living, since none of the English ladies had any money. But she smiled at her companion and promised never to buy shares in a gold mine which wasn't demonstrably there. And they went on to talk about Margery Mollison, who had been ill with pleurisy since she rashly undertook to exercise somebody's dog in the park. The dog had gone into the Serpentine and Margery Mollison, trying to haul it out, had somehow gone in too, and she had been so ill that the doctor had insisted on her having a nurse. By an extraordinary coincidence the nurse had turned out to be Sister Wainsford whom they had known at Rouen in the old days, and who was now doing private nursing from one of those agencies.

"She was always a brick to us," Mrs. Gamalion declared. "Not like some of those bossy hospital Sisters! All of us V.A.D.s used to tease her like anything and she never minded a bit!"

Charlotte did not pay much attention to Sister Wainsford because she had suddenly noticed the time and realised she must hurry away. There were plenty of later trains to Marston but they were not for her; she had to be back early so that she could collect Alison from The Laurels and take her home and put her to bed.

"Oh, you silly girl, you don't have to go yet!" Mrs. Gamalion protested. "Why, we haven't settled anything about our holiday. Can't your mother have Alison for the night?"

"No, I promised I'd be back on this train."

A watchful eye on the clock, a hurried departure, a feeling of oppression as the train carried her towards Marston; these were as much part of a day in London as wearing one's best clothes. Travelling homewards Charlotte began to dream of a different day when Alison would be old enough to accompany her or to be left by herself, when each of them would be free to come and go, and neither would ever promise the other to be back at a fixed time. At first she found it easy to picture this golden age, but as she drew nearer to Marston the dream faded and changed – there were other people in it, not just her and Alison. And the dreamer was awakening to her everyday self, the self that Marston and

Mrs. Field had trained to be docile, trustworthy, and considerate. And also to be punctual. "Qui s'excuse, s'accuse," Mrs. Field used to say warningly, and this applied to trains being late as well as to every other kind of excuse. Unpunctuality was held to occur through loitering.

Charlotte approached The Laurels at a fast trot. But it was all right, the train hadn't been as late as she feared, and Alison and Mrs. Field were still absorbed in a fairy story. It was so lucky that Alison always enjoyed the stories her grandmother thought suitable; but she was, in all ways, an ideal grandchild and the apple of Mrs. Field's eye.

Though not yet sixty Mrs. Field had already acquired an elderly appearance; not elderly and shrivelled, but elderly and majestic. She had abundant grey hair and a stately figure, she inspired awe as well as admiration, and even her lighter remarks sounded portentous. It was with a light remark that she now greeted her daughter.

"I never really liked you in that hat," she said. "Still, I suppose it's fashionable even if it doesn't suit you."

"Mummy come home," said Alison, stating it as a fact and showing no particular enthusiasm.

"I hope you enjoyed your day, Charlotte."

"Yes. . . . Yes, it was very nice."

"Alison has been as good as gold," Mrs. Field said fondly. "But then she always is – aren't you, my precious?"

"I hope she'll keep it up when she comes to stay with you."

"Of course she will. Though you must remember, Charlotte, that you are not to count on my being able to have her. Not absolutely. I told your aunt Edith I would go to her if she needed me, and I must stick to that. So I can't *promise* to have Alison to stay."

A promise was sacred; but no promise was being given. Charlotte suddenly realized that no promise would be given even if Aunt Edith recovered from the mild malaise at present afflicting her. The threat of not-being-able-to-have-Alison was being held over her because her mother disapproved of her going to Italy.

Like the threat of appendicitis, which had been used to bring her back from Italy last year. No, not like that, she thought penitently. The appendicitis must surely have been a real scare; her mother couldn't possibly have – have imagined it.

Nevertheless her reaction to the new threat was a small, cold surge of rebellion, as oddly bracing as it was unexpected. It braced her to sit up and smile calmly at her mother, and to answer her in a voice as firm as her own.

"It will be a pity if you can't have Alison, because she does so enjoy being with you. But I dare say she could stay with the Smiths instead."

Mrs. Field stared hard at her daughter as if she wasn't sure she had heard her aright.

"And who are the Smiths?" she demanded, when staring had produced no results.

"They live quite near us, and Evvie Smith is the same age as Alison. They have a nanny. I'm sure Mrs. Smith would have Alison to stay if I asked her."

The Smith nanny was only what Mrs. Field would have called a nursemaid and for a moment Charlotte was quite appalled at having so blithely promoted her. But the other Charlotte, the new, rebellious one, observed the effect with satisfaction. "Nice Evvie," said Alison, inadvertently coming in on her mother's side.

"Or I might take her with me to Italy," said the new Charlotte. "Would you like that, darling?"

This time the effect was electrifying. Alison did not get a chance to reply, she was snatched up and held very firmly on her grandmother's knee, as if menaced by kidnappers. "Take Alison abroad!" Mrs. Field exclaimed in horror. "Why, Charlotte, how can you suggest it! And I don't like the sound of these Smiths either. It will be *far* better if she comes to me."

Plans that were far better were also, if Mrs. Field had anything to do with them, as good as settled, and 'as good as settled' had all the force of a promise. Charlotte perceived that her Aunt Edith's malaise would not be allowed to require a personal visit – good advice, after all, could be imparted by letter – and that her mother would positively insist on having Alison under her own roof.

It seemed at the time like a victory.

CHAPTER VIII

"ONLY *German* measles," said Mrs. Gamalion, "but her mother said it unsettled her. They thought she'd got over wanting to be a nun, but as soon as their backs were turned she packed a bag and went straight back to the convent! Luckily the Mother Superior was a brick and sent her home again but of course it gave her parents an awful fright. Wanting to be a nun is a bad thing at that age!"

"At any age," Sister Wainsford said with a jolly laugh.

Mrs. Gamalion turned to the hovering waiter and ordered three cups of coffee, for herself and Charlotte and Sister Wainsford. Then she went on explaining about Veronica Crabtree, whose mother had decided at the last moment to keep her at home. She was quite recovered from the measles but still dreadfully rebellious – even the Mother Superior's discouragement hadn't really put her off.

"Discouraging her might be part of their game," Sister Wainsford said sceptically. "They're very cunning, you know."

Three nuns crossed the piazza, looking as guileless as doves. The façade of Santa Maria Novella glowed in the sunshine, dominating the mind by its beauty, and the dark cypresses in the cloister beside it pointed the way to heaven. In Italy the way to heaven was inescapably through those doors, into that cloister, and church doors and cloisters were everywhere, an easy step from every crowded street.

"Italy is so beautiful and that's why they thought it too risky," Mrs. Gamalion explained. "Her mother said she wouldn't have a moment's peace if Veronica was in Florence seeing churches all the time!"

"And nuns," said Sister Wainsford. "I do think they ought to shorten their skirts," she added critically. "All the dust of the streets, and the mud, it's terribly anti-hygienic. And now that everyone else is showing a bit of leg, why shouldn't they?"

Charlotte thought it would have been better if Sister Wainsford had shown a little less leg, even none at all like the nuns. She was large and plump and her scanty summer dress was far too revealing, of fat arms bare to the shoulder as well as of muscular legs.

But Italy seemed to present itself to Sister Wainsford chiefly as a place in which to acquire 'a gorgeous tan'. In the pensione she spent much time sunning herself on Margery Mollison's bedroom balcony and at café tables she scorned the sheltering umbrellas, though her arms looked painfully red. Charlotte, who hadn't taken to Sister Wainsford, fancied that Mrs. Mollison also found her something of a trial, in spite of the bond of the past, the shared experiences of the Great War. "She was wonderful when I was ill," Margery Mollison had remarked thoughtfully, and there was an implication that she wasn't, on any reckoning, wonderful now.

But what did it matter? They were in Florence, and it still seemed a minor miracle that Charlotte had got there, and a whole month of freedom and happiness lay ahead. Sister Wainsford was a misfit, with her total lack of interest in the arts and her contempt for foreign food, scenery, and customs, but in that ample air there was room for both of them to breathe. Sitting in the piazza, talking to Mrs. Gamalion, and presently walking beside her on the shady side of the street (with Sister Wainsford on the opposite pavement, not missing a moment of sunlight), Charlotte felt the satisfaction of being there as a kind of triumph. Just to have arrived, to have faced and overcome the Marston opposition, was for the moment happiness enough.

At the pensione Mrs. Mollison was waiting for them, cheerfully resigned to their lateness. Mrs. Gamalion and Charlotte had arrived only the previous day and at lunch they still had to share the table which had been allocated to Mrs. Mollison and Sister Wainsford. It was not a 'good' table but the Signora had promised Mrs. Gamalion a better one, for the four of them, as soon as the Stubbinses left.

"And she said they were leaving today," Mrs. Gamalion declared. She turned round and peered across the dining-room at the better table near the window. "Are you sure that's him, Margery? He had a wife last night."

"His wife had a headache, he told me so before lunch. But I'm afraid they're not leaving till tomorrow."

"The Signora ought to let us have that table *now*. It's too big for just a couple."

"It will hardly be big enough for all of us if the Cokers come. We shall need one of those tables in the middle of the room."

"I haven't heard a *word* from them," Mrs. Gamalion said indignantly. "She seemed so keen at first and then next time I saw her she was shilly-shallying, saying she hadn't been well and mightn't feel up to it! She said Harley might come by himself, and he said it would depend on how she was, whether he could leave her."

"He's a devoted son," Margery Mollison observed.

"But she's a very good mother – she brought him up so well – really he owes everything to her. We could have a bigger table put in the window if they do come," Mrs. Gamalion decided. "I'll speak to the Signora about it tomorrow."

"The Stubbinses haven't definitely decided to leave tomorrow," Mrs. Mollison said later, when she and Charlotte were alone. "It all depends on whether Mrs. Stubbins feels like travelling to Rome. But I didn't tell Minnie, because I didn't want to upset her. She does so count on getting a table in the window."

Charlotte could not accustom herself to hearing Mrs. Gamalion referred to as Minnie; nor did she aspire to address her as Minnie. It seemed an inappropriate name. Safe of course. Mrs. Mollison used it because they were very old friends. They had known each other for years and years.

"I was her bridesmaid, you know," said Mrs. Mollison, who had an uncanny knack of coming in pat on one's thoughts. "Well, we called it that, but in fact I wasn't dressed as one because it was a very quiet wedding, because of the war."

A war wedding, Charlotte remembered, recalling Mrs. Gamalion's account of her brief but happy married life.

"People said all those war weddings were a mistake but I've never regretted mine!" She knew it could not have been quite as Mrs. Gamalion described it for Mrs. Gamalion must have been rather older than she made out, not the girl-bride recklessly defying her parents who thought her too young for marriage. No, but she must still have been fairly youthful, all those years ago in the Great War.

What puzzled Charlotte now was that Mrs. Mollison had been her bridesmaid. Surely she must have been a little old for that role. She was, surely, a lot older than Mrs. Gamalion. She must be getting on for sixty, Charlotte thought, eyeing Mrs. Mollison covertly and comparing her with that standard of maturity, her own mother. The comparison was difficult because they were not at all alike. Mrs. Mollison was small and wiry and wrinkled, with none of the dignity of Charlotte's mother. She dressed rather untidily, she wore spectacles with thin gold frames, and no make-up at all. She reminded Charlotte of an elderly Cairn terrier, faithful and still active but far, far removed from impetuous puppyhood.

"Ancient history to you, my dear," Mrs. Mollison remarked, again coming so close to thought-reading that Charlotte felt very uneasy. "And better forgotten, anyway. Dear Minnie should never have married him."

"But it was in the war," Charlotte said, summarising the romance and snatched-at happiness and tragedy that surrounded that brief marriage.

"Oh yes, it was in the war."

There was a pause. Margery Mollison looked at her watch and then at Charlotte, her head a little on one side, more like a Cairn than ever. "Sister was 'in the war' too," she said. "That is how we came to meet her."

"Yes. . . ."

"It's an odd thing about wars, Charlotte. People seem perfectly splendid in them, whom you would never feel drawn to in peace time."

"I see," said Charlotte, not really seeing, because Mrs. Mollison had met Sister Wainsford since the war, only last Christmas, and had presumably felt drawn to her then.

"Oh, but I was ill," said Mrs. Mollison, answering the thought.

"I suppose she is a good nurse."

"An excellent nurse. And that's all one notices when one's ill – the comfort and reassurance good nursing provides. But I admit it's my own fault. I talked about Italy. I inspired her with the idea of this reunion. Of course she hadn't forgotten Minnie in

Rouen – Well, what I really came to say was, will you come out with me now? A little walk, and perhaps a visit to the cemetery?"

The cemetery was their name for a much-decayed palazzo in which lived an English couple, husband and wife, who were as much a fixture as the crumbling walls that surrounded them. They never went out but they expected to be visited, and the obligation to visit them was passed on from one acquaintance to the next. Neophytes were warned that the Hudsons lived in a slum, and their palazzo had become known as the cemetery because it struck most people as being little better than one – a cemetery of dead hopes and splendours and scandals, a last resting-place for two people who could only doubtfully be counted as still among the living.

"They are parasites," Mrs. Mollison said. "They live on us – on the news we bring them, and on the fresh air that seeps in when we open their door."

But it was evident to both of them – no need for thought-reading – that a visit to the cemetery was preferable to an afternoon with Sister Wainsford, and that they had come out to escape her. Charlotte might have escaped her in any case, but Mrs. Mollison had a top bedroom with a balcony (just like one's own private sitting-room, as Sister had enthusiastically proclaimed), with a splendid view of the Arno and the terraced hill beyond; a balcony which she was too generous to keep to herself. She had even offered her balconied bedroom to Mrs. Gamalion for her own – a gesture which for an Old Faithful could fairly be regarded as obligatory – but Mrs. Gamalion had preferred a larger bedroom on the floor below, without a balcony but with space for all her clothes to be unpacked and hung up, some in the wardrobe and others from strings stretched across the room's corners, rows of pique skirts and dressy blouses and striped washing-frocks and bosomy cardigans, all getting rid of their creases after the long journey in the bulging suitcases, lisle stockings and gloves getting dry after being washed in the pensione's only bathroom, much against the Signora's wishes. Mrs. Gamalion also had a view of the Arno, her room was a front one with a nice big window. But Sister Wainsford had a room at the back.

She and Margery Mollison had arrived a week before Mrs. Gamalion and Charlotte, and during this week Sister had spent every afternoon sitting on the balcony, sometimes nodding off but more often not. It wasn't surprising, Charlotte thought, that Mrs. Mollison had handed her over to Mrs. Gamalion and made excuses for not accompanying them. Even an Old Faithful had her limits.

"It isn't far from the Casa Guidi," Mrs. Mollison said, leading the way out of a narrow street into a still narrower lane. "But I suppose you've been here before with Minnie?"

"I came once, two years ago, but we didn't get in. The Hudsons were 'not at home' that day."

"They never go out, you know. There must have been some domestic crisis."

"How dreadful – to live in Florence and never to see it."

"Oh, they see it as it was."

The great door of the house stood open. Inside was an empty, echoing hall and a stone staircase rising into darkness. "It isn't really a palazzo," Mrs. Mollison said, "but it pleases them to call it one. They live on the first floor and the rest is all let off to tenants. Don't touch the wall, dear."

Charlotte had been told about the cemetery, she was prepared for the semi-darkness of the sala with its broken windows boarded up, for the smelly little dog, a spiritual descendant of Flush, for the frizzy blonde wig of her hostess and the crimson velvet jacket of her host. It was all much as she had expected, comic and pathetic both at once, and at first a decided improvement on an afternoon with Sister Wainsford. But as time passed she began to feel depressed and wished with increasing desperation that Mrs. Mollison would bring the visit to an end. The impossibility of taking the initiative was another reminder of her own youth, her subordinate position in a world where everyone else had suddenly begun to seem very old.

The Hudsons were of course acknowledged to be old, though with wigs and finery they tried to conceal it. They were reputed to be in their nineties and to have known, as children, the last Austrian Grand Duke. They were old, but terrifyingly vivacious.

Mr. Hudson was continually falling into a feeble rage, reminding Charlotte of a puppet jerkily imitating the anger of a human being, while Mrs. Hudson maintained a perpetual show of good humour, smiling and nodding at every remark with emphatic amiability. Their conversation, ranging back over the years, was chronologically topsy-turvey.

"I have not seen the Duchess since the autumn," Mrs. Hudson informed them. "She is wintering in Rome as usual, and invited us to join her for the New Year. But we prefer our own palazzo to that monumental edifice. It can be just as cold in Rome."

How many New Years ago?

"Young Hetherington should be getting leave about now," Mr. Hudson piped shrilly. "I expect his mother will bring him on her next visit. If she deigns to remember our existence down here in the city."

How long since old Colonel Hetherington had retired from the army and settled in his cheap back room?

Other names were mentioned, other enquiries made, and by Margery Mollison's evasive replies Charlotte perceived that many of the people mentioned were dead, or no longer capable of travelling to Italy.

The dark, musty room where they sat was as sinister as its owners. It imprisoned her in the past, it loomed dimly round her as a temple consecrated to the venerable and the vast. Furniture on a heroic scale crowded against the walls, a refectory table filled up the space in the centre, threadbare velvet hung in twenty-foot petrified cascades at the side of the three long windows, where half the panes were boarded up. At a higher level were rank on rank of pictures of which little could be seen but their frames, and above them on the high coved ceiling some shadowy goddesses were faintly discernible among painted clouds, patches of damp, and crumbling plaster. It was a room that absorbed light and sound as greedily as blotting-paper absorbs ink, a room without echoes or reflections. When the quavering voices ceased one felt the silence of the tomb.

Charlotte's circling glance had been noted. "A lifetime among the arts," Mrs. Hudson fluted, leaning forward to tap her on the arm. "Oh yes, we have our treasures, our triumphs over wealth and fashion. A Correggio, Mrs. Moley, above the chimneyplace. And our own Florentine here beside me."

A good copy, certainly an antique, Mrs. Mollison said afterwards; and if it pleased them to suppose it genuine one must humour them, it was as nearly a Leonardo as the house was a palazzo. But to Charlotte, still shivering in the warm evening sunlight, the sepulchral house appeared as the last step in a long, daunting path – venerable Hudsons at one end and herself at the other.

Behind her on the Lung' Arno stood the hotels and pensiones, where in a hundred bedrooms a hundred English ladies were brushing their grey hair, putting on their modest semi-evening dresses, assembling their embroidery and the books they would read after dinner. A hundred English ladies all much older than herself, all halfway or more along the path that ended with the Hudsons.

"Even Mrs. Gamalion," she thought, and turned away from the thought quickly.

A walk in the sun banished the Hudson shivers but the mood of discontent persisted. It was ungrateful of her, and ridiculous. Wasn't she, after all, in Italy – and wasn't it enough simply to have escaped for a season from Marston and to be enjoying the freedom and beauty of Florence, with a benefactress who never made her feel inadequate and stupid? But somehow, this evening, it didn't suffice; she was tormented by a sense of fleeting time, of the brevity of youth and the long path ahead. And it was no good counting one's blessings, for they like youth were transient, and would soon be later memories of a vanished summer. Not even shared memories, next winter in Marston.

When Alison is older I shall bring her with me, Charlotte thought. But this led back, as in a maze, to the thought that she would then be older herself. Like Margery Mollison, wiry and alert. Or like Sister Wainsford – oh no, please not, that would be much worse. Surely I couldn't turn into someone like that!

"Poor thing, she's tired out," Mrs. Mollison said, as they watched Sister Wainsford cross the hall. She had announced her intention of going to bed immediately after dinner and now she was off, plodding up the stairs because she did not trust the shaky lift, suffering from sunburn, swollen feet and a surfeit of sightseeing. Mrs. Gamalion, who looked rather tired herself, remarked crossly that Sister had aged a lot since the old days at Rouen – what were a few churches compared with all the walking she did *then*, on the go all the time and anyway the sunburn was her own fault and if she couldn't stand the heat it was a pity she had come.

After this they settled down quietly, Mrs. Gamalion in an armchair and Mrs. Mollison and Charlotte on a stiffly upholstered sofa, in a corner of the big room near an open french window. The pensione was on the upper floors of the building and the windows of this room led out on to a loggia, where there were more chairs grouped among pots of lilies and geraniums and begonias, with an admirable view of the Arno below the high parapet wall. Charlotte had suggested they should all go out there but her companions pointed out that they would not be able to read; something had gone wrong with the exterior lamps and the loggia was in darkness. So they sat indoors, but close to the window because it was a hot night. Mrs. Gamalion read an English newspaper, Mrs. Mollison read a novel from the English library, Charlotte attempted to read a novel but soon gave it up. She sat with the book on her knee, looking about her.

There were not many people in the room that evening. A few groups like their own, reading or talking in low voices, Colonel Hetherington and Miss Owen playing bezique in the far corner, another elderly man perusing the pages of a long letter. Two old men, several middle-aged ladies . . . all sitting indoors on this hot summer night.

She looked out through the dark rectangle of the open window. The light from the room dimly illuminated the part of the loggia just outside, she could see the line of the parapet and two of the pillars that supported the sloping roof, and a couple of cane chairs and a shadowy group of pot plants on the right. And beyond the plants, where the loggia stretched away into darkness, there was a pinprick of red light that glowed and faded as she watched, and then glowed again. Then she discerned the figure of a man leaning on the parapet, smoking a cigar and watching the scene below.

The Arno and its bridges were hidden from Charlotte by the parapet. The man was silhouetted against the distant lights on the hill beyond the river and the luminous haze of the night sky. When he turned to gaze upstream a faint reflection from the street lamps fell on his face, and it was an unknown face. Even Mr. Stubbing might have appeared to advantage, seen on a balcony against the romantic background of a Florentine night by someone looking out from a lighted room, but this was not Mr. Stubbing. Charlotte was quite certain of that. She looked out from the lighted room at a man standing in darkness, and afterwards it was as if she had seen Harley Coker quite clearly and recognised him at once. Tall and slender, with a long oval face that had something mediaeval about it – a calm nobility which would have looked well in marble – and those long-fingered delicate hands that were so eloquent in gesture. The characteristic expression, touched with melancholy as he contemplated the imperfections of the world, was as visible in retrospect as the gleam of lamplight on the fair head.

So she saw him – or thought afterwards that she had seen him – when he was still a stranger to her. He lingered a little longer in the darkness and then walked into the room, and into her life.

CHAPTER IX

HARLEY Coker had once lived in Nything, with his Mama. Mrs. Coker had been a friend of Mrs. Gamalion and her name used to be mentioned when Mrs. Gamalion talked about her life at home, and was sometimes given the adjective 'poor' – which was a tribute more generally bestowed on those who were both unfortunate and dead. Poor Canon Cowper, poor Lady Ansdell: these were hierarchic figures looming in the dim chronicles of Mrs. Gamalion's girlhood, so far away now that their misfortunes hardly concerned Charlotte; they were indubitably dead. But she wished she could remember why Harley's mother had been dubbed 'poor Mrs. Coker'.

And what had happened to her? Her name had simply dropped out of Mrs. Gamalion's letters and neither her death nor her departure from Nything had ever been mentioned. Once again Charlotte reminded herself to ask Mrs. Bateman about them; Harley Coker and his widowed mother, who had lived somewhere near by, but not – she recalled with certainty not on the Green, and had attended the Parish church and sat in the pew immediately in front of Mrs. Gamalion.

"Mrs. Coker feels the heat in church dreadfully! She sits in the pew just in front of me and I've often had to lend her my smelling-salts. Of course she's not at all strong. But I tell Harley he ought to speak to the verger about it – there's a grid in the floor just beside their pew and since we had the new furnace put in the crypt the heat comes up in *waves*! It's like sitting over a volcano!"

Something must have happened to the new furnace since those days, perhaps just old age, for it seemed to Charlotte an extinct volcano now. But the simile recurred to her on the cold, foggy day when she went to tea with the Wakelins – when, after crossing the deserted public gardens and walking the length of Church Street, she arrived at their house. The rosy glow from its windows shining through the fog, and the warmth she felt as she stepped into the porch, were a foretaste of what was to come – when Bart opened the door the comparison to a volcano was inescapable.

"Come in," he said, rather peremptorily, and as soon as Charlotte was across the threshold he shut the door and drew a heavy curtain across it. "The house gets cold so quickly if the door's left open," he explained.

"I suppose it does," said Charlotte. It was the hottest house she had ever been in.

"That's the whole secret of keeping warm, not to let the cold air penetrate. We have double-glazing in all the windows, and the roof is insulated and the walls too. You can walk through the whole house and the temperature hardly varies, it's much healthier like that, you know."

"Is it?"

"Oh, yes," said Bart, helping her off with her coat. "It's going from one temperature to another – indoors, in one's indoor things

– that gives one a chill, don't you see? When one goes *out of doors*, of course one wraps up properly. Not that Lily and I go out much in this sort of weather . . . Hope you didn't find it very cold, coming here."

He led her into the drawing-room, where Lily greeted her and besought her to sit by the fire. It was an electric fire, imitating a grate piled with coals, flickering and glowing with mechanical efficiency. But as Bart explained, she would be equally warm wherever she sat; the fire was just to make the room look cosier.

"Oh, but she will *feel* warmer by the fire," Lily insisted. "I always do. I sometimes wish we could have a real one."

"But you don't need a real fire, with central heating," said Charlotte, edging away from the splendid imitation. She had no wish to feel warmer.

"We had lovely log fires at Warley. We sawed up the wood ourselves, it was such fun."

"Hard work too. Kept us fit."

"Not always, Bart. Don't you remember the time when you cut your hand?"

"And the time when the log rolled over and crushed your toes."

"They weren't really crushed, just bruised. I was wearing thick gardening boots, luckily," Lily explained to Charlotte.

"Might have had to have them amputated," said Bart.

"And you might have got blood-poisoning from your cut hand."

"Tetanus."

"Yes, tetanus as well. Or are they the same thing?"

"Not sure. I must ask Elliott. Doctor Elliott is our doctor. If you haven't found a doctor yet, Mrs. Moley, do call in Doctor Elliott when you need one. He's such a nice, sympathetic man."

"Up to date too. He's very clever about injections. Gives them to all his patients."

"I'll remember the name. Doctor Elliott. But I'm hardly ever ill so I hope I won't need any injections."

"But they're to *prevent* your being ill. Awfully good idea, especially nowadays with so much illness everywhere. Tell her about them, Lily, while I brew the tea."

The Wakelins were injected against colds, influenza, anaemia, chilblains, and rheumatism. Dr. Elliott also kept them informed of any local outbreaks that deserved special precautions; there had been a case of diphtheria last year and two or three cases of paratyphoid the year before that, and as soon as he heard of them he had come round to warn Bart and to offer innoculations, which of course they had had, just to be on the safe side. Neither the paratyphoid or the diphtheria had spread into an epidemic but they might have done. Having injections, Lily pointed out, saved one a great deal of worry about catching things.

"I suppose so," said Charlotte. "But don't the injections themselves make you feel ill?"

"Some of them do, just at the time. But we don't mind because we know it's only the injections and quite safe. The real worry about feeling ill is wondering if you're going to get worse and have something really serious, isn't it?"

"Yes, I see. But you both look very fit," Charlotte said reassuringly.

"Oh, we are. Of course we take good care of ourselves. Bart says it's very stupid to wear yourself out trying to pretend to be young. There he is with the tea."

The tea was wheeled in on a trolley; a more sensible arrangement, said Bart, than carrying a heavy tray. Afterwards they both escorted Charlotte on a tour of the house and showed her the numerous labour-saving devices it contained, and how they had planned everything to be as easy as possible. She had already noticed the absence of ornaments and pictures in the sitting-room – to save dusting – and the rest of the house was just as bare. But very comfortable, except for the oppressive heat. Thick carpets and heavy curtains enveloped Lily and Bart in cosiness, shut them off from the outer world of November fog and deepening gloom. The darkness was kept at bay; in their warm, brightly-lit house the Wakelins were well protected against the hostile season of winter. They took good care of themselves. They could stand a long siege.

"The ceilings don't *look* low do they?" said Lily. "But we had them made as low as possible, because it makes the house warmer."

"We learnt that at Warley. Great high rooms – impossible to keep them comfortable in winter. Heat rises, you know. There we'd be, sitting by a roaring fire, and all the warmth in the room was up near the ceiling. No good to *us*."

"But they were such beautiful ceilings," Lily said wistfully. "Lovely old plasterwork, some of them very elaborate. The dining-room had a pattern of grapes and vine leaves, and the drawing-room had painted medallions all round the frieze. And the rooms themselves were beautiful, so dignified and well-proportioned, the staircase went up in a long curve." She gestured, then stopped. "No, I can't explain. I'll take you to see it one day."

"Can't do that, Lily. It isn't our house now."

"But it's standing empty, Bart. And we want to look at the garden."

"Gardens are different. Not like going inside."

"We should do no harm, and I'd like to see it again."

For a moment Lily looked rebellious, like a child forbidden a treat, and in her faded blue eyes Charlotte seemed to glimpse the high-ceilinged rooms, the dignity and spaciousness of Warley Hall.

"Wouldn't like to go back there, would you?" Bart asked. Lily blinked and smiled, shaking her head vigorously, though she knew it was only a joke. "When I think of the dusting – !" she cried gaily,

"And the draughts!"

"And how damp it was in wet weather."

"We're much more comfortable now, and we don't get ill or over-tired."

"There's really nothing to do in this little house, it's so beautifully planned."

A light in the porch was turned on when Charlotte left, so that she could see her way to the gate. She heard the door shut firmly behind her, and pictured Bart pulling the curtain across and carefully adjusting its folds. She walked away down Church Street past the vicarage, past the lych-gate and the low wall of sea-rounded stones embedded in shelly mortar, behind which lay the crowded, overgrown churchyard, hidden now by darkness and sea fog.

All the Ellans were buried there, in the family vault which was also Mrs. Gamalion's resting-place. She was the last of them, there were no Ellans now in Nything. Warley Hall had seen them depart long ago, as it had seen the Wakelins depart last year. Driving away with all their possessions, leaving the house empty; or dying in a high-ceilinged bedroom with the darkness becoming dawn. One way or another, Warley had seen them go.

Charlotte walked slowly, for the fog was quite thick. But from each street lamp she could see the one beyond, a pale blur in the gloom. She decided not to attempt the short cut through the public gardens and before she reached the entrance she turned off down another street that led towards the sea front. Or so she hoped, for she had not been that way and it did not run in a straight line. It seemed to curve to the right, in the direction from which she had come; then, as she paced on, it began to curve left again. She crossed the end of another street that joined it, and the curve seemed to become a sharp bend. She could only see one lamp ahead and it was impossible to judge her direction. A car came towards her, moving very slowly, but when she turned to look after it the rear lights were invisible. Perhaps it had turned the corner and gone down the street she had crossed. Perhaps she ought to have gone that way herself.

It seemed ridiculous to be lost in Nything quite close to her own house. The sea front could not be far away; or was she walking parallel with it, towards the public gardens? The street lamps were far apart here and the houses were set back from the street behind fences or privet hedges. Peering through the fog Charlotte arbitrarily decided that it wasn't the kind of street that debouched on the Green; it hadn't the air, it curved about too much, and the houses, or at least their fences and gates, looked too modern. She turned round and traced her way back, lamp by lamp, to the street whose end she had crossed, and set off along it.

She could hear a fog-horn, somewhere out in the estuary, and the sound convinced her that she was walking towards the sea. This street too seemed to curve but by now it was difficult to be sure; at any rate there were no sharp bends. She walked on. The fog-horn boomed away, faint and hoarse like an exasperated

Leviathan with a sore throat, penetrating the fog which muffled all other sounds . . . even her own footsteps sounded strangely muffled. Under the next lamp post she paused to look down, and saw why. The paving stones were thinly covered with sand, not deep enough to be felt but enough to deaden the ring of footsteps. A small drift of sand lay against the base of the lamp-post, and there was more in the gutter at the edge of the road.

"How very odd," she thought.

It was just odd – nothing more, or she might feel frightened.

For where could she be? The pavements on the landward side of the Green would not be covered with sand, and she had not crossed the Green to the esplanade. She had walked along streets all the way, from lamp post to lamp post, so she could not have crossed the Green. Anyway, this wasn't the narrow esplanade with its asphalt surfaces, this was a proper road, just visible in the hazy circle of light from the lamp overhead. But outside that circle there was nothing but fog, the road came from nowhere and led nowhere, and she could not even see across it.

She stood on the edge of the pavement under the lamp, looking at the patch of road and wondering why it seemed different from the streets she had traversed. There was the sand, of course. But there was something else, a difference in the atmosphere, a sense of space and openness. It was as if she stood on an unknown shore, far away from Nything. "Nonsense," she said aloud, contradicting the whispers of alarm.

On the other side of the road there would be houses; as there were on this side, she supposed, somewhere behind the wall at her back. She couldn't really be standing on the edge of nowhere. Her suspicion that the other side of the road was different (a wilderness, a desert) was sheer imagination.

"Nonsense," she repeated. And she stepped off the pavement and marched straight ahead.

Imagination proved right. There was nothing on the other side of the road. No wall, or gates, or houses. Nothing but sand-hills. The fog seemed to be lifting a little, or perhaps she could see better now that she wasn't concentrating on the street lamps; at any rate she could make out in the darkness the slopes of sand, beginning at her feet and rising to shadowy dunes. They looked enormous. Far away beyond them, at an unguessable distance, the fog-horn blared forlornly.

It was the strangeness of it that was frightening. Charlotte was hardly aware of thinking until she found herself back on the other pavement and walking rapidly onwards.

But it was pointless to hurry on, when she was already utterly lost. The return of conscious thought checked her, and the next instant she saw – quite literally – the light.

She could only have walked a few yards but they had brought her to the end of the high wall that bordered the pavement. There was a gateway here, the gates standing open, and the light shone out from the house behind the wall. It had just been turned on. It was a powerful lamp hanging from a bracket beside the door and it illuminated the door itself, the white steps leading up to it, and the short drive to the gate. As Charlotte watched, the door opened and a woman came out and stood on the steps. An elderly woman wearing a dark dress and hugging a shawl round her shoulders and somehow conveying at the briefest inspection an air of extreme respectability.

Charlotte could hardly believe it. The house and the woman looked solid enough but they seemed to have sprung out of the darkness like a transformation scene in the theatre. She rushed forward before they could vanish again.

There were two steps up to the door. She stood on the lower one and could see into the hall. It had a red turkey carpet and was quite a large room, containing some wicker chairs and small tables and a lot of brass ornaments, some on a high shelf, others hanging on the wall at the back. Among them, looking oddly out of place, hung a large oil painting in a heavy carved frame. Italian, too dark and dirty to see properly but obscurely familiar, perhaps a copy of a Florentine masterpiece. One part of her mind continued to puzzle over it while she listened to the woman in the shawl.

"Moss Bank," the woman was saying. "That's where you are." She raised her voice as if addressing a foreigner. "Moss Bank."

"Moss Bank," Charlotte echoed. She had heard the name before but she couldn't immediately place it. "Can you tell me how to get to the Green?" she asked.

"Why, straight back along the front, of course. Moss Bank isn't the ends of the earth!"

It had struck Charlotte as being almost that; the edge of nowhere, remote and forlorn. But she saw that this respectable woman would be quick to resent an imputation of remoteness. She was resenting it already.

"I expect I walked a long way round, in the fog," Charlotte said hastily. "I've only recently come to Nything – that's why I don't know where I am."

"This *is* Nything. The Moss Bank end of the front."

At one side of the hall another door opened slowly and a man appeared and walked across to the staircase at the back. He was younger than the respectable woman but not a great deal, he was bald, and stooped, he carried a book and wore a velvet jacket of faded crimson. He did not pause or turn his head to look at them but walked slowly upstairs and disappeared. He had exactly the same effect on Charlotte as the picture: an apparition somehow out of place in that setting, unknown and yet obscurely familiar.

"Oh – the end of the front," she said, pushing the puzzle aside. "But it's very foggy. Could you just explain which way I'm to go?"

"It's clearing now. I came out to look because I'm expecting people. They won't be long now, I hope. Fog's going out with the tide."

Charlotte turned round. She could see several street lamps above the garden wall and she realised why the house had stood out so clearly when she first approached it.

The fog had already begun to lift.

"Then I expect I can find my way back," she said.

The woman gave a grudging smile. "I'd better show you or you'll be going a long way round again. Not that it is so long by the Avenue," she added firmly. "But you want to get to the Green, don't you? Come along and I'll show you."

It wasn't really far to the end of the front. They crossed the road and walked past a short stretch of sand-hills that flattened into a patch of rough grass. A chain fence edged the grass, with an entrance to an asphalt path. There was even a lamp post by the entrance, and a sign saying, 'To The Esplanade'.

"There you are, just follow that path. You can hardly miss it," said the woman, sounding as though she had her doubts. "There's the lights over there, all the way along the front. Fog doesn't last long in Nything, it always goes out with the tide . . . Are you at the Pennine?"

"I beg your pardon?"

"The Pennine Guest House. I thought you might be staying there. People come for the winter, it's so mild – no frost and snow like they get inland. The Pennine's on the Green, but they make you pay for it. Just for the address – the climate's the same at Moss Bank! So if you're staying long –"

"But I'm not at the Pennine. I have a house on the Green."

"Oh, I see. Well, I'll be getting along."

There was no mistaking the tone of vexation, and Charlotte's gratitude was spoken to a retreating back.

CHAPTER X

THE fog went out with the tide but it came in again with the next one. Not so thick though – well, of course it wouldn't be so thick in daylight. And I suppose it wasn't really so bad last night, Charlotte thought. In daylight she felt ashamed of herself, of her incompetent wandering and the moment of panic and her enormous relief when the light shone out from that house.

"I passed dozens of other houses. Why did I go on and on instead of ringing someone's bell and asking where I was? Because I didn't want to admit that I was lost? But I didn't really believe I was lost until I came to the sandhills. That was awfully stupid of me, when I must have walked miles. But that's stupid too, it wasn't many miles. Moss Bank is only at the end of the front. Though I didn't realise how long *that* was until I walked back the whole length of it. I must buy a map of the town. Alison would have brought a map straightaway, and by now she'd know her way everywhere. But then Alison is good at reading maps."

Charlotte's breakfast-table thoughts were not uninfluenced by the letter lying beside her plate. She hadn't yet opened it, but even unopened it made its effect. Alison's handwriting resembled her grandmother's in its clarity and decisiveness; the envelope was a sharp reminder of that Marston household where stupid blunders were rightly rebuked. Mrs. Field would have made short work of excuses ("Qui s'excuse, s'accuse"), and Alison would never have got lost in the fog.

Not even if we'd stayed at Rivermead, Charlotte thought. In that unwholesome part of the town there had often been fog, and it had been one of Mrs. Field's satisfactions that Chamberlain Avenue was 'well above it'. Charlotte smiled, picturing The Laurels with the fog lapping at its garden walls but stopped from infiltrating by the force of her mother's convictions.

Then she opened Alison's letter.

"There isn't a good evening train so I shall travel on Saturday. There will be plenty of time to discuss things. . . . I've got Monday and Tuesday, though I shall have to leave early on Tuesday afternoon. . . ."

There was more to the letter than that; Evelyn's love, an inquiry from the library about a long-overdue book ("Evelyn thinks you took it with you"), and the time the train would arrive at Nything on Saturday afternoon. P.m., *afternoon*, wrote Alison, as if she feared her foolish mother might come to meet a train arriving in the small hours. But for Charlotte the word that mattered was Saturday.

Next Saturday. She looked round the untidy kitchen and thought of the rest of the house. She tried to imagine how it would look to Alison, and despaired. What had she been doing all these weeks since her arrival? Pottering about, poring over the treasures, going to tea with Mrs. Bateman and Robert, with the Wakelins, with a nice woman Mrs. Bateman had introduced her to; gardening on fine afternoons, walking across the Green and watching sunsets, looking in the dowdy shop windows and wondering about a winter coat. It amounted to nothing. What had she been doing?

"But you enjoyed yourself, Charlotte. It's a long time since you've had a holiday like this. This is *your* house – Alison isn't going to live in it!" The imagined voice of Mrs. Gamalion was warmly encouraging. "I always knew you'd love Nything – it's just the right place for you – that's why I left you the house! You're independent now, you needn't ever go back to Marston. You've only got to be firm!"

"But poor Alison," said Charlotte. "She's going to have a terrible shock."

She knew that would not have mattered to Mrs. Gamalion, who had administered many shocks in her time and was an expert at ignoring pained surprise, protests, even threats. "Alison will soon get over it," Mrs. Gamalion would have said. Old Faithfuls had surprisingly soon got over things, accepted a changed plan, San Remo instead of Bagnio di Lucca this year, forgotten their threats of leaving the party and settled down to enjoy the new situation. One only had to be *firm*.

And I can be firm, Charlotte thought. Very firm. Poor Alison, the shock of seeing the house would be doubled by the shock of finding a firm mother living in it. For a moment she thought of writing to tell Alison that she needed her winter clothes, and asking her to pack them in a suitcase and bring them with her. My thick coat, that dark blue dress, my tweed skirt . . . But no, it was no good. Alison wouldn't bring them because it had not yet been settled that her mother was remaining in Nything. That was what she was coming to discuss, and even Charlotte could see the illogicality of bringing winter clothes to a mother you hoped to take back with you to their starting-point, her proper place. For something about Alison's letter now convinced Charlotte that her daughter meant to take her back to Marston.

"I'll buy a winter coat before she comes," she decided, "I need a new one anyway. And later on they can post some of my other clothes. I'll make a list of what I need."

'They' meant Evelyn. Charlotte could not quite envisage Alison meekly packing up that parcel.

She bought the new coat that morning. There was not much choice, which was just as well because she always found it so hard to make up her mind about clothes. But faced with only three coats that fitted her she had little difficulty in rejecting the bright red one and the black one.

The brown tweed was quite suitable and a friendly shop assistant helped her to find a hat to go with it. Hats were even more difficult than other clothes and Charlotte felt triumphant, finding a nice hat so quickly seemed a propitious omen. The weather was encouraging too, the fog had cleared and the sun was shining out of a pale blue sky, cloudless and calm. It was much warmer than yesterday and the friendly shop assistant remarked that they were in for a fine spell and she wouldn't be needing her new thick coat just yet.

A fine spell for Alison's visit, sunshine to light up the dark little house, warm afternoons so that they could walk on the esplanade and sit looking at the sea; and high tide in the afternoon so that the estuary would appear truly sealike. Charlotte wasn't sure about the tides but she felt confident that the weather would support her. She would have gone for a walk that morning, but she suddenly remembered that she had promised to help Mrs. Bateman clean the brasses in the church. She was a little late – no, not really late, but there would not be time to go home first. Carrying her parcels, the coat in a very large bag and the hat in a smaller one, she set off along Church Street.

"You're not late but I was early," Mrs. Bateman assured her. "I thought you might have forgotten about taking Mrs. Tarrant's place, so I came early in case you didn't come at all. To give myself plenty of time, I mean."

"But you've nearly finished!"

"Not quite, there are still those tiresome knobs on the banner – oh yes, and the vicar's frame."

Mrs. Bateman looked relieved as her eye fell on the list of incumbents, framed in complicated brass. With a gesture she offered it to Charlotte, as if to placate her for some injury.

"If you could do that, but it's a horrid, fiddley thing – oh dear, yes, it's my own fault, coming early like that, and you mustn't think – Well, Robert said you wouldn't forget."

"As a matter of fact I nearly did. I was shopping."

"So I see. What have you been buying?"

"A winter coat, and a hat. Alison is coming next weekend."

"At last," cried Mrs. Bateman, before she could stop herself.

"At last," said Charlotte, rubbing away at the vicar's frame.

"Oh dear – I didn't mean –"

"Yes, you did. And I quite agree, I thought she would have come before now; though at the same time I'm glad of the delay."

"It has given you time to get things straight – to get the house ready?" Mrs. Bateman hazarded.

"It ought to have done but it hasn't. Well, the house is a bit more habitable, I suppose, and the garden is *much* better, thanks to Robert, but I'm afraid they're not really up to Alison's standards. And never will be," Charlotte added truthfully.

"Then I don't see why – Wait a moment, I've just remembered Lady Ansdell's tablet behind the pulpit."

Charlotte was gathering up the cleaning rags and brass polish to return them to the cupboard in the vestry, but Mrs. Bateman took them from her and hurried off down the aisle, "It can hardly be seen, that's why I forgot it. I shan't be a moment. . . ."

Charlotte followed more slowly, looking about her.

She attended the church on Sundays but this was the first time she had walked round it. There was a great deal to look at.

The church dated from the early nineteenth-century, like so much of Nything, but at various later dates it had been enlarged, restored, and improved. All the windows were now filled with very gaudy stained glass, reds and blues predominating, and the floor of the chancel and the centre aisle had been laid with encaustic tiles in red, blue and yellow.

At intervals along the sides of the aisles were the grids for the heating, and attached to the outside of each pew was a bracket with a little tray on the floor underneath it, for wet umbrellas. All these must have been improvements in their day, together with the 'new' organ that bulged out on one side of the chancel, and the rather primitive electric lighting, and the Art Nouveau railings round the font at the west end. But the improvements all belonged to the past. The church looked rather shabby now, and the zealous parishioners who had enlarged it had been wrong about Nything's future. The present-day congregation were almost outnumbered by the memorials of their predecessors.

It was these memorials that Charlotte looked at as she walked. The walls of the nave were covered with tablets and scrolls and bas-reliefs in the shape of urns or shields, commemorating the generations of the dead. Most were of marble, white and grey, but there were also brass tablets with black gothic lettering, difficult to read, and some of these later ones had been fixed on the square pillars that divided the centre of the church from the side aisles – perhaps because there was no space left on the outer walls. The same surnames recurred in memorials clustered together but spread out in time, with the epitaphs growing briefer as the years of the century lengthened. Some of the names were not unknown to Charlotte, she had heard them when Mrs. Gamalion talked about the old days in Nything, and now the sight of them stirred faint recollections – faint indeed, the remembrance of a recounted remembrance, wavering in the reflections in a pool, faded as the earliest photographs in the Book. But the Ellans and their friends did not detain her; the tribute of shadowy recollection was tribute enough. She was looking for another familiar name, and she could not find it.

"It's quite interesting, isn't it?" Mrs. Bateman had been back to the vestry and came to meet her in the north aisle. "I always enjoy walking round and reading the names. The Ellans are over there, on the south wall."

"Yes, I saw them. Do you think Mrs. Gamalion would have liked a brass tablet? Perhaps I could –"

"No, I'm afraid you couldn't. The vicar won't allow any more. He says churches shouldn't be cluttered up with private memorials, and if you were to ask him he would tell you to give the money to the Bell Fund instead. For having the bells re-cast," Mrs. Bateman explained. "They're all cracked, and two can't be rung at all."

"I suppose it's a better idea," Charlotte said doubtfully. "More useful," she added, looking about her at the profusion of fields and scrolls, the dusty archives of congregations gone to dust themselves. Mrs. Bateman gave a snort of indulgent protest, "More useful, yes – and more fitting, he would say, I expect Robert would say the same, or else he'd want you to send the money to missions and not bother about cracked bells. Oh, I dare say they're right," Mrs. Bateman conceded, with the air of making allowances for masculine and clerical principles, "only they simply don't understand that for ordinary people – Mrs. Gamalion, for instance – a twentieth-part of a new bell wouldn't seem at all like a memorial!"

Charlotte agreed that it wouldn't. Not for Mrs. Gamalion, who would certainly have argued that a memorial must be visible – her name on a brass tablet where people could see it and preferably adjacent to all those Ellans, her kinsmen, in the south aisle. But privately she now felt more sympathetic than Mrs. Bateman to the idea of an *audible* memorial; a share, however small, in the music that would ring out over Nything when the bells were restored.

"Can you tell me –" she began. But Mrs. Bateman was in full spate, talking about memorials in general and pointing out particular examples as she passed them. As she had said, she enjoyed walking round the church, and it was even more enjoyable to have someone with her, a newcomer who was interested in the past and to whom she could act as guide.

"Mrs. Farrant isn't interested," she explained, half apologising for her own eloquence.

Mrs. Farrant, it appeared, had four children, and one or other of them was always ailing. At present three were ill with measles, which was why she hadn't been able to come today; but even when things were more normal she was always in a hurry, not caring to look at the church but anxious to finish the brasses and get home. Charlotte felt quite sympathetic towards Mrs. Tarrant and thought it very natural that with four children in poor health she should not care to linger over all those reminders of mortality.

"And here are the Ellans – but you've looked at them, did you say?"

"Yes," said Charlotte. "But that window at the end, is that an Ellan memorial too?"

She stepped forward, though the window at the east end of the south aisle hardly required a close inspection and probably looked better at a distance. The reds and blues were particularly vivid and there was a border of leaves and fruit (oranges? pomegranates?) to add more colour to what was already a very colourful design. Entwined with the foliage at the base was a scroll, gothickly illegible. "To the Glory of God and in loving memory . . ."

"I can't make it out," said Charlotte.

"Canon Cowper," said Mrs. Bateman.

"Oh, of course!" She could read the name now, but she did not read on because she knew about Canon Cowper. He had been vicar of Nything for years and years – but long ago when Mrs. Gamalion was quite young. He was a name, perhaps a photograph in the Book, a much-loved man; but that was all she knew about him. Or was there something else? For a moment a dormant reminiscence stirred in Charlotte's mind, faintly muttering, "Poor Canon Cowper". Then it was gone.

"He was a former vicar," Mrs. Bateman said briefly, and led the way down the south aisle to the porch.

Charlotte had the impression that Mrs. Bateman did not like Canon Cowper, for she had been ready to linger over the other memorials and now she seemed to be hurrying away. But perhaps it was just the window she did not like; or perhaps he simply did not interest her. Just the wrong period, poor Canon Cowper, not remote enough to seem romantic and yet long before the Batemans' arrival in Nything. Just one of a long string of past incumbents.

But – "Wait," she called to Mrs. Bateman's retreating back. And when she had caught up with her – for Mrs. Bateman did not wait but marched out into the sunlight – it was to ask the question she had tried to ask at the beginning of the guided tour.

"Can you tell me – is there a memorial to a Mrs. Coker, who used to be a friend of Mrs. Gamalion's and lived somewhere in Nything? I think she must be dead, because Mrs. Gamalion never

mentioned her in her later letters. But I don't know, I thought it
– the memorial, if there is one – would say –"

How ridiculous. Naturally a memorial would be evidence of
Mrs. Coker's decease. But Mrs. Bateman did not laugh, though the
face she turned towards Charlotte was bright with another kind
of feeling which even then struck her companion as being largely
relief from tension. Whatever Mrs. Bateman had been expecting
– whatever she firmly hadn't waited for – was now behind her in
the church. She had her back to it. and the change of subject was
as welcome as the cheerful midday sun.

"My dear. I never realised you knew them! Mrs. Coker and
Harley! How extraordinary you should mention them now,
when only the other day – But never mind that now – Of course
they *were* great friends, Mrs. Gamalion and Mrs. Coker, until the
dreadful falling-out and after that I don't believe they ever spoke
to each other again. That's why, I suppose, Mrs. Gamalion didn't
mention her in her letters."

"Oh, was that it? But I wonder why she didn't mention the
falling-out."

"Perhaps because it was all her fault. Though I shouldn't say
that – I only heard about it from Mrs. Coker so it may have been
a biased account. You can't imagine Mrs. Coker admitting that
anything was *her* fault, can you?"

"I don't know," said Charlotte, though she felt that in a sense
she had known Mrs. Coker and that unblamability must have
been an essential quality in Harley's perfect mother. "I never met
Mrs. Coker, but Mrs. Gamalion often talked about her. And –"

"– wrote about her, until they quarrelled." Mrs. Bateman
finished the sentence with a laugh but as they passed under the
shadow of the lych-gate her first exuberance seemed to subside.
"Such a pity when old friends quarrel, especially when they are
getting on. No time to put things right. People die so suddenly."

"What happened to Mrs. Coker? Did she die suddenly?"

"No. Yes. I mean, she died but I don't think it was very sudden.
No, I remember – Harley had the house full of nurses, so she must
have been ill . . . Now when was it?"

They were standing on the pavement where Charlotte had walked yesterday evening in defeating fog, so different from today's clear sunlight that she wondered why she should suddenly recall the whole sequence of her misadventures. *A house full of nurses* ... but she was seeing the house at Moss Bank and a very respectable woman – and yes, she might once have been a nurse, she had just that air, but she wasn't the link. And yet there was one.

"Some years ago now," Mrs. Bateman continued. "How tiresome it is not to remember when things happened." She pondered another minute before adding, "Of course it doesn't matter. Especially as you didn't really know them after all."

"I did know Harley."

"But I thought you said –"

"I never met Mrs. Coker, but Harley came to Italy with Mrs. Gamalion."

"Did he? I wonder Mrs. Coker let him go without her. They were very devoted, you know. Poor Harley, I think he still misses her."

Charlotte heard the tone of pity tempered with mockery before she realised what Mrs. Bateman was actually saying.

The neighbourly comment might have been in a foreign language, so long did it take her to understand what it meant.

Then she cried out. "But does he still live here?"

"Oh yes," said Mrs. Bateman. "Well, not quite in Nything but where they always lived. It's – how can I describe it –"

She didn't need to. The house at Moss Bank was as vivid to Charlotte as if she were still standing on its threshold. In the foreground was the respectable woman and behind her in the hall a door opened slowly and a man entered and crossed the scene and went upstairs.

He was bald and he stooped, but she had had plenty of time to look at him. It seemed incredible to Charlotte that she had failed to recognise Sir Galahad grown old.

Chapter XI

A DETERMINATION that Alison should not spend her weekend spring-cleaning the legacy drove Charlotte to prodigious tasks, that afternoon and the next day. She spent the afternoon cleaning the kitchen, the afternoon and all evening, with a short break when she hurried out to buy drawer paper, a washing-up mop and the kind of household detergents Alison would expect to find on the shelf by the sink. The next morning she began in the bedroom Alison would occupy, which contained, among other things, twenty-nine cardboard boxes complete with hats and three rolled-up carpets complete with moths. There was also the furniture (all such too big for the room), the wardrobe full of clothes and the chest of drawers full of Christmas presents, Mrs. Gamalion had treasured the presents she received; she had opened the parcels and then done them up again in their wrappings of tissue and ribbon, with the cards from their donors, and put them carefully away in cupboards and drawers. Too precious to use.

Charlotte found a cache of her own gifts, ranging from the hemstitched handkerchiefs of first acquaintance to the quilted bedjackets and warm gloves she had thought suitable for an old lady; and in the next drawer another cache from Margery Mollison, who had chosen frivolous items such as boudoir caps and lace jabots. But Margery Mollison had been dead ten years, and the latest of her presents were smaller and cheaper.

"She got swindled too," Charlotte reflected, thinking of Miss Glyn-Gibson, that snake in the grass, and seeing the humble calendars and painted matchboxes as evidence of poverty.

The house was tall and thin, all landings and steep stairs. But there was another tiny bedroom on the first floor as well as hers and Alison's, and into it she wedged the carpets and the hat-boxes, the clothes and the Christmas presents. It was already crowded but she got them in somehow, and locked the door and removed the key to keep Alison out. The attic bedrooms were even worse, but attics were a natural repository for junk; Alison might be scornful but she would not be outraged, she would not say, "But Mother, it's quite impossible!" and insist on their moving to an hotel.

She concentrated on thinking about Alison, partly because it was important to recapture her point of view, to remember the things that would earn her approval and show her that her mother was capable of living alone, and partly because she did not want to think about Moss Bank and Harley Coker. Not yet, while there was so much to be done; she had wasted enough time already and she knew how easily she could be distracted from these urgent, necessary tasks.

Alison would notice the hole in the landing carpet and see it as a potential danger, and she would also condemn the rattling windows (though they weren't exactly dangerous) and the big wardrobe in Charlotte's room that tipped forward if one opened the door wide. Alison was scornful of people who suffered accidents in their homes simply because they were too stupid to notice obvious hazards or too lazy to deal with them.

Dim lights, worn carpets, wobbly pans, broken-legged chairs ... from Alison's point of view, Charlotte thought sadly, the whole house was strewn with death-traps, like an illustration in some admonitory pamphlet on What to Avoid.

She turned the landing carpet round so that its hole was near the window and not at the top of the stairs. The dim electric bulbs must be replaced by more powerful ones, the wardrobe door must not be opened if Alison was in the bedroom. But she might forget – it would be better if she could prevent the wardrobe tipping by putting wedges under its front feet, so that it stood more upright. She was considering how to manage this when she heard the squeak of the front gate, followed by the rattle of the door knocker.

An interruption, but she could not bring herself to ignore it. She ran downstairs, ready to explain to some stranger that the empty house next door was no concern of hers. People often came asking to look over it.

"No, I haven't got the keys. It doesn't belong to me . . ." The formula wasn't needed, for it was Robert Bateman who stood on the doorstep.

"Oh, Robert! Good afternoon."

"Good afternoon. I'm sorry if I'm interrupting. I'd wondered –"

"No, of course you're not. Come in." Charlotte hoped she had not worn the expression of one who is being interrupted. "Come in," she repeated. "I was surprised – that's all. I didn't expect it to be you at the front door."

Mrs. Bateman and Robert usually approached through the back garden, which was nearer for them than walking round to the Green. But as Robert pointed out, they had come that way in the beginning only because the front door could not be opened.

"And now that it can be," said Charlotte, "you intend to be more formal?"

"It wasn't intentional today – I'd been for a walk and was coming back along the esplanade. And I wondered whether there was anything I could do to help?"

"You've helped a great deal already. The front door and the front garden –"

"But that was fun," said Robert. "Especially the garden. And it gave me 'something to do'."

A quotation from Mrs. Bateman. Charlotte could hear her saying it, though not to Robert; but he was perceptive enough to have discerned his mother's anxiety that he should not be idly bored. She nearly asked him point-blank why he was thus unemployed and in danger of being bored; for a moment they seemed to be on terms when such a question could be asked and answered. But the moment passed, swept away by Robert's talk of what still needed to be done in the garden and by her own Intrusive thoughts of what needed to be done in the house. For although she had denied it, and although she liked him, Robert's presence *was* an interruption. It didn't matter whether she liked him or not, just by being there he was stopping her from preparing herself and the house for Alison.

He had already done more work in the garden, since the first day when he had cleared the ivy. It looked very nice, Charlotte thought, as nice as any little plot could look in November, which wasn't a time of year when anyone expected a garden to be gay. And that was all that mattered – that it should look nice now. But men were idealists, and Robert like his mother was a keen gardener, he was thinking of the future and picturing the garden in the Spring, an idealist's vision of daffodils followed by tulips and summer annuals and roses, bright and orderly as an illuminated picture in a Book of Hours. Charlotte sighed for the vision, and for Robert's enthusiasm which made him look like the boy in the photograph.

"I'll buy some bulbs," she said. "Next week, when Alison has gone. I shan't have time to plant them until then."

"They ought to go in now," said Robert. But he spoke absent-mindedly, looking at the kitchen into which he had followed Charlotte. She filled the kettle and put it on the gas-stove, resigned now to the interruption or at least not sorry that it offered a reason for sitting down and drinking a cup of tea. She had had no lunch and it suddenly seemed a long time since breakfast.

Robert was in the way. He should have been led into the drawing-room and left there, but since he generally arrived at the back-door he was no stranger to the kitchen and it was quite natural that he should simply have followed her. It was her own fault that he was here instead of in the drawing-room, but it was his fault that he was so tiresomely in the way, always standing between her and whatever she needed. He stood between her and the larder door, having moved there from his first halt in front of the stove, and after she had made a detour to reach the larder he seemed to realize – but too late – that he was blocking the approach and stepped aside into the narrow space at the end of the table. It was the end with the breadboard on it and Charlotte was carrying a loaf and a plate of butter – wasn't it obvious that she was coming there to cut the bread-and-butter? It became obvious to Robert, and he walked round the table and propped himself against its other end, where the drawer was.

Charlotte pursued him; to herself it seemed that she had been hustling him out of her way ever since they entered the kitchen. "The breadknife in that drawer," she said in a patient voice.

"I'm sorry." Robert moved again, hesitantly towards the dresser, then away from it as if he had guessed that cups and saucers and plates would be Charlotte's next requirement. "Shall I cut the bread-and-butter?" he asked helpfully.

"No, thank you." Even to herself Charlotte sounded brusque. "You can fetch the jam," she said hastily, trying to make up for it and show Robert that his assistance wasn't unappreciated. But of course he did not know where to find the jam. "It's in the larder – no, don't bother, I'll get it when I put the loaf back –" She just stopped herself from adding, "It will be quicker."

A man hanging about, getting in the way, offering to do things one could do much quicker oneself – how exasperating it seemed, on this particular afternoon when she was in the thick of preparations. Yet at the same time the scene was oddly domestic and recalled a long-ago past when offers of masculine assistance – however ill-timed or unneeded – could be absolutely counted on. Of course there had been a maid in those days, it was only when she was out that Charlotte had cooked supper and Gabriel had hung about offering to help, poor Gabriel who was so competent a civil servant and so clumsy in the kitchen. In justice to Robert Charlotte reminded herself that he hadn't so far broken anything or even dropped anything, though he had taken the china from the dresser and set it out on the tray. She felt quite penitent when she noticed that after doing so he carefully stepped back from the table and stood in the corner by the door.

She made the tea. Robert opened the door and carried the tray into the drawing-room. He placed it on the round table and pulled up a chair for her.

"Sit down," he said. "You're looking very tired."

All thoughts of justice and penitence left Charlotte in a flash. To be told that one is looking tired is never a compliment; at that moment it simply meant that she was looking revolting. Tactless Robert, to remind her that she had rushed downstairs to answer the knock without pausing to remove her apron or glance at her hair.

"I'm not tired," she said. "Not really. Do you take sugar?"

"No, thanks. You must be. When I looked at the kitchen –"

"Oh, but I haven't been scrubbing the kitchen. I did that yesterday."

"And what have you been doing today?"

Charlotte did not answer. She felt that her appearance answered for her; her apron was dirty, her hair was tumbling over her forehead, and she was almost sure there was a black smear on her cheek. After a moment she stood up and removed the apron and cast it on a small chair behind her, though there was nothing she could do about her face and hair.

Standing up, after so brief a spell of sitting down, showed her that she was much more tired than she had thought. In a bemused way she forgave Robert, telling herself at the same time that there was nothing to forgive. But she had been horrid to him. He was looking quite anxious.

"Sit down," said Robert. "Drink your tea. Have some bread-and-butter."

He held out the plate and Charlotte obediently helped herself. She ate it in silence and when Robert urged her to drink she drank. Then she ate some more bread-and-butter.

"I'm sorry there isn't any cake," she said at last, feeling the strangeness of this silent tea party as partly due to a lack of the proper provisions,

"Cake doesn't matter but food does. Didn't you have any lunch?"

"No, I was too busy."

Robert said nothing. Charlotte said nothing because the strangeness had worn off and it seemed quite all right now just to sit in silence, eating bread-and-butter, drinking very strong tea – the second cup poured out by Robert was powerfully restorative – and resting. Then, quite gradually and without any feeling of awkwardness, the silence ended and conversation was resumed. She could not remember afterwards which of them broke the silence or how they knew that the time had come to begin talking again. But presently she was telling him about the death-traps, the hole in the landing carpet and the dim bulbs and how strongly Alison felt about foolish people who let these hazards exist in their homes – that they almost deserved to fall down and break their legs because they hadn't looked after their possessions or kept their houses in proper repair.

"So that's what you were doing," said Robert. "Trying to remove the hazards."

"Trying to hide them. They aren't really hazards – only Alison is rather particular. And of course I want her to approve of the house."

"As a suitable place for you to live in?"

"Yes. And then too I had to get her room ready. The spare room – but I don't think Mrs. Gamalion ever had anyone to stay."

She told Robert about the hats and the hat-boxes, the carpets and the Christmas presents. He saw, as she had seen, the pathos of those presents, all looked at and wrapped up again and put away. Wasted – yet in a way not wasted, since Miss. Gamalion had had the pleasure of opening the parcels and knowing that her Old Faithfuls remembered her. But she was old and poor; she could have had some comfort from bedjackets and warm scarves. The real sadness was in thinking of her forgoing them because she valued them too much, thought them too precious to use.

"Yes," said Robert gently, "but you must remember that they *had* a value. Possessions meant a great deal to her, didn't they? So a house well-stocked with gifts would make her feel happier."

"Possessions? Yes, I suppose so. She was a great hoarder. But a lot of the things – not blankets and clothes of course – were hoarded because of their associations." Charlotte looked round the room at the worthless, battered treasures. "She valued people more than material things . . . she loved being alive, and having a lot of friends, and going to Italy where everything was more – more vivid. She could still feel young in Italy. And in the end, I think, when she had given up the pretence with other people, she could look at her treasures and get back there, with her friends and her youth, and that's why she cherished them."

"Yes, I see. But what about the hazards? Have you finished whatever you were doing upstairs?"

"I think so – well, almost. I must get some brighter lamps tomorrow, and there are one or two things, no, nothing much, truly, and I shan't do any more this evening."

Robert stood up, staring about him with a critical eye.

"This room doesn't look dangerous, anyway."

"Of course it isn't! Nor is the rest of the house. After all, Mrs. Gamalion lived in it for years without damaging herself. It's just, as I told you, that Alison minds about such things."

"And she'd mind still more, if you were to fall down and hurt yourself."

"Oh, but I shan't," Charlotte said confidently, "I feel perfectly at ease in this house." To reassure Robert, who appeared not to share her confidence, she added that of course she knew about the hazards and would be careful to avoid them.

"I shan't need to open the wardrobe door more than half way," she said.

"What's the matter with the wardrobe door?"

"It's the wardrobe itself, the one in my bedroom. It tips forward if you open the door wide, and it's rather heavy. But –"

"Really, Charlotte! How can you feel safe when you're daily confronted with a wardrobe that tips forward?"

"Only when I open the door wide. And I shall be specially careful –"

"I'd better have a look at it," said Robert.

Afterwards Charlotte remembered that she herself had planned to prop up the wardrobe. Of course she could not have managed it single-handed, and of course it was kind of Robert to have taken so much trouble, hunting in the shed for bits of wood and a saw to cut them up with, testing the door repeatedly until he was satisfied it could be safely opened. And unlike Alison, not reproaching her for her foolishness.

His sole comment – "All I can say is that Mrs. Gamalion must have led a charmed life" – had been made at the start, when he first pulled the door open and nearly brought the wardrobe down on top of him.

But people – even kind Robert – were so fussy, there was nothing wrong with the house and nothing in it to hurt her; on the contrary it gave her a feeling of strength and security, difficult to analyse but extraordinarily comforting. It was only to placate Alison that she had tried to hide its deficiencies and so-called dangers. Alison would look at the house with a hostile eye, quick to see what it lacked, quick to despise it. A horrid little ruin, full of absurd souvenirs of the past – someone else's past – is a dull little town that nobody had ever heard of.

"My house," Charlotte thought sleepily. She lay in bed, exhausted but tranquil, listening to the soft murmur of the sea as the tide came in and the waves broke gently against the sea wall. Nything on Sea, Moss Bank at the end of the front, with Harley walking across the hall, not looking at her. Well, we're all growing older, Robert isn't any longer that boy in the photograph, he must be about the same age as I am. Is it selfish to want to have a life of my own and get away from Marston at last?

CHAPTER XII

PEOPLE who remembered Mrs. Field in her active years had often remarked on the resemblance between her and Alison. When Alison was growing up Charlotte used to explain that they meant it as a compliment, that they were all very fond of Granny and naturally noticed any little likenesses and made the most of them. For at that time she thought a schoolgirl might not care to be told she looked like her grandmother. And there was another reason for minimizing the proclaimed resemblance; she did not want Alison to be forced into a mould, or encouraged to think of herself as 'her grandmother over again'.

But it was much too late by then. Alison had been moulded long ago, by association as well as by heredity.

She was Mrs. Field's pupil as well as her grand-daughter, and from babyhood she had shown herself marvellously responsive. ("So different from you at that age," Mrs. Field used to say as Alison's capacities revealed themselves.) She did all the proper things at the proper time, from enjoying being read aloud to (and never having nightmares afterwards), right through learning to read to herself and learning to swim and opening a bazaar. It was a bazaar Mrs. Field should have opened, but she was imprisoned by a sudden attack of lumbago and since it was in aid of a children's charity she was inspired to send little Alison as her deputy.

Alison managed beautifully; sympathetic visitors assured Mrs. Field she could be heard all over the hall and was word-perfect although she had had only that morning in which to learn her speech. She had been managing beautifully ever since.

She resembled Mrs. Field more in character than in appearance, Charlotte thought, or rather, though the physical likeness existed, it was at present least obvious. As a plump child she had had something of her grandmother's solid dignity, but it was gone now – she was shorter than Mrs. Field and the plumpness was a thing of the past, and perhaps of the future when middle-age would bring out the latent resemblance.

"When she's as old as I am," Charlotte thought, but the idea seemed fantastic.

It was impossible to imagine Alison any older than she looked now, sitting in the window with her fair hair shining, her young body so pliantly adapting itself to the angular seat. It was typical of her that she should be up and dressed; less typical that she had waited there instead of coming to see whether her mother was awake.

Charlotte was still in her dressing-gown, but this too was passed over by Alison. She had been passing over things ever since her arrival yesterday, treating everything to the same cheerful smile and deliberate avoidance of comment.

She had talked about Marston, about Evelyn, about the journey, even when she was being shown round the house. Charlotte had realised in the end that Alison meant to say nothing until the time came to discuss things properly.

Which wasn't just yet, obviously. Alison ignored the dressing-gown until Charlotte apologised for it and then she brushed the apology aside.

"Oh, I'm not ready either. I haven't done anything to my face. And you did say breakfast at nine, only it's such a promising morning that I had to get up and look at it."

Alison was precise, she did not say 'beautiful' because the beauty of the day was hardly yet apparent. A mist lay over the estuary, just beginning to dissolve in the early rays of the sun. Promising though it looked, this was a November day.

"Are you cold?" Charlotte asked anxiously. "I'll light the gas fire. It looks very antiquated, but it works."

"I'm sure it does, but I'm perfectly warm."

Charlotte knew Alison did not feel the cold, but she could not help taking this as a tribute to the mildness of Nything. "Then I'll run and get dressed," she said.

"Are we going to church?"

"Well—"

"You do go, don't you?"

For a moment a familiar note sounded, polite but probing, as if Alison suspected her of backsliding.

"Oh yes, every Sunday. But I thought perhaps this Sunday, as you're only here for two days. . . ."

"We'd better go," Alison decided.

Charlotte was an attentive churchgoer as a rule but that morning her thoughts wandered. She kept pulling them back and reproaching herself for allowing them to stray, and the next moment they were off again, carrying her away to a different church and a different time.

The Sundays of small childhood, sitting between an unforgettable mother and a father who was no more than a name and a bristly moustache. Later Sundays, when her mother had worn mourning and had somehow gained in importance. A succession of still later Sundays when church had been nothing but misery and anxiety – fear of feeling sick, of fidgetting, doing something that would earn a rebuke afterwards. She had known that rebukes were necessary, that bad behaviour deserved to be punished, only it sometimes puzzled her now that after so many rebukes and so much tedium she had survived to be a Christian. She did not know when she had finally become a committed Christian, not just a regular churchgoer.

Alison was a fairly regular churchgoer in Marston but a highly critical one. She had escaped the rebukes and the punishments; indeed she had never deserved them because she was not a child who fidgetted or felt sick. She had accepted the convention of churchgoing but she was always finding fault with the services –

the sentimental hymns, the archaic language of the prayer book or the limitations of the vicar's sermons.

She fidgetted inwardly, Charlotte thought, and perhaps it was a greater hindrance to worship than the mere inability to keep still. But no one could be sure, least of all her mother. She was young, she had years ahead of her – as Charlotte had had once – in which to learn not to fret and fidget.

Once again a sermon had gone unheeded. The final hymn brought the congregation to its feet, Alison reached for her hand-bag and Charlotte remembered too late that she had nothing but sixpences and had meant to ask her daughter if she could change them for half a crown. But Alison was an observant daughter, she noticed the sixpences being laboriously delved for and thrust half a crown into her mother's hand.

The little man with wiry upright hair came round with the brass plate, on which a cluster of sixpences would have looked like five mean people. They walked out of the church into a day radiant and golden.

Charlotte looked for the Batemans but could not see then. She was not allowed to linger, Alison took her arm and guided her briskly down the path and through the lych-gate, knowing very how easily her mother got herself involved with dim little women who simply could not stop talking.

"What a gorgeous day! I don't wonder the church was half empty."

"Thank you for the half-crown. I'll give you the sixpences now –"

"Oh, not now. Mother. I'll remind you when we get indoors."

Alison stopped herself from saying 'home' because it would not have been accurate.

But she was at her charming best – lively, friendly, uncritical. It was a day of peace, without a cloud in the shy; even if clouds had appeared in the real sky Charlotte felt that Alison's deter-mination would have sent them scudding away. She felt too that Alison welcomed the note that had come through the letter-box in their absence, a note from Lily Wakelin inviting them both to go for a drive that afternoon. "We will call for you about three o'clock – do hope you will feel able to come. We shall look forward to meeting your daughter."

"That will be fun," Alison said with enthusiasm, and Charlotte understood at once that the serious discussion was not scheduled to take place till tomorrow.

They drove out to Warley. Charlotte wondered whether the Wakelins ever went anywhere else; she imagined them starting off in a different direction but always ending up at Warley, the ponderous car turning this way and that in the network of narrow roads and like a compass needle gradually swinging to rest, pointing to their real objective. She would have preferred not to go to Warley today, in case it led to talk of the Ellans and Mrs. Gamalion and put a strain on Alison's bright neutrality. But she need not have worried; the Wakelins were not interested in ancient history.

Warley belonged to their own past, its history had begun when they bought it. They had cut down a lot of trees, made a new rose garden and restored the long herbaceous borders. The recital of all they had done left no time for any mention of the Ellans.

"It's a beautiful place," said Alison.

"Was. Shockingly neglected now, though."

"Well, I can see that. But I can imagine how it looked when you lived here. A great mass of colour on this side, and the beech hedges framing it. It must have been quite marvellous."

Alison had a special manner for old people, courteous but youthfully animated; in such company she seemed to become younger in every way as if she had slipped back into being an adored and *bien-élevé* grand-daughter. It was a success with the Wakelins from the start. Charlotte left them chattering together and strolled off by herself, to see what lay beyond the ragged beech hedge.

Ruin worse than the rest. She walked through an almost closed gap and found herself in a narrow path, with another beech hedge on the other side and another overgrown gap further along it, leading to nothing but another narrow path. The paths were of rank grass, between the high walls of the hedges where the brown leaves still hung thickly, as concealing as they would be in high summer when they were green. The sun that had shone so splen-didly all day was now low in the sky and the paths were all in shadow and much colder than the garden she had left. It seemed a sad place to Charlotte, and nothing to do with the Wakelins. Unhappy Ellans had walked here, telling each other bad news or more likely escaping from the rest of the family to face it alone. Being jilted, or hearing of the untimely death of someone one had loved in secret and could not mourn for openly; or knowing that poor graceless Dick had had his last chance and was to be shipped off to Australia. The best of brothers, in spite of all his failings.

"Stop inventing," Charlotte told herself, though in fact the story of the wild young man who had been sent to Australia was not invention but one of Mrs. Gamalion's legends – and what made it even more poignant was that he had died of fever six weeks after arriving in Melbourne. But although she stopped her catalogue of grief she still felt very sad. She turned round – for all this time she had been walking slowly along the meandering paths – and began to look for the way back into the rose garden.

"Where has your mother got to?" asked Lily's piping voice.

"Time we were moving," said Bart's voice.

Alison's voice said cheerfully that Mother seemed to have got lost.

The odd thing about the voices was that they sounded so close, although their owners were invisible. They sounded as if the speakers were standing in the path from which Charlotte had just emerged; or else they must be in the next path beyond the gap she was approaching. She pushed through it, but the path was empty.

The disembodied voices spoke again, but now they were much fainter. Charlotte realised she was walking away from them although she had thought she was walking towards them. She stood still and called.

Lily's piping was just audible. "She's in the maze! Go to the entrance, Bart, and tell her how to get out."

When Charlotte had been extricated from the maze she was a little in disgrace. It wasn't part of the Wakelins' restored garden (she had been right about that) and they could not understand why she had gone to look at it. Moreover she had delayed their departure.

"It's so gloomy in there," said Lily. "I never cared for it at all."

"Who wants to get lost in a maze? Come on, Lily, you're shivering."

The long blue shadows of the trees stretched across the lawn and the trees themselves seemed nearer, as if they were closing in on the shuttered house. "It will soon be night," Lily said reproachfully.

But back in Nything they forgave her and insisted on taking her and Alison to tea at the Pier Hotel. "Nice old things," Alison said afterwards, watching the car nosing cautiously out into the quiet street. "You didn't really want a lift, did you? I thought it would be fun to walk back along the front."

The esplanade was deserted. On a November evening Nything attached no importance to being a seaside resort.

But Alison admired the chain of lamps twinkling away into the distance and the shadowy glimpses of the sea below the sloping wall.

"We must come and sit out here tomorrow," she said. "I'm sure it would be warm enough to sit out, in one of those glass-walled shelters, if it's another sunny day."

Monday morning looked less promising than Sunday, the mist was thicker and took longer to disperse. But by midday the sun was shining again. They went for a short walk in the morning, down Beach Street to the centre of the town, where they looked at the shops, and then back by the public gardens. It was while they were walking across the gardens that the sun broke through the mist.

Charlotte quickened her steps, feeling slightly more cheerful. Last eight, and again this morning, she had felt anxious and oppressed. The visit was half over and outwardly it was being very successful; but why hadn't they, before now, been allowed to raise the subject Alison had come here to raise? There was something unnerving about Alison's silence – not that she was silent about other matters, but her easy talk kept resolutely to safe subjects. She admired some things – the esplanade at night, the view of the Green – but in a cool, non-committal way, and about the many defects and inconveniences of the house she was quite alarmingly uncritical. As though they didn't matter because the whole house was doomed anyway.

The visit was going according to plan, but it was Alison's plan, not Charlotte's.

It was still Alison's plan after lunch. The day was quite warm now and brilliantly sunny. They had finished washing up and come into the hall when Alison mooted her plan. It was quite time, she said, they talked things over.

"Yes," said Charlotte, walking ahead of Alison.

"Where are you going?"

"In here."

She opened the drawing-room door. The past flowed out to meet her, not sad, distant memories but as it were vivid yesterday, or only last week, and fall of strengthening gaiety and enthusiasm. In here she could defend herself from the claims of Marston.

"No, let's go out. We can sit in one of those shelters and look at the sea."

Charlotte saw her defences slipping away. "We could sit in the garden," she offered as a compromise. But Alison shook her head.

"No, it wouldn't be the same. I want to look at the sea."

Robert had done wonders with the privet hedge but one couldn't see the sea from the garden.

"We could sit upstairs in my bedroom," Charlotte said wildly.

Alison laughed at her. Yes, upstairs one could see the sea, but why not go out and be nearer to it, on this glorious afternoon?

But Alison knew why not. As they walked across the Green Charlotte wondered whether Alison had consciously felt her authority diminished in the house. Few of the Old Faithfuls could have stood up to Alison but collectively they were formidable. (My house, and I can see it from here.)

No, it was nonsense, Alison was impervious to such influences; Marston would rightly have ignored them. No, it was much simpler than that. Alison wanted her own way – this was her plan, she had decided last night that they would sit in the shelter. Only the weather could have deflected Alison.

A serious talk always took time, it could not be hurried because due consideration had to be given to all aspects of the problem. Mrs. Field had been splendid at serious talks, at discussing the whole thing sensibly and considering every detail. Charlotte's heart had often been, as they say, in her boots, sinking there by degrees as the folly of her proposed course of action was revealed to her.

But it wasn't in her boots today, although Alison was being just as conscientious as her grandmother in asking pertinent questions and pointing out the flaws in the replies. Something in the air of Nything, in the sight of the esplanade and the pier and the house across the Green, gave Charlotte confidence and kept her heart in its proper place.

How sweet Alison looked, sitting in the corner of the glass shelter with the sunlight on her hair. She had such pretty hair. "Dear child," thought Charlotte, hoping Alison would grow out of being so excessively efficient. Perhaps she would marry soon. "It might have been all right with Mother if Father hadn't died," Charlotte thought, remembering how tyranny had grown on Mrs. Field like a more durable kind of mourning.

"Even if it was a *good* idea," said Alison, "you must see you can't afford it."

"I think I can."

"But Mother, we've just been discussing what it would cost you to live in that house. It's practically falling down, and it's simply not worth repairing even if you could afford it. Especially when you've got a perfectly good flat in Marston."

"I thought I'd give you the flat. The title deeds, I mean," Charlotte added, for the flat itself had seemed to be Alison's from the start.

"But it's your home! It always has been!"

"Yours too, and Granny's. And now you've got Evvie so you'll be quite all right, the two of you together."

"Are you jealous of Evelyn? Is that it?"

Alison spoke very earnestly but Charlotte laughed.

"Of course not, don't be a goose. I'm very glad you've got a nice friend like Evelyn."

"I'm not a goose."

"Of course not. I was only teasing you, and telling you not to become one. I didn't say you *were*."

"I can't think what's the matter with you," Alison said sharply. She didn't like being teased, she wasn't accustomed to it, Charlotte thought. Flippancy was inappropriate in a serious talk and it was years since Charlotte had dared to laugh at her capable daughter.

"Nothing's the matter with me; I'm quite well and I haven't lost my wits. It's just that I've decided it's quite time I left Marston. And it's perfectly possible, now. You've got Evelyn and I've inherited this house, and I'm staying here."

"But we've just discussed it all! We've talked it over!"

That had always been the point of a serious discussion; whether it was instigated by Mrs. Field or by Alison, its aim had been to prove to Charlotte that she was wrong. Misguided, ill-informed, incapable, too impoverished; but anyway, wrong. And now at last a serious discussion had failed in its purpose.

No wonder Alison looked bewildered as well as angry. After a moment she fell back on an argument she would have scorned in the security of Marston.

"'But you can't abandon me – I'm your daughter."

Charlotte took it calmly; all her young life people had been reminding her that Alison was her daughter, all she had to live for, her sacred charge. After so many repetitions she could hear the phrase with detachment.

"I'm not abandoning you, Alison dear. You're grown up and very capable. You have a good job, a home you're fond of, and Evvie. I mean, you're long past the age when people could reproach me for abandoning you. Judging by what one reads, lots of girls of your age leave their parents – they leave home and set up in flats in London with their own friends –"

"That's absolutely different, Mother."

"Not really. If you'd left home and gone to live in London I shouldn't have complained of being abandoned. I don't think you should complain, because I'm leaving you and staying here."

Chapter XIII

THE train had come from the bigger town up the coast and it included a through coach that would be attached to a main-line express and take Alison straight to London. But it wasn't an express at present. The station was at the back of the town, almost in open country, and from the wooden footbridge Charlotte could still see the departing train chugging slowly away, past the gas-works and the new cemetery and along a low embankment between fields, until she remembered that it wasn't lucky to watch a train disappear from view. She walked on, and came down into the station yard.

The taxi that had brought them to the station had gone, there was no one in sight, and the whole place looked shabby, dreary, and dilapidated. Like Nything itself, as Alison had pointed out.

Charlotte hadn't argued; it was not a suitable moment for defending Nything and she had not reminded Alison of how brightly the sun had shone yesterday. The Green, the esplanade and the sea, which Alison had admired before they had the serious talk, would earn no praises now, they shared in the general disapproval poor Nything had incurred simply by being the scene of her mother's rebellion. It was quite fitting, Charlotte thought, that today should be cloudy and that the weather forecast predicted rain.

She walked away from the station, along the rather depressing street that linked it with the centre of the town, past the shops and the little square with the drinking-fountain polished granite, indestructible and hideous – and down Beach Street to the Green. In her mind's eye she could still see the train slowly pulling out and Alison sitting in her corner seat, giving her one brief wave and no smile. But they had kissed each other goodbye on the platform. Alison's disapproval was mitigated, in public at any rate, by her strict regard for the conventions.

A peck on the cheek, good wishes for the future (rather vaguely worded) – then Alison was in the train, and the train was bearing her away, and the visit was over.

It had not been a success, even the smooth beginning seemed in retrospect unnaturally constrained, and the last phase had been extremely uncomfortable. If Charlotte had won a victory she felt no sense of elation. She could only remind herself, rather wearily, that she had been *firm*.

So here she was, still in Nything instead of on her way back to Marston, which had been the intended finale to Alison's plan. It was early afternoon, just twenty-four hours since Alison had led her out of the house to sit in the shelter and discuss the whole thing sensibly, but the display of firmness seemed to have been going on for weeks.

"How did I manage it?" Charlotte wondered, standing on the Green and slowly taking in her achievement – the simple fact that she was still here. With no thought but the mere wish to continue looking at Nything she crossed the Green and set out along the esplanade. The shelter where they had sat yesterday was now occupied by three people and a black poodle. She walked past it, marvelling at her firmness.

But it had not been too difficult in the shelter; she had felt quite calm, even confident, then, and she had even hoped to be able to explain her own point of view and to gain Alison's approval, or at least to come to some amicable arrangement. It was afterwards, in the evening, and again at breakfast this morning, that the weight of Alison's displeasure – with all Marston behind it, Mrs. Field and The Laurels and the ghostly advisers jostling for position – had made her continuing firmness so peculiarly exhausting.

She thought now that but for Mrs. Bateman and Robert she might have crumpled under the strain and turned back into the dutiful, irresolute Charlotte who allowed other people to know what was best for her.

Mrs. Bateman and Robert had given her a breathing space. They had called in the middle of the morning, looked in just for a moment, as Mrs. Bateman explained, because they so wanted to meet Charlotte's daughter and it seemed the only chance.

"Lily Wakelin told us your daughter is leaving this afternoon," said Mrs. Bateman, "and I know that means the two-fifteen train and you'll be having lunch early, so we won't stay long."

"Of course you must stay – come in and talk to Alison while I make some coffee."

"You mustn't bother," Mrs. Bateman protested, but Charlotte took no notice. She left them with Alison in the drawing-room and thankfully retired to the kitchen where the Marston atmosphere was less dense.

When she returned with the coffee they were talking about gardening. Or rather, Robert and his mother were talking and Alison was listening with a fair show of attention.

"Oh Charlotte, you shouldn't have bothered," Mrs. Bateman said.

"The privet hedge really ought to come up," said Robert. "It's taking all the good out of the ground."

"And it keeps the sun off too. Not as much as it did, of course, you should have seen it before it was cut," Mrs. Bateman told Alison. "It was as high as the bedroom windows!"

"On the other hand," said Robert, "it does protect the garden from the wind –"

"– and the sea winds do so much damage. It's the salt," Mrs. Bateman explained, seeing that Alison wasn't enough of a gardener to understand. "Even in Church Street where I live, the garden suffers terribly in a gale, and I'm further inland than your mother."

"I think I'll keep the hedge," said Charlotte.

"It will protect the house too," said Alison. "The gales might blow it down if it didn't have some protection."

"Oh, but it's a very solid house. These old houses may look rather – er, ramshackle, but they're very solidly built." Mrs. Bateman thought it was Charlotte, not the house, that needed protection and she good-naturedly set herself to supply it. "There's nothing much wrong with the house," she continued. "Of course it was in rather a state when your mother first arrived, but –"

"It still is," Alison said coldly.

"Well, she hasn't been here very long, has she?"

"Quite long enough, I think."

"I expect you miss her," Mrs. Bateman said chattily. "But it will be nice for you to visit her here – and your friend too, the girl who shares your flat, perhaps she'll come with you next time. At

Christmas, perhaps? And for a longer visit, I hope. You can't have seen much of Nything yet, but when you come again –"

Alison had had enough of the Batemans. "There isn't much to see, is there?" she asked, in such a parody of her polite voice for the elderly that Charlotte trembled.

"It's not very big," Mrs. Bateman agreed doubtfully.

"Or very interesting. Oh no, I shan't be coming for Christmas, I'm going away with Ev – the friend you spoke about."

"Where are you going?" Charlotte asked. This was the first time Alison had mentioned Christmas. The first time, perhaps, she had thought about it, for the pause that followed the question suggested that her destination wasn't settled.

But – "Bournemouth", said Alison, producing it like a trump card she knew her mother had not expected her to hold.

The Smiths, Evelyn's parents, had retired to Bournemouth and Evelyn usually spent Christmas with them. Charlotte wondered whether they knew yet that they were having Alison as well.

Christmas at The Laurels had never been very enjoyable. In Charlotte's younger days a faint but definite sense of grievance had hung about the house, along with the small bunches of holly which were all Mrs. Field allowed in the way of decorations – and only in the hall and on the stairs where they would do least damage to the wallpaper. There were also a few sprigs of holly on the dining-room table, and a good deal more in the servants' hall because they expected it. Suitable fare was provided, but never a Christmas tree.

Naturally they went to church on Christmas morning, and later in the day the maids came into the drawing-room and were given their presents. The parlour-maid and housemaid got lengths of black alpaca for afternoon dresses, the between-maid got a length of striped print and the cook a pair of strong, thick-soled black shoes. "She likes them for the floor," Mrs. Field would explain, alluding to the stone-flagged kitchen. And she would point out that the maids were also getting a good dinner, a goose all to themselves as well as plum pudding and mince pies and a bottle of tawny port and dessert. They had their dinner on Boxing Day, when the family had cold turkey and did not expect to be waited on. (Though of course Cook had to cook the servants' dinner, and the family's meal had to be set out and later washed up.) And after Boxing Day things quickly returned to normal, the sense of grievance disappeared together with the holly, and Charlotte's new doll took its place with the old dolls in the nursery instead of being permitted to sit on the drawing-room sofa.

The truth was that Mrs. Field did not care for undisciplined excitement and gaiety any more than she liked the clutter and mess of evergreen decorations. "People make so much fuss," she would complain, and only her respect for convention compelled her to have holly in the hall. In later years the holly was omitted altogether, for as the two remaining maids grew older they came to share her dislike of anything that interfered with routine and were quite content with a token decoration in the shape of a paper bell that could be folded up between Christmasses and left no mess at all. Even for her grand-daughter Mrs. Field would make no concessions, though she insisted on Charlotte and Alison spending Christmas under her roof. It was of course an excellent excuse for detaching them from Rivermead.

Naturally Alison, who admired her grandmother so much, had accepted her view of Christmas festivities as a squandering of money and time. The war and Mrs. Field's long illness had fixed the pattern irrevocably; Christmas at The Laurels, now as in the past, was celebrated with the minimum of fuss, and there was a perceptible feeling of relief when it was safely over.

Charlotte wondered what Christmas at Bournemouth would be like. Would Alison find a house garlanded with holly, crackers on the table, even a Christmas tree shedding its messy needles on the carpet and scenting the room with resin? The Smiths, in the old Rivermead days, had always had a party and a tree for Evvie – they were the kind of parents who positively enjoyed turning the house upside down and ensuring bilious attacks for other people's children. After one particularly bad bilious attack (not Alison's fault, poor darling, if she was *encouraged* to eat creamy cakes) Mrs. Field had artfully arranged for a tea-party at The Laurels always to coincide with the Smiths' annual Christmas party, so that Alison could not go to it.

"But she's going to it this year," Charlotte thought.

She looked across the esplanade railing. The grey sky had grown darker and she could see the rain approaching, blotting out the distant opposite shore while she watched. She glanced back, surprised as usual by the distance she had walked; somehow a walk along the sea front never seemed far, until you looked round. Even the nearest glass shelter was some distance behind her, for she had nearly reached the end of the long esplanade. She turned and began to walk back.

She reached the shelter just in time. The first drops of rain were becoming a steady downpour and she took refuge on the side that faced inland, with a glass partition, between its seat and the one that faced the sea. She had her back to the sea but she could look through the glass end of the shelter at the esplanade, deserted now except for one hunched figure advancing towards her from the direction of Nything. But this *was* Nything – "the Moss Bank end of the front." Of course. She watched the hurrying man draw nearer. She recognized him at once, almost as though she had known who it would be. This was the Moss Bank end of the front and here was Harley Coker, hurrying home.

At the shelter he stopped. He was directly behind Charlotte now and she could not see him, but she heard him enter the front part of the shelter; like herself he was taking refuge from the rain. She glanced the other way, through the glass partition, and saw that he was sitting at the far end of the seat that faced the sea. A tweed cap concealed his baldness (how odd that Harley should wear a deerstalker when he had so despised the kind of men who stalked deer), and the profile now presented to her had changed very little except in the way of a few wrinkles and darkening where all before had been smooth and delicately pale. A panama hat, artistically wide-brimmed, had protected that alabaster skin from the suns of Italy.

"Harley," said Charlotte though the glass screen.

He could not hear her. They were separated by a glass partition, and by layers of intervening time. It was as if the young Charlotte in Florence had spoken his name and expected her voice to reach him across the years. Besides she knew perfectly well –

the knowledge had been painfully acquired – that Harley never heard what he did not wish to hear. At a closer range than this he would still have ignored a voice that sought to call back yesterday.

Charlotte looked away and the spell was instantly broken. The absurdity of it was what struck her now – of feeling herself a girl again, of experiencing in rainy middle age the poignant emotions that belonged to youth and Italy. It was rather like seeing a ghost, she thought; one would be tricked for a moment into thinking it was a living human being and then realize it was a phantom, dead long ago. It was the young Charlotte, not Harley, who was the ghost.

She stared straight ahead, waiting for the rain to stop; already the downpour was less heavy and in a few minutes she would be able to go. Harley Coker must be going too, she heard the shuffle of his footsteps on the concrete floor and supposed he was resuming his homeward walk. Then a shadow briefly obscured the glass end of the shelter and he was standing in front of her.

"Charlotte Moley it is! I knew I could not be mistaken."

Charlotte stood up. Spontaneity was impossible and she hardly knew what to say.

"How clever of you to recognise me, Harley."

It was a banal response but the right one, for it assured Harley Coker that he had been recognized himself. His relief was touchingly visible and now he was able to lift his deerstalker cap, which had concealed the baldness that might have hindered recognition, and stand bare-headed in the rain for a short – a very short – moment while relief remoulded itself as triumph. Then the cap was on his head again and both hands were free to grasp Charlotte's. Like all his gestures it was beautiful and she regretted that it was a little spoilt by the hesitancy of her response.

"Don't speak of cleverness, Charlotte – it wasn't needed and never will be. You are proof against time."

"And you knew I was in Nything?"

She couldn't stop herself asking the deflating question. It was ridiculous of Harley to imply that he would have recognized her anywhere if he hadn't been forewarned of her presence. But he wasn't deflated, it crossed her mind that he had not even seen the point, let alone felt it.

"I have known it for three whole days," he said solemnly.

"I've know that you were here a little longer than that."

He took no notice. Perhaps it was an admission he did not choose to hear.

"I would have sought you out before," he continued, "but I judged it better to wait. Mrs. Bateman told me you had a visiting daughter."

"A visiting daughter – yes, she left today."

"That babe you used to talk about. How impossible it seems!"

"Well, children grow up," said Charlotte. She could not recollect talking to Harley about Alison but no doubt she had mentioned her occasionally.

"And we, alas, grow older."

She agreed it was so.

"Not you, Charlotte. I repeat – it's too wonderful to see you again, to see you still the true Florentine, la Fiorentina on the marble staircase with the lilies at her feet."

"Oh rubbish," Charlotte thought. But she did not say so because there was something pathetic as well as ridiculous in Harley's nervous gallantry. It was his own youth, not hers, that he was striving to re-create.

"It isn't true – we're all older," she said gently, not wholly rejecting the gallantry but wishing she could indicate that it wasn't required.

It was he who abandoned it, quite suddenly and with an effect of changing from knightly armour into something a good deal more comfortable. One moment he was standing outside in the rain admiring her, the next he was under the shelter's roof and advising her to sit down again because the storm was not yet over. Charlotte obediently sank down on the bench and Harley seated himself beside her, furtively patting the sleeve of his overcoat to find out if he had got very wet. He seemed reassured, and spoke magnanimously of the rain as having been the cause of their meeting.

"Though of course I should have called on you," he added.

"You know where I'm living? But of course Mrs. Bateman will have told you."

"Mrs. Gamalion's house." His voice conveyed the wonder of it.

"She left it to me. Oh yes, I suppose Mrs. Bateman told you that too."

"She had no need to. I knew you were Mrs. Gamalion's appointed heir. Her will was in the local paper and I must confess to reading it with uncommon interest. But it never occurred to me, Charlotte, that the legacy would bring you to Nything."

"Didn't it? Well, no, it didn't occur to me either, when I first learned about it. It was only when I got here –"

"But it's precisely that – your getting here – that I failed to envisage. I imagined you in another life, your own sphere, happily settled and multitudinously occupied, and all your links with the past – our absurd fantastical excursions with our absurd, fantastical commander – long ago severed."

"But Harley –" she began, forgetting that one couldn't stop Sir Galahad in full flight.

"I imagined a chain of intermediaries extending itself on your behalf. Solicitors, valuers, house agents, instructing one another and instructed from – oh, so far away, by you. But you remained remote. How could it be otherwise, when remoteness had been for so long your quintessential quality? In short," said Harley, neatly folding his wings and planing to earth, "I imagined you would simply put the place up for sale."

"Without even seeing it?"

"What was there that could interest you? It belonged, surely, to a past you had altogether relinquished."

"Didn't you wonder *why* Mrs. Gamalion left the house to me? If I had, as you supposed, lost touch –"

"My dear Charlotte, when did Mrs. Gamalion ever need the support of a good reason for her actions? It would so entirely like her to bequeath her property to someone she had not seen or heard of since the golden age."

"I don't agree," said Charlotte. "She never said anything about it in her letters but I think she chose me just because I *was* still in earshot."

"Her letters!"

"Yes. You see, I wasn't so remote as you imagined. I'd never been to Nything, and I had no idea she was leaving me the house, but we did keep up. So I think, there was, after all, a reason for the legacy."

The last of the Old Faithfuls – for she could certainly count herself as that – wondered why Harley looked so remarkably taken aback. Then she remembered the quarrel, the absence of any reference to Cokers in all the later correspondence. It was he that was out of touch, he probably had not spoken to Mrs. Gamalion for years, presumably he was now conjecturing what Mrs. Gamalion had written about him, imagining himself blackguarded, his mother's sacred memory besmirched. He did not guess, and there was no immediate way of telling him, that they had simply ceased to be mentioned. (And conceivably 'being dropped' might strike him as more painful than being libelled.)

"A reason indeed," he said at last. He stood up, clutching at his scattered self-esteem and somehow appearing much older and rather forlorn. "Well, the rain seems to be over, and I must be on my way."

"I must be going too." Suddenly Charlotte felt sorry for Harley and wished she had not made him so uneasy. "But you'll come to see me, won't you?" she continued. "There's so much to talk about, so much I don't know and should like to."

"But you kept up," he said stiffly.

"We kept up, yes, but not up to date. You see, Mrs. Gamalion lived in the past. Most of her letters were about – what did you call it? – the golden age. I didn't even know, until Mrs. Bateman told me, that you were still living in Nything."

He looked happier as he remarked on the strangeness of it. Strange, and yet natural too (she could see the likelihood occurring to him) that an old lady should concern herself exclusively with the distant past. Then his expression grew solemn and after a portentous pause he asked whether Charlotte knew of his loss.

"I learned of your mother's death from Mrs. Bateman," she answered truthfully.

Chapter XIV

Harley Coker's house at Moss Bank had a name as well as a number. It was called Bank House. Harley explained that formerly it had been the only house in the district – not counting a few old cottages at the end of the road, long ago pulled down. There had been an orchard at one side of the big garden, with fields behind, and the road had been a gravel lane, rather muddy in winter but blessedly quiet and private. When he was a boy they used to walk to church across the fields at the back, by a footpath that brought them out at the end of Church Street just beyond the vicarage paddock.

The description of this vanished paradise made a sad contrast with the present. Moss Bank was still on the very edge of Nything but you could no longer walk to church across the fields. The orchard had gone too, there were houses all along the landward side of the road up to the garden boundary, and the road had been widened and surfaced. There was street lighting now, and the houses were numbered. "Quite suburban," said Harley mournfully.

"But it's all open in front, and beyond you," Charlotte protested. "And you've got your big garden as well, between you and the new houses. It's quite a walk to this end of the road."

"You found it tiring?" he inquired anxiously.

"Not at all. I enjoyed it – I like walking."

"I have no car, you understand, or naturally I should have fetched you. Of course I shall escort you home when you leave."

"You needn't bother to escort me," she said. "I often go for a walk along the esplanade in the evening. I shall be quite all right."

"But you cannot walk home by yourself on Christmas Day. When you have ventured so far to enliven my solitude! No, Charlotte, I positively cannot allow you to walk all that way back by yourself."

In spite of the suburban surroundings Harley seemed to think he lived a considerable distance from Nything, whereas his housekeeper had insisted this *was* Nything – the Moss Bank end of the front. But Harley Coker and Miss Rimmer were two very different people. Charlotte had been aware of their disparate personalities as soon as she entered Bank House.

Downstairs, the house seemed to have been taken over by the housekeeper. The orange-yellow wicker chairs and shiny ornaments in the hall, the 'contemporary' decoration of the drawing-room, the plastic flowers in their plastic vases, were recent innovations. Upstairs in Harley's sitting-room his own taste prevailed – or more likely his mother's taste slightly modified by her son's artistic nature. For this had been her boudoir and the room next door had been her bedroom. It was Harley's bedroom now. The rooms were reached by a short corridor, which could be likened to the moat between a castle and its potential assailants. The simile appealed to Charlotte; here was Sir Galahad besieged.

"Christmas Day," said Harley. He looked round the room as if conjuring up visions of the past, then rose to his feet and carefully adjusted the folds of the damask curtains across the windows. "My mother disliked it if they weren't drawn properly."

"But this is an upstairs room, no one could see in."

"That wasn't the point. She disliked the untidiness of it, if one was careless and left a gap in the middle. She would have noticed it long before we'd finished tea."

"Not if she'd been sitting where you're sitting. You didn't notice it yourself until you looked round."

"Ah, but she always sat on the other side of the fireplace. Where *you* are, Charlotte. That was her chair."

Charlotte immediately wished she had not been given the seat of honour. There was something distasteful about sitting in Mrs. Coker's hallowed chair – in being an inadequate substitute, or understudy, for Harley's matchless mother.

But kindness compelled her to respond to his reminiscent tone, and to the sense of change and impoverishment that permeated the room and indeed the house.

It hardly needed a question to release the memories of other Christmases, of Mrs. Coker's custom of entertaining a few friends to tea, and of the pleasure her invitations gave to the honoured few. Her Christmas tea party had been famous, Harley said with a smile. She could not manage a dinner party; even the tea party had taxed her strength, for she had always been delicate. But it happened only once a year and she had always insisted it was worth the effort – because of the pleasure it provided for her friends and for him.

"And I expect she enjoyed it too," said Charlotte.

"She enjoyed it in her own way," he replied solemnly.

Charlotte wondered how Mrs. Coker's way of enjoying a party differed from other people's. "Did you have it in this room?" she asked.

"Oh no! This was Mother's boudoir, you know – a place for rest and renewal, for seclusion and study." (What did she study? Charlotte asked herself.) "Of course we often sat here together; she used it more and more as she grew older. But in those days we used the whole house. Indeed we should have been uncomfortably crowded in this room – large though it seems in one's solitude. But I am speaking of a gathering, an assembly, not numerous, indeed, but cheerful and enlivening. In fact the numbers varied from year to year. But the tradition, the spirit of the thing, that was what counted. I miss it still."

Charlotte perceived that she was doubly a substitute; the occupant of a hallowed chair and also in a sense a substitute for the cheerful and enlivening gathering of former days. That was why she had been asked; it was a pathetic attempt to revive the tradition. But why was no one else available but a newcomer to Nything?

She had not seen Harley since their meeting on the esplanade. But she had received two notes from him, the first explaining that a bad cold had prevented his calling on her, the second inviting her to tea on Christmas Day.

He wrote that he was quite recovered but that his housekeeper had also had a cold and since she was still enfeebled his hospitality must be of the simplest. Perhaps that was the explanation; his housekeeper wasn't equal to providing tea for a larger number.

"Our Christmas tea party was always held downstairs in the drawing-room." Harley gave a deep sigh. "Of course it looked quite different then."

<u>In those days we used the whole house.</u> Charlotte was back with the moat, the castle, Sir Galahad besieged and his kingdom under enemy rule.

"Different?" she asked cautiously.

"*Very* different. My dear Charlotte, you can have no notion, now, of that room's elegance and charm. All gone, all destroyed, vulgarized by the late so-called improvements. I should never have permitted it, but that I failed to visualise the horrors that would result when I gave Miss Rimmer what it pleased her to describe as a free hand."

"You let her choose the wallpaper?"

"Wallpaper in the plural; did you notice that there is a different pattern on every wall? Yes, yes, I left it all to her – the chair covers, the paint, the revolting accessories. Did you observe the ashtrays and the floral arrangements?"

"But why, Harley? Why did you let her choose everything?"

"She insisted the room needed redecorating. Of course she was right," said Harley, in the magnanimous tone Charlotte remembered so well. "I admit it – in recent times the room had been somewhat neglected – in fact it was many years since we had last had it done. So I agreed that redecoration was necessary." He sighed again, more deeply than before. "Miss Rimmer persuaded me to take a holiday, to avoid the discomfort of a disorganized household while the work was in progress. I think she knew I would have put a stop to it, had I been there."

"Miss Rimmer sounds formidable."

"A good soul, a very good soul. She nursed my poor mother most faithfully."

So she *was* a nurse, Charlotte thought. The enfeebled house-keeper had not been visible that afternoon; Harley had opened the door himself and after showing Charlotte the drawing-room to demonstrate that it was too cold to be comfortable, he had led her upstairs; he had left her in his sitting-room, where the tea table was already set out, and had then brought up the tray with the silver teapot; another journey had been necessary because he had forgotten the milk jug and the sugar basin. Perhaps Miss Rimmer was too enfeebled to attend to things, or perhaps, good soul though she was, she had refused to co-operate in the entertainment of even one visitor on Christmas Day. Poor Harley with his ghost of a tea party!

"And so you're grateful to her – well, naturally," Charlotte said aloud. She was beginning to see Miss Rimmer as another Sister Wainsford, excellent in her proper sphere but a sore trial otherwise. "Is she staying on? I mean, doesn't she want to go back to nursing?"

"It was my idea." Poor Harley gave the deepest sigh of all – almost a groan. "My idea, that is to say, that she should remain as housekeeper. I had not then realised, I had not begun to consider –"

His voice died away, sighing or groaning into silence. After a respectful pause Charlotte gently prodded him into speech again.

"What hadn't you considered?"

"The expense."

She echoed him sympathetically. "Oh dear, yes – the expense." But it hardly struck her at first as a sufficient reason for all those sighs and groans. She had somehow taken it for granted that Harley was comfortably off, and if he could afford to keep up this big house then surely he could afford the wages of a housekeeper. Besides, he had recently spent a good deal on having the place redecorated.

"But I don't understand," she said, as this thought occurred to her. "Why did you give Miss Rimmer a free hand in the drawing-room, if you're worried about expenses?"

"I had to. She insisted. She had this plan. A strange ambition, but perfectly genuine – not just a sudden whim. She was so competent – so confident – she had no doubts of her own ability. And I was distraught, with grief and worry – and then the discovery of how bad things were, much worse than I had anticipated. It seemed absolutely the only solution."

He spoke jerkily, sometimes in whispers as if Miss Rimmer's strange ambition were too bizarre to be mentioned aloud. But little by little Charlotte made out the story.

Miss Rimmer had always aspired to own an hotel. It was her dream to settle down in a respectable neighbourhood and build up a good-class business which would provide her with a home, an interest, and of course a living. She fancied a seaside resort, but she was particular; such opportunities as had presented themselves were never quite suitable. Moreover she had no money. She had had 'expectations' once, but they had failed her. The dream remained a dream, the strange ambition incapable of fulfilment – until the day when Harley, distraught and desolate, had confided to her how bad things were. He had invited her to stay on as a house-keeper but he now had to confess he could not run to a housekeeper. Indeed he would not require one, because he would have to sell Bank House. What distressed him most of all, what mattered far more than the actual catastrophe of turning out, was that he had faithfully promised his mother he would never leave it.

It was then that Miss Rimmer had told him of her lifelong ambition, and of the expectations that had never materialised. She could not afford to buy an hotel now.

Harley could not afford to remain at Bank House. But something could be arranged to suit both of them; it was just the kind of place she fancied and of course he would have his own rooms and be quite separate from the visitors. It would still be his home but he would have some help towards the upkeep if Miss Rimmer took in paying-guests.

Only he would have to do some repairs and redecorating first. The place needed brightening up and he must give her a free hand in the drawing-room and the hall.

"It seemed absolutely the only solution."

"A very good idea," said Charlotte.

So it was, considering the circumstances, and she went on reassuring him while they walked back along the esplanade, for Harley, having unbosomed himself, could not stop talking about the changes at Bank House. He had been shocked, horrified, outraged by Miss Rimmer's innovations, yet he had to admit that the good creature had done her best to please him – it was she who had suggested that his mother's rooms should be turned into a private suite, with a bathroom in the old dressing-room, where he could live undisturbed even when the house was full. He had stipulated from the beginning that those rooms must not be used for paying-guests, but it was Miss Rimmer who had seen that he could fittingly occupy them himself.

Very sensible of Miss Rimmer, Charlotte thought, to persuade Harley himself to occupy two otherwise unusable rooms. "And was the house full, in the summer?" she asked.

It had been full for a week in August. At other times there had been few guests or none, but Miss Rimmer was not discouraged because after all it was her first season and the place as yet unknown. And two people who had stayed there in June had returned for another week quite recently, which pleased her very much.

Charlotte said good night to Harley at her front door. He would not come in but he waited till she had opened the door and switched on the hall light, and she thought he looked with keen though melancholy interest at the scene the light revealed. That at least had not changed, though it must be a long time since Harley had last glimpsed it.

I must ask him to tea, she thought. She turned on the lights in the drawing-room and revived the smouldering fire and sat down to think about Christmas Day, now nearly over. The cold church at seven o'clock that morning, with the black shapes of the windows gradually assuming their familiar reds and blues as darkness gave place to daylight. The crowded church at matins, looking as it must have looked in the past and with the heating also suddenly and mysteriously restored to full vigour, coming up in *waves*, just as Mrs. Gamalion had described it. Harley had been at church but she had not seen him. She had known the Batemans would not be there, for Robert was doing duty at a country church which lacked an incumbent, and Mrs. Bateman had gone with him.

But Charlotte was acquainted with several other people by now, with whom she exchanged greetings after the service. Today it seemed to her that she was no longer a stranger in Nything.

The Wakelins never came to church, not even on Christmas Day, but she joined them afterwards. They had insisted on inviting her to a festive meal at the Pier Hotel where they always went for celebrations – their birthdays, their wedding anniversary, Christmas and the New Year.

"We like celebrating," Lily explained, "but it's no fun if you have to do a lot of cooking, is it?"

"And all the washing-up afterwards." (Bart seemed to have forgotten he had a machine to do this for him.) "All that toil and moil – it's exhausting, not fun at all. Lily and I manage things better. Book a table – walk in – eat a good meal – walk out again. Can't think why everyone doesn't do it, instead of fussing with roasting a turkey and making mince-pies and so on."

Charlotte wondered what the Wakelins would have done if Christmas Day had brought frost or snow, since they never ventured out in cold weather. But no doubt they had foreseen such hazards and provided themselves with an alternative, a feast in tins that only needed opening. It was kind of them to have invited her. How lucky that her winter clothes had arrived last week, so that she had her dark blue dress to wear for this festive occasion. Lily too wore a blue dress, but a lighter colour and much more elaborate than Charlotte's.

It matched her faded blue eyes and had a soft deep ruffle of lace at the neck which was very becoming. It was an old-fashioned dress that she might have treasured for years because Bart had always admired her in it.

"Two little girls in blue," Bart said, lifting his glass. "The compliments of the season to both of you!"

Sitting by the fire, Charlotte looked down at her own blue dress and recalled the arrival of her winter clothes. They had been packed in a suitcase, not locked but tied up with yards of strong cord and a great many knots. They had arrived without warning and without her having asked for them to be sent, but she had known by the knots and the labels that the sender was Evelyn. The letter – Evelyn's Christmas letter – had followed a day or two later. It was lying on the table beside her, and she picked it up and read it again.

Evelyn thanked her for the cheque just received and said it would come in very useful. She explained that she was writing straightaway because she would not have much time for letters at Bournemouth – only four days' holiday and there was sure to be a lot going on. Mummy was so pleased Alison was coming and it would make Christmas even better, though it was always fun anyway.

The next paragraph was rather disjointed. Charlotte could imagine Evelyn frowning at the paper, changing her mind about what to say.

"I hope you are having fun too. Alison told me about the house and about your staying on. It does sound a good plan, if you like it I mean. I sent off your thick clothes at the weekend, it's been rather cold here so I thought you might need them, Alison said. Well, in fact it was my idea, but she agreed. We are managing beautifully. Sorry this is such a scribble, I just wanted to send my best wishes for Christmas. And a really happy new year. I do understand. Let me know if there's anything I left out."

Below Evelyn's sprawling signature there was a postscript; "It's just that Alison never feels the cold so it didn't occur to her."

Alison's Christmas letter had been much shorter and less informative.

Charlotte had not expected encouragement from Evelyn, whose views on most subjects were a loyal echo of Alison's. Perhaps Evvie knew that Alison was beginning to relent; was it wishful thinking to read in the letter an assurance that all would be well? Anyway it was nice to know that they were managing beautifully.

I hope you are having fun too. Well yes, I enjoyed it, Charlotte thought, wondering too whether Alison was enjoying the Smiths' traditional Christmas revels at Bournemouth. She thought about her companions today, the Wakelins and Harley Coker, poor Harley shut up in Bank House with his ruthless housekeeper, fighting a losing battle against the invasion of paying-guests. Still, they were a disagreeable necessity, they enabled him to go on living in the style to which he had been accustomed. And Miss Rimmer, Charlotte thought, could hardly be more ruthless or strong-minded than the late Mrs. Coker. All his life Harley must have been ruled by his mother.

Long ago in Florence when he had come from the dark loggia into the lighted room – a dramatic entrance which at this distance of time could be seen as carefully planned – Mrs. Gamalion's first delighted shrieks had almost at once become injuries for Mrs. Coker. Where was she? – *how* was she? – had the journey exhausted her? His mother was at home in Nything, Harley had explained, and seen now Charlotte thought she could distinguish a genuine astonishment in Mrs. Gamalion's cries as she took it in. She had not expected – not really expected – that Harley would be able to get to Italy without his mother.

He had smiled and made some teasing reply; gallant badinage was always his note with Mrs. Gamalion. It had not occurred to Charlotte – but it did now – that Harley Coker's Italian holiday, like her own, had been an escape from bondage.

Chapter XV

In Florence Harley had never considered the expense of anything. He had a lofty attitude, a soul well above niggling accountancy. To talk about money was rather vulgar, or so he seemed to think, when the question of economy came up, as it often did.

Mrs. Gamalion and her friends were always discussing the cost of things. They had to keep a careful eye on expenses, for none of them was rich and it was important to get good value and not to spend too much – as one so easily could – on non-essentials. Sitting in the loggia after dinner they would exchange information about little shops where they had bought cheap presents, the embroidered handkerchiefs and tooled leather book-markers which it was obligatory to take back to relations at home, or they would compare the prices in various cafés, item by item, and argue about which was best.

"But didn't you think it was good value? Such a nice clean place, and much cheaper than Doney's."

"Not really. The cakes are cheaper but they're very small, and the coffee actually costs more."

The arguments were good-humoured, for at heart all the ladies were on the same side, anxious to help one another to save money, grateful for warnings or advice. Mrs. Gamalion was probably the most expert economizer, but though none could equal her talent for bargaining they enjoyed hearing of her successes. A few lire saved here, a rapacious cab-driver defeated there, were a kind of collective triumph for the whole circle.

But Harley laughed at them, or gently shuddered, according to his mood. He seemed to have enough money not to bother with such petty economies.

It was that summer, the second summer in which Harley joined Mrs. Gamalion's party in Florence, that Charlotte allowed herself to think about marrying again. It had not been a thought, or even a dream, last year, for nothing had happened then to disturb the settled pattern of her existence, the role she had long accepted as permanent. But something was happening now. Perhaps after all it had begun last year, at the very moment when Harley had walked out of the darkness – a moment of mysterious significance which she had not tried to understand. It had come and gone, all in her own mind, and better forgotten. He was charming, but he charmed everyone; the happiness she felt in his company was shared by all of them. She would have been foolish indeed, if last year she had allowed herself to dream of marrying him.

But this year it was different. Charlotte was humble about herself but she could not help being aware of Harley's admiration. It took her back to the brief time between leaving school and marrying Gabriel, when one or two young men had flattered her by their attentions, had sought her for a partner at the tennis club and even invited her to dances. Her mother had minimized the importance of the young men, they were 'just boys' and not to be taken seriously. Anyway there was Gabriel, so reliable, so kind, so clearly destined to be her husband that no other choice had ever really existed. But the young men had taught her the pleasure of knowing herself admired.

She had forgotten what it was like, for although Gabriel had loved her he hadn't, as her mother would have put it, tried to turn her head by excessive flattery and admiration. For one thing, he hadn't needed to, since their marriage was a foregone conclusion; for another, he wasn't a young man. But now, catching Harley's gaze fixed upon her or listening to the special tone of voice he used when they were together, she felt the forgotten pleasure reviving, and bringing with it a confidence she had barely begun to experience in the tennis-club days. Admiration gave her confidence and confidence enhanced those qualities that had evoked the admiration. Harley Coker wasn't the only man to notice her now, and Mrs. Gamalion's friends agreed that Charlotte was looking 'wonderfully well' that summer.

"And so Italian," they were saying a little later. But again it was Harley who had launched Charlotte in the role; not by comparing her with the female inhabitants of the city but by proclaiming her to be the original model for that picture in the Hudson palazzo, a reincarnation in whom they could all discern the classic Florentine features and the true Florentine grace. He made so much of it that the Hudsons received an unusual influx of callers, some brought by Harley himself. Naturally he insisted on Charlotte's accompanying him so that he could demonstrate his discovery.

The picture hung on the far end wall of the sala, suspended above a painted, worm-eaten chest (the famous marriage-chest alleged to have belonged to a Medici bride) which stood on a shallow plinth or step that extended the width of the room. Less fame attached to the picture; it had perhaps been hung there because it was so big and needed half a wall to itself, and even the Hudsons had found no name for the painter. For them he remained Pictor Ignotus, a man who had once disregarded the doubts imagined for him by Robert Browning and let his soul spring up to achieve a masterpiece. Fortunately for his reputation the dusty windows with their many boarded-up panes left the masterpiece in decent obscurity.

But it could bear more daylight, all the same; there were hidden merits, as well as faults, waiting there for illumination. Moreover there was Charlotte, who needed no merciful dimness to preserve the illusion of beauty. Harley removed a leather screen, then pulled the threadbare velvet curtain back from the nearest window and tucked it over a chair against the wall, and prized away a piece of board that had stood behind it, letting in more light and also a current of unfamiliar fresh air and the faint, genial sound of Italian voices rising from the street below, where the hour of siesta was over and women were beginning to emerge from dark doorways and resume their conversational existence. The presence of a number of people, added to the noise floating in on the warm summer air, brought the Hudson sala to life in a way Charlotte had not thought possible. And there she was, standing on the shallow step beside the bridal chest, facing the window as Harley directed and then, again at his command, turning her head a little towards the spectators. "That's it," he cried. He stepped aside, waiting for the audience to applaud his perspicacity, and Charlotte looked at their respectful upturned faces and burst out laughing.

"No, no, you mustn't laugh! La bellezza on the wall there isn't laughing. Imagine yourself in the picture – the girl standing on a staircase with the lilies at her feet."

"Oh dear, I can't. I'd rather not," Charlotte cried gaily. "Think of being stuck on the lowest step of a marble staircase and knowing that if you turned your head you'd see the long climb in front of you, a hundred and umpteen steps up to your uncomfortable seicento future. No wonder she looks pensive!"

Nevertheless she tried for Harley's sake to check her laughter and allow him his triumph. It was hers too, of course – an agreeable moment of being looked at and admired – but chiefly his whose artistic eye had discerned the likeness and who was now waiting to impress his friends.

But they had all seen it. She was permitted to descend from her little stage and Margery Mollison carefully replaced the board and let the window curtain fall down into its folds, shutting out the street sounds and bringing back the customary dimness, although the presence of Harley's audience diminished the customary resemblance to a tomb.

Heaven knew what the Hudsons made of it – the surprising influx of visitors, some of whom had never ventured there before, newcomers blinking their bewilderment, Mrs. Gamalion flying about pointing out the chief treasures of the collection, Margery Mollison patiently bringing up a succession of strangers to be introduced. But whatever they thought, the Hudsons appeared to be mildly enjoying the stir and bustle, perhaps imagining themselves back in an earlier age when more celebrated visitors had thronged the room, arriving and departing in carriages that lined the narrow street, announced by a major-domo whose voice could be clearly heard enunciating their names and titles. His absence today, and their inability to recognize the names uttered by Mrs. Mollison, were puzzles they seemed content to leave unsolved.

"We were all Archdukes and Archduchesses," Mrs. Mollison declared afterwards. "It took them back, you see – right back to the beginning."

"But they weren't grown up then. They can only have been small children in the Austrian regime."

"They're like children now and they've lost track of time. They think they were grown up in the world their parents knew – much grander and more exciting even than their own. The golden age is always the longest ago past."

"I don't understand," said Charlotte, "why they remember it alike. Did they both grow up in Florence?"

Mrs. Gamalion could answer that question. "Oh yes, they're first cousins. Their mothers were sisters. His father was killed in the Crimea but he and his mother were already living here because of her lungs, because all her family were dreadfully liable to consumption though I was told it was the shock of his death that really finished her!"

"Whose death?" someone asked in perplexity.

"Mr. Hudson's father's, of course! He was killed in the charge of the Light Brigade and she never smiled again," said Mrs. Gamalion, brilliantly dovetailing two familiar fragments of history. "And the boy – *our* Hudson – was brought up by his uncle and aunt here in Florence and married his cousin – I believe he went home and was in the cavalry like his father, but not for very long as it didn't suit him as he was so artistic and not used to the climate. So he sent in his papers – of course there weren't any wars then so it didn't matter – and came back and got married. Someone told me she had all the money – he'd hardly got a penny of his own – but then they were cousins so it wasn't like fortune-hunting!"

"But is a man who marries for money less blameworthy if he picks on a cousin?" Margery Mollison wanted to know.

Harley Coker thought it depended on the cousin – a pretty one would make the man seem less mercenary, though on the whole he agreed with Mrs. Mollison that it was just as bad to marry a cousin for her money as to seek out a rich widow.

"Like you," he whispered to Charlotte, teasing her under cover of the hubbub that had now developed. Some people were echoing Mrs. Mollison, someone else was protesting that the Hudsons had no money at all, while Mrs. Gamalion was loudly explaining that it wasn't fortune-hunting when the money was in the family and no brothers or sisters to share it.

"I'm not a rich widow," Charlotte said lightly, "nevertheless, people seek you out. What other explanation could there be for it? That man at the corner table – does he dream of being comfortably supported by your wealth, or has he a reason wholly unconnected with avarice?"

It was an awkward question to answer. "He's lonely," she said, for loneliness was a plausible explanation of John Sefton's behaviour and also, she hoped, a defence against any accusation Harley might make of her having encouraged him. Poor Mr. Sefton, he was lonely and naturally one was sorry for him . . .

"Poor fellow, it's not surprising, with those dangling arms and short little legs. A man who scuttles about like a crab feeling its way is eternally doomed to be lonely."

And that was the end of her admirer John Sefton, he had turned into a crab and she could not see him as anything else. He scuttled in vain, always arriving too late and finding her surrounded by other people or committed to an expedition he had not been invited to join, and at last gave up and packed up and took himself off to Bordighera ("He'll be in his proper element there," said Harley) and was forgotten. The room he had occupied was now taken by Margery Mollison, who was persuaded to move from her old room because it would do very well for Miss Glyn-Gibson.

"You can afford that front room with a balcony and she can't," said Mrs. Gamalion.

It was difficult to fit Miss Glyn-Gibson in as she had not booked her room in advance like the rest of Mrs. Gamalion's party, and the cheaper rooms were all taken when she at last wrote to say she would join them. But the letter stirred Mrs. Gamalion to excitement and after fluent arguments and discussions with the Signora she found this solution; after all, Margery Mollison had always had a front room in the past and it wouldn't hurt her to pay a little more for the short time that remained. Half the visit to Florence was already over.

"Oh well, it won't hurt me *much*," Mrs. Mollison said to Charlotte. "But I do rather grudge the expense, even in a good cause."

"It's a much nicer room than the other," Charlotte replied consolingly. They were standing in it, having just finished transferring Mrs. Mollison's things from the bedroom at the back of the house – a bedroom, it now struck her, of a much humbler kind than any hitherto occupied by her companion, who in former years had been insistent on a good view and a comfortable mattress.

"Views don't matter so much when one gets older," said Mrs. Mollison, answering the thought as if it had been spoken. Then she answered the question behind it, saying in her brisk voice, "I'm not as well off as I was, so I decided to economize on views this year."

"Oh dear, I'm so sorry. So does Mrs. Gamalion know? It seems a shame you should have to pay more so that Miss Glyn-Gibson can pay less."

Mrs. Mollison laughed. "It's the kind of arrangement one gets accustomed to, travelling with Minnie! And it evens out, you know. I've had splendid rooms in my time, with one of her protégées – or so I suspected – sharing the cost, one of those girls with wealthy parents who don't seem to exist any more."

Charlotte remembered Menaggio, the lovely room Mrs. Gamalion had obtained for her, and Alice and Muriel grumbling about theirs. "Don't look so worried – I'm not ruined," Mrs. Mollison continued. "In fact I'm probably no worse off than anyone else. Things go up all the time, and my income tends to go down, that's all. But I think everyone is feeling the pinch. That's why Minnie and all of us are hoping Miss Glyn-Gibson's scheme will come off."

"What *is* her scheme?"

"But haven't you been approached? Asked to contribute to the Fund?"

"No. Oh – yes, I remember now, Mrs. Gamalion did talk about a Fund, last winter when I saw her in London. But all my money is in trust, tied up, you know, so that I can't get at it."

Careful Gabriel. How justified he was in his belief that women should be prevented from getting at their capital.

Miss Glyn-Gibson arrived that evening, as meek and dowdy as Charlotte remembered her, with a battered suitcase bearing someone else's initials and a small black bag like an old-fashioned doctor's which she carried everywhere, locked up and with the key on a string round her neck. It contained Important Documents relating to the Scheme, the promised contributions to the Fund scrupulously set down in a stiff-backed ledger, a very modest bill for expenses, and a full, even lyrical, description of La Residenza, written by somebody else and therefore, as she was at pains to explain, quite unbiased.

Mrs. Gamalion was both elated and disappointed. It was exciting that Miss Glyn-Gibson had actually found a large villa which she hoped to purchase, but disappointing that it was not in the near neighbourhood of Florence and that she would not reveal its whereabouts. But as she explained, everything – the whole future – might be imperilled if she did. She was negotiating for it privately and no one else knew it was for sale; once let the place be mentioned, a whisper get about, and rival buyers would appear and push the price up.

"She's quite right. If we knew the name one of us might easily mention it in the hearing of the servants."

"Oh, one can't trust Italian servants! But she's already told *someone* about it, the person who wrote the description," Mrs. Gamalion pointed out. "She could get us all together and tell us when there aren't any servants hanging about and then we'd never mention it again. In a church! Why not all of us meet in Santa Croce after tea?"

But Miss Glyn-Gibson was adamant. As for the lyrical description, it had been written by an Australian acquaintance who had now returned to the Antipodes and who had no idea she was seeking to buy a house. They had visited the place together, but in the guise of sightseers, and the Australian had written an account of it at her suggestion, ostensibly as a test of memory.

Everyone was satisfied. Miss Glyn-Gibson, in spite of her meekness, had a strange authority, an almost hypnotic power of inspiring confidence. It must be remembered too, as Charlotte remembered afterwards, that they all longed for the Scheme to succeed and were looking forward to la Residenza as a haven to shelter them from old age and increasing poverty.

La Residenza was not yet the villa's name. That was the name it would have when they had bought it; they, the contributors to the Fund and founder-members of the Scheme, who would live there permanently and very cheaply, a colony of English ladies who had left behind them the discomforts of English winters, who were no longer worried about the cost of the annual railway journey and the way pensione tariffs went up every year. Living in one's own villa would be *far* cheaper; moreover there would be the paying-guests, English ladies like themselves but not permanent residents, who would flock to the place once it became known, attracted by the modest terms and the friendly English atmosphere, and who would help to pay for the upkeep.

"It will be self-supporting in no time – we shall live there for practically *nothing*!" Mrs. Gamalion cried enthusiastically.

Miss Glyn-Gibson had a deprecating smile for such optimism. "You mustn't pitch your hopes too high," she said. "I don't want anyone to be misled, or to join the Scheme without studying the figures." The figures, pages of estimated costs, were fished out of the black bag and passed from hand to hand, inspiring fresh confidence by being so detailed and business-like.

"But just suppose there should be a war," someone murmured anxiously.

"Oh, but there won't be. You mustn't go by the papers – someone who really knows told me Hitler isn't half as strong as they make out."

"It's just bluff. All those tanks in the pictures are really made of cardboard!"

"And Mussolini wouldn't come in anyway! I know for a fact he doesn't want a war. The Italians would *never* fight against England!"

Mrs. Gamalion's vehemence raised a laugh, but everyone agreed with her. The Italians were on our side last time. The Berlin-Rome Axis meant nothing, Mussolini was much cleverer than Hitler, he had no intention of getting involved in a real war. Abyssinia didn't count, it was a long way off; Mussolini had saved Italy from anarchy and he would never risk exposing it to the horrors of war. Only there wasn't going to be a war.

"Thank God Glyn-Gibson is leaving," Harley said next morning. "Of course she's right about the war-mongers – it's just political bluffing – but being right does not excuse her appalling dullness."

"Do you distrust her?" Charlotte asked on impulse.

He shook his head. "I wasn't questioning her probity – she is, I am sure, depressingly honest and conscientious. Think of those brown eyes, staring at you like a devoted dog's, and the supreme sense of responsibility that compels her to wear that key on a greasy string round her neck all day, and, one assumes, all night as well. Honest, sincere, hard-working, she deserves every epithet of respect. But I've had quite enough of her."

"She'll be going away first thing tomorrow."

"Let us go away today ourselves."

He was not suggesting an elopement, merely a day at Fiesole. Just the two of them, blessedly alone up there on the hillside, sitting in the Roman amphitheatre, watching the lizards and smelling the wild thyme. They would slip away quietly, separately, so that Mrs. Gamalion would not guess they were deserting her before she had settled the plan for the day. Charlotte would pretend to be going back to her bedroom in search of a book or some writing-paper, while Harley would stroll out to the loggia and so, by the other door, downstairs. They would meet each other in half an hour's time, outside the Palazzo Vecchio by Neptune's fountain.

He was not suggesting an elopement, but everything he said, and most of all his way of saying it, told Charlotte what her heart hoped to hear. Even their meeting by the fountain had the character of a romantic assignation, achieved as it was by stealth and secrecy. Heptane's tritons tossed their heads, the plumes of falling spray shimmered with tiny rainbows, brilliant as happiness in the bright morning.

"Oh look," Charlotte cried. "Look at the rainbows!"

And Harley looked at them and allowed the whole fountain to be beautiful, for he would have denied her nothing just then and had forgotten his critical objections to Neptune. Just as he had forgotten his mother in Nything, to whom he owed so much and whose approval – seeing that Charlotte was not after all a rich widow – would be essential if he were to contemplate matrimony.

But Mrs. Coker must have been aware of his forgetfulness, and of the danger to which it exposed him. Her warning voice, inaudible to both of them at that moment, reached Harley only just in time but reach him it did, with an effect as startling and immediate as if she herself had appeared at his side in the great half-circle of the amphitheatre, where he and Charlotte had till then imagined themselves alone. It was a tremendous triumph for telepathy and mother love.

CHAPTER XVI

"Is Margery Mollison in this group?" Robert asked. Charlotte leant over the back of his chair and looked at the photograph in Mrs. Gamalion's Book. Mrs. Mollison was at the end of the row, she said, and that was Harley Coker next to her.

"I don't think I'd have recognized him," said Robert. He picked up the magnifying-glass and had another look. "Yes, of course it is. Harley Coker before he went bald. Oh well, I suppose I shall be unrecognisable in old photographs by people who've only known me since I went bald."

"But you're not bald!"

"I shall be one day. I meant, people who know me then won't recognise photographs of me as I am now."

"But of course they will," she said indignantly, before she remembered that she had not recognized the handsome young curate of Mrs. Bateman's photograph. But no, she *had* recognized him; only it had been a shock to discover that he was no longer young. Pondering on the changes wrought by time she found herself saying rather irrelevantly that Harley Coker was only ten years older than herself.

"He looks a great deal more," said Hebert, "but it's his baldness. He must have gone bald when he was still fairly young. He was certainly bald when I came home after the war – that's why I'd forgotten till I saw that photograph what he used to look like before."

"What were you doing in the war? Were you away all the time?"

"I was an army chaplain. Mostly in the middle east, and then in Burma. That's why I didn't get home."

"I suppose Harley just stayed here."

"Yes, I think so. He was an air-raid warden or something." Robert spoke absent-mindedly, still turning the pages of the book. "That's a nice photograph of you with Mrs. Gamalion," he said, holding it out for her to see. "How happy you look."

"So I was. We both were. That's an early one, she's written the date underneath it. The second time I was in Italy with her."

"Before the arrival of the snake in the grass?"

"Oh yes, it was long before that. Look at us beaming away . . . I don't think I've ever felt so carefree since!"

Before Harley's arrival too, she thought. The girl standing beside Mrs. Gamalion was simply glorying at being in Italy, at having escaped from Marston. Dazzling sunlight everywhere, two lemon trees in tubs flanking the steps, Mrs. Gamalion's parasol propped against the wall, waiting to be unfurled when they set off for wherever they were bound for.

"But you're happy now?"

"Yes," said Charlotte. She thought of her house, the legacy which had finally set her free. Of course she was happy; to admit to doubts would have been, in this room, an insult to her benefactress. "Oh yes," she repeated confidently.

"Good," said Robert.

He closed the Book and stood up, turning to the window for another look at the garden. He had been working in the garden that afternoon and as usual had stayed to have tea. It wasn't the first time either that he had amused himself by glancing through the Book.

He knew a lot about the past by now, and sometimes surprised Charlotte by the extent of his knowledge – by the way he remembered an incident or a name and fitted them into the pattern. "I talk too much about the past," she would say apologetically; but Robert's interest led her on to begin again. Bit by bit it had been revealed to him, from the meeting at Menaggio to the closing scene at La Residenza.

He had learnt why Miss Glyn-Gibson was known as the snake in the grass, and why Colonel Hetherington's poor watercolours were hung in a row on the wall. It did not occur to Charlotte that he had also learned a good deal about herself.

"I've pruned the roses pretty hard," Robert said, still surveying the garden. "It's a bit early but I wanted to get them done. I hope they'll be all right."

"I'm sure they will be."

"That little mowing-machine isn't really any use. I've given it a good oiling, but the blades are eaten away with rust."

"I'm not surprised, since it's been lying all these years in the shed. Perhaps I'd better buy a new one. But I see you've managed to mow the lawn with it."

"Grass grows. It will need mowing again."

"All right," said Charlotte. "I'll buy a new one before next time."

"I think it would be a good idea. But be sure to get a small one, something quite light and easy to push. You don't need a big one for this patch of lawn."

It was at that point, in the middle of a trivial and even domestic discussion about lawn-mowers, that she became aware of something wrong. Or at any rate, different.

Robert's back was still turned to the room, his face was hidden and he was addressing all his remarks to the window or the garden; he had been standing like that for five minutes, not even turning his head.

"What are you looking at?"

"Nothing," he said. "I mean, just at the garden."

"What's wrong with it?"

"Nothing."

"Well –" said Charlotte, half exasperated, half alarmed.

"I'm going away tomorrow so I was just having a last look. No, there's nothing wrong, but there are various things I'd intended to do and haven't."

"You're going away!"

"There's that hollow in the path. I'd meant to re-lay the paving-stones – there's always a puddle there, just by the gate."

"But why didn't you tell me you were going away tomorrow?"

"I'm telling you now," said Robert. He was no longer address-ing the garden, he had turned round and they were face to face. But he was smiling at her, looking just as usual; it was her own voice that had sounded agitated and protesting.

"There's nothing to tell, anyway," he went on. "I have to be in London for a few weeks – perhaps longer, I don't know yet. I heard about it only yesterday – I knew I should be going, but I didn't know when . . . in fact I thought I'd have to wait some time. It seems silly to tell people one is going away and then not go, doesn't it?"

Charlotte felt obliged to agree. What seemed silly now was her own alarm and the proprietary tone it had produced; as if she thought she had a right to be told of his plans.

She felt thoroughly ashamed of herself.

"But I'm sorry I didn't look at your mowing-machine till today," Robert was saying. "If I'd known you needed a new one I could have helped you to choose it. You must be sure to get a lightweight one, if you're going to use it yourself."

He was making conversation, covering up her own embar-rassed silence, filling in the minutes that remained.

Now they were at the back door and there was a momentary pause in which alternative hopes that he would enjoy himself – take care of himself – have an interesting time – fairly fought for utterance, but they fought a losing battle with Charlotte's pride. Any such hopes might have sounded like an attempt to find out what he was going to do in London.

"Good bye," she said austerely.

"Good bye," said Robert.

He took two steps down the path and then stopped. Perhaps he too felt the bleakness of their farewell and hoped to mitigate it by a parting joke. "You'd better get Harley Coker to do the mowing," he said.

"What?"

"Persuade him to take my place. He won't need much persuading, will he? Good night, Charlotte – take care of yourself."

He was gone. Charlotte stared blankly at the door in the garden wall. It was just a not very funny joke.

Naturally Robert had not been told anything about Harley Coker. He knew Harley had been in Italy, that she had met him there long before she met him again in Nything, but that was all. He knew nothing about the cult of La Fiorentina, the flattering performance in the Hudson sala – or the epilogue up at Fiesole. If he had known those things he would not have suggested – even jokingly – that Harley Coker should be persuaded to mow the lawn.

Looking back, Charlotte could not imagine why she had taken Mrs. Bateman to be another too-zealously doting mother, like Mrs. Coker. First impressions weren't reliable. But Mrs. Bateman wasn't reliable either, at least in her maternal role, though utterly reliable in other ways. One could not count on her, where Robert was concerned, to behave consistently – at first she had seemed over-fussy and Coker-ish, and now she was almost callously indifferent. Of course she wasn't callous, Charlotte thought; but it was as if, with Robert's departure, she had thankfully resumed her independence and did not want to be reminded of the relationship and whatever it held of strain and anxiety.

"Oh yes, he'll be away for several weeks," she said brusquely.

Further inquiries, carefully spaced out, produced much the same sort of replies, with never a hint of why he had gone. Charlotte gave it up, reminding herself again that Robert's doings were no business of hers. What was there to worry about anyway? – surely his mother would have betrayed her anxiety if there was anything to be anxious about.

But Mrs. Bateman remained briskly matter-of-fact, giving not the slightest impression that she was beset by private fears.

"Tell me about Alison," she said, on the last occasion that Charlotte asked after Robert. "How are they getting on in that flat? Is she coming here for Easter?"

"I don't know – I don't think so," Charlotte answered vaguely. She was vague because she was still thinking about Robert, wondering whether Mrs. Bateman had deliberately changed the subject because she positively disliked being questioned; or was it simply politeness, turn and turn about to talk of one's offspring? (Only Mrs. Bateman never did talk of Robert.)

"You don't know? But doesn't she write and tell you how they're managing?"

She sounded quite perturbed, obviously Robert must write to her or she would not think it unusual that Charlotte did not hear from Alison.

"No, I meant that I didn't know whether she would be coming for Easter," Charlotte explained. "As for the flat . . . oh yes, she writes to me, but she doesn't say much about it."

"Children never tell one the things one wants to know." Before Charlotte could make anything of that Mrs. Bateman had expanded it. "My Mary is a maddening correspondent, she writes pages about the flower-show or the Women's Institute and never answers any of my questions. I expect your Alison is just as bad."

"Well, yes. Alison doesn't write *pages*. But I heard from Evvie recently and it – it sounded as though they were getting on quite well."

"It would be nice if they could both come down for Easter. You would have room for both of them, wouldn't you?"

Charlotte thought of the third bedroom and the attics, she pictured Evvie (it would have to be Evvie) wedged in a tiny clearing among hat-boxes and rolls of carpet. She could hear Evvie saying placidly that she could sleep anywhere and not to worry about a bedside light; but Alison's reactions did not bear imagining.

"I could put one of them up, if you can't manage it," Mrs. Bateman offered. "The other girl – Evvie – perhaps, and I would give her breakfast and she could spend the rest of the day with you."

"It's very kind of you. But I don't know – I don't think –"

"Of course you don't yet know their plans," Mrs. Bateman interrupted. "But there's no need to settle things now – I shall be at home at Easter and there's a spare room available."

Charlotte thanked her, wondering as she did so whether Mrs. Bateman had failed to notice Alison's attitude to the legacy and her harsh criticisms of Nything, which made any future visits seem highly unlikely. But probably by now Mrs. Bateman had transformed the whole scene in her mind, blotting out the bits that conflicted with her conventional picture of a visiting daughter. Just as she blotted out looming unpleasantnesses in her own life: old age, failing strength . . . and other disagreeable things.

In a way, but for different reasons, Alison was taking the same line. No quarrel officially existed, they wrote to each other at intervals and her letters contained neither arguments or reproaches. Nor, of course, did they contain any reference to Nything, or any comment on the local news recounted in Charlotte's letters. Nything had been blotted out, expunged from Alison's map of England – except for the address on the envelopes Charlotte might have been living in limbo. No quarrel existed; therefore there could be no reconciliation. The Marston method had always been to ignore disputes and Alison was ignoring this one.

But Charlotte found herself less able to ignore it, as the weeks went by. She had escaped from Marston, but she had never meant to cut herself off from Alison.

The weeks went by quite rapidly, bringing the spring, the mild sunny weather Mrs. Gamalion had extolled in so many postcards. The daffodils, planted much too late, were confounding Mrs. Bateman's predictions by appearing in the garden, and after a prolonged hibernation the Wakelins were appearing in the street, muffled to the ears and clutching mysterious metal objects that gave off heat and warmed their hands.

At first they only walked across Church Street to visit Mrs. Bateman, then they ventured as far as the nearest shops, and on a particularly sunny day they came all the way to the Green. They seemed surprised and triumphant at having got so far.

"It's the furthest we've been yet," Lily said. "Bart thought we might go across the Green to the esplanade but I thought we'd better have a rest, if you were at home."

"You must stay to tea," said Charlotte, helping Lily to unwind an immensely long scarf.

"Oh no, we couldn't do that, thank you. Dr. Elliott wants us to get out more, but only while it's sunny and warm. If we stayed to tea we might get cold going home."

"Doctor's orders. Told us to take more exercise. Must admit I prefer the car," Bart remarked.

"But it's to stir up our circulations after being indoors so much during the winter. We're having injections for it as well, but he said walking was important, so long as we were careful to get back indoors before the sun lost its heat. So if we could just sit down for a quarter of an hour."

Charlotte made up the fire and pushed the chairs forward; her drawing-room must be arctic compared with theirs. But the Wakelins had removed only an upper layer of their wrappings and they seemed quite comfortable. How pale they both looked, blanched by their sojourn in the house, pale and a little shrivelled, as if during the winter their ever lasting quality had diminished. The dried flowers of the set-piece had wilted, the leaves and stems were brittle.

"How nice it is to have a real fire," Lily exclaimed. "Look at the flames, Bart! It's like being back at Warley."

"Oh come, Lily, think of the size of the room. Nice little room" – he turned his head stiffly towards Charlotte – "but not like *Warley*."

"I meant the fire. Of course we burned logs at Warley and the fireplace was much bigger –"

"Should think so! Remember what a lot of wood we got through."

"And those pretty red and blue flames. The apple wood was the prettiest."

"But we used up the old orchard a long time ago. No, Lily, the oak burned best. Nothing like oak, for firewood or anything else."

"That lovely oak staircase . . . I do miss going upstairs to bed."

"Can't have everything in a bungalow."

"Those wide shallow steps and the curve of the banisters. Do you remember when you fell down the top flight?"

Neither head turned towards Charlotte now, the Wakelins had forgotten her and were back at their endless contemplation of Warley. Preparing for old age had begun as a game, had carried them to Church Street and a bungalow carefully planned for survival, but survival was all that the present had to offer. Everything else, the excitements, pains and pleasures that make up life, existed only in the past.

Like the Hudsons, Charlotte thought, they had outlived their real lives. Yet they weren't really old – not nearly as old as the Hudsons. It was an attitude of mind, perhaps; a premature putting on of blinkers, a too exclusive concern with oneself – the self whose thoughts and actions stretch behind one like a shadow and can only be seen when one pauses and looks back at the way one has come.

Like me, she thought in a panic. It was absurd, but for a moment she saw herself standing on the staircase – a marble staircase of course, not Lily's oak one – and forever looking back at the way she had come. Standing there like the girl in the picture or the other girl who ever so long ago had copied the pose at Harley's bidding. Umpteen steps still ahead of her but she had already become a person who preferred to look back at the past.

There was no clock to measure time in Mrs. Gamalion's drawing-room, but Bart and Lily wore watches and were under doctor's orders. They had rested for fifteen minutes and must now set off for home before the sun lost its heat. Wound up again in their mufflers, buttoned up and belted and gloved, they walked down the path and out of the front gate. Charlotte went with them, though they wondered at her coming out without a coat.

"But it's lovely and warm – almost summery."

"You're like Mrs. Bateman," Lily said. "She talks about summer as soon as we get a fine day. But then she's like that about everything, isn't she? Always so cheerful and unfeeling."

"Unfeeling? Do you mean callous?"

"Not exactly," said Lily. "We're very fond of her, aren't we, Bart? Only she's always so – so –"

"Selfish," declared Bart.

"Impatient, if we're ill or anything. Not callous, exactly, but unfeeling, like I said. As if she simply couldn't understand, or didn't want to have to think about illness and sad things."

"Yes," said Charlotte. And she added, "I thought she might miss Robert, as cheerful as ever."

"Oh yes," Lily agreed.

Bart was walking away and in a second Lily would follow him. But the Wakelins were Mrs. Bateman's oldest friends and might easily know why Robert had gone to London. It was none of Charlotte's business, she hadn't been told and she already had cause to feel ashamed of seeming inquisitive. Besides, it was wrong to try to find out obliquely what you hadn't been told by the person – the people – concerned.

But she moved a step forward, half blocking Lily's path. "I wonder if he'll be back for Easter," she said.

"Who?"

"Robert."

"Come on, Lily! Time we were moving."

"Robert," Charlotte repeated, for she perceived that Lily had already detached her mind from the conversation. "He's only in London temporarily – isn't he?"

"I didn't know he'd gone to London," said Lily.

"Oh yes, Mrs. Bateman did tell me, but I'd forgotten. Yes, but she'd be cheerful anyway, and of course it doesn't make any difference. She's quite used to living alone."

It was no good, Lily wasn't interested in Robert and neither knew nor cared what he was doing in London.

She was only interested in rejoining Bart, who had stopped a short distance away and was giving peremptory halloos.

Charlotte stepped aside and let her go. She watched the Wakelins' slow retreat, and was ready with an answering farewell wave when they paused and looked back. They were probably too far away to see her face but she smiled as well, just in case they were exceptionally long-sighted.

Then she went back into her own garden and behind the safe concealment of the privet hedge expressed her disappointment by slamming the gate.

CHAPTER XVII

GRASS grows, and in springtime it grows remarkably fast. A nice sight, said Mrs. Bateman – for when the grass started growing fast it showed that winter was really over. Her own lawn had been cut two or three times before Easter but from now on it would need mowing every week or even twice a week; she hated to see it shaggy and luckily her jobbing gardener Albert felt the same and he would come round after tea to give it an extra mowing if necessary. Tuesday was his day for her but he often turned up on a Friday evening as well.

"And he'd be there all day if I let him," she said. "But I can't afford a gardener two days a week and anyway I don't need one. I managed without a gardener at all until a year or two ago. Then Robert and Mary made a fuss, and I had to promise to get someone to help with the mowing and the digging. Oh well, I suppose Albert is useful in lots of ways, but he's so obstinate and tiresome in others. The lawn is really the only thing we agree about."

"Your lawn is lovely," said Charlotte. "I'm just going to cut mine," she added defensively, aware that her own little patch looked decidedly shaggy. But the new mowing-machine was standing in full view, proof positive of good intentions.

"That won't take you long." Mrs. Bateman looked at the new mower with interest. "If I had one like that I could manage without Albert."

"But your lawn is much bigger than mine."

"Yes, I suppose it is. And there'd still be the digging, and clipping the hedges. . . . I fell off the ladder one autumn, and that's what really started Robert and Mary fussing. Though I only sprained my wrist and it was better in no time. Well, I'm keeping you from your mowing."

"It doesn't matter a bit."

Mrs. Bateman snorted gently; a shaggy lawn mattered more to her than it did to Charlotte. But as she turned away from the front gate she remembered why she had stopped there. She turned back, gesturing towards the house on the other side of the dividing wall.

"Have you seen that For Sale board?" she asked.

"No!"

Charlotte joined Mrs. Bateman on the pavement. The house next door, twin to hers, was up for sale; a large board had been erected beside the gate and a smaller one could be seen in one of the upper windows. The house had been standing empty for months, ever since she first saw it, and now looked much more derelict than her own.

"I heard a lot of banging while I was having breakfast," she said. "That must have been the estate agent's men putting up the board."

"I wonder why they've waited so long. It belonged to Mrs. Gamalion, didn't it? Who did she leave it to?"

"I don't know. I've had several people inquiring about it, but I don't know who owns it now."

"I must find out," said Mrs. Bateman.

Charlotte did not have to wait for Mrs. Bateman to pursue her researches. Harley Coker, taking his customary walk along the esplanade that afternoon, saw the For Sale board and came across the Green for a closer look, after which he called on Charlotte to inform her of what was happening.

"Yes, I know. The boards were put up this morning." She barely hesitated before adding, "Won't you come in?"

Harley did not hesitate at all. (She had known he wouldn't.) He came in and settled himself in what had become his customary chair, stretching out his legs and looking very much at his ease. He always contrived to find some reason for calling on Charlotte and today he had been presented with a brand-new one which would justify a lengthy visit.

She guessed it would even justify his staying to tea and risking annoying Miss Rimmer.

"So you're not going to have the cats as neighbours after all," he began. "I incline to congratulate you, Charlotte; except that cats might have been in themselves a defence against boisterous children. Or rather, a preferable alternative."

"What cats? What are you talking about?"

"Why, the house next door and its future." A little mystery suited him and he was in no hurry to dispel it. "Not a cattery, one may now assume, since they themselves, the custodians, have presumably authorised its disposal. No doubt they are right in holding that their poor charges will benefit more from the purchase price than from actually residing in a place which, salubrious as it may be for human beings, has no particular advantages – so far as I am aware – for cats."

"But whose cats? I don't understand."

"No one's cats. That was precisely the point. It was their plight – homeless, unwanted, abandoned to starve in gutters and maintain themselves as best they might from imperfectly impenetrable dustbins – that touched our late commander's heart. Knowing her as we do, we may surmise her displeasure at this rejection of the proffered asylum. But all things considered, I rather agree that –"

"Do you mean Mrs. Gamalion left the house next door to a lot of cats?"

"To their custodians," he gently corrected her. For a moment the picture of the cats themselves as beneficiaries still hung before Charlotte's eyes, she imagined them moving in, putting butter on one another's paws, giving large orders to the milkman and celebrating their arrival by a grand mouse hunt all over the house. When she listened to Harley, who was explaining that Mrs. Gamalion had bequeathed the other half of her property to a society – the exact title of which temporarily eluded him – dedicated to the rescue and rehabilitation of stray cats.

"Mrs. Bateman didn't know that," she said.

"Then she cannot be a careful student of the local paper. I read the wills every week, and naturally I pay special attention to the wills of people I knew. Though no doubt one would have been informed, long before reading of it in cold print, if one had been left any legacy oneself."

No doubt one would; but Harley's voice betrayed a wistful hope that it might not always be so. Charlotte thought of him opening the local paper week by week, reading about the wills, reading about the Stray Cats who had been so generously assisted by Mrs. Gamalion. And about herself too, another undeserving beneficiary.

Not that he was deserving himself. Compared with Mrs. Gamalion the Cokers had been prosperous, or at least they had appeared to be. Moreover they had quarrelled with her, and although Harley seemed to regret the quarrel he had done nothing to bring about a reconciliation; he had sided with his mother and neither of them had spoken to Mrs. Gamalion again. How could he have hoped for a legacy?

But he was poor Harley in another sense now – just as his mother had been "poor Mrs. Coker." At last Charlotte thought she understood about poor Mrs. Coker. There was something in both of them, Harley and his matchless Mama, that aroused a reluctant, exasperated pity. She felt it within herself as she listened to him, and did not doubt that Mrs. Gamalion had felt the same at times as she listened to Mrs. Coker.

"You'll stay to tea, Harley?"

"I ought to get back. Miss Rimmer will be expecting me."

"Oh, do stay," She knew very well that he meant to, and out of pity she spared him the tiresome business of having to manoeuvre her into repeating the invitation.

"Do stay this time – you pander too much to Miss Rimmer's feelings."

"One doesn't like to disappoint the good creature."

"Then you'll disappoint me instead."

She was overdoing it, almost demanding that Harley should look gallant and knightly, which he immediately did.

It was her own fault that he now saw himself as a man inescapably doomed to disappoint one or other of his female entourage; a man, however, who could also confer happiness merely by staying to tea. Visibly rejuvenated, he became correspondingly less pitiable, but she reminded herself that it was her own fault and received with due appreciation the speech that followed, in which Harley, though showing a proper concern for Miss Rimmer's solitude, made it beautifully clear that he could not bear to disappoint his present companion. How, indeed, could she have imagined otherwise?

She imagined nothing. A curtain had fallen, long ago, on that particular stage, the romantic play was ended and would never be revived. Mrs. Bateman's growing interest in what Harley Coker might be up to went unobserved, because Charlotte saw him only as poor Harley. His occasional lapses into gallantry meant nothing, they were routine responses of the kind he had learned to make in the past, pathetic leftover snippets of bygone charm. He had been gallant with everyone (when he wasn't being supercilious) and the wonder was really that they had managed, he and she, to ignore the painful last act of the play and to strike up a new friendship, based on her pity, and on Harley's side – as she could not fail to recognize – on his need for a female figure to replace the one he had been so thoroughly trained to regard as irreplaceable.

"Oh, he just likes to talk about the past," she expressed it to Mrs. Bateman. "About Bank House, you know, and his mother and how they lived . . . the tea party she always gave on Christmas Day and so on."

"They were dreadful occasions," said Mrs. Bateman, temporarily forgetting her real interest and Charlotte's quite maddening reserve. "One shouldn't speak ill of the dead but Mrs. Coker's Christmas Day tea parties were – well, just dreadful."

"In what way?"

"It's hard to explain." Mrs. Bateman paused and snorted, indignantly surveying the past. Then after another pause she got going.

"Of course no one wanted to turn out on Christmas Day for tea in that icy drawing-room with Mrs. Coker in purple silk and a kind of lace shroud that went over it, at least it always made me think of a shroud though of course it wasn't really. And to feel one was the object of a good deed – for that's how she saw it – when really we had only gone to please *her*. To keep the thing alive."

"I suppose it had become a tradition and you didn't like to stop it?"

"Yes, but it was her tradition, the Bank House tradition, not ours. You see we weren't the original guests. Either they'd died or else she'd given them up – as *she* put it, they'd failed her. Morally, not at the last minute by having colds, I mean."

"Like Mrs. Gamalion, I suppose. She must have been one of the original guests, until they quarrelled."

"Yes, they'd offended her or died off and she had to get new people to take their place – especially, I think, to replace the ones she'd quarrelled with, so that she wouldn't seem like someone who quarrelled with all her friends. Of course you never knew Mrs. Coker, but she was like that. She had to demonstrate, all the time, that she was blameless. Poor thing," said Mrs. Bateman, half laughing, half snorting.

"And of course you were sorry for her," said Charlotte. "That's how you got roped in, for the Christmas day tea parties."

"Well, yes, I suppose so. Though 'roping in' rather describes it. I mean, she was very insistent – she used to waylay people after church on Sundays and look as if she would have a heart attack if she was thwarted."

"How very disagreeable."

Charlotte was thinking of Harley, threatened by heart attacks if he dared to thwart his mother, but Mrs. Bateman was thinking of the tea parties. "Yes, they were," she said. "I don't quite know why, but I simply hated those parties. Partly because Mrs. Coker was so gracious, like lady Bountiful ministering to the poor. I suppose it hadn't always been like that. We were replacements for the original guests – definitely second-best. And partly – oh, I don't know."

I was a replacement too, Charlotte thought. It seemed sad that Harley should have striven to re-create a Christmas tea party which no one had really enjoyed. (But Mrs. Coker had enjoyed it in her own way.) Filial piety carried to extreme lengths, or possibly a form of protest against Miss Rimmer and the new regime . . . the drawing-room, the scene of those parties, was now enemy territory and of course he grudged it her. Thinking these things Charlotte failed to notice Mrs. Bateman's sudden ending, which might otherwise have struck her as marking a hasty suppression of further comments, presumably adverse, on the Coker treatment of second-best guests. She hadn't in her whole account of it mentioned Harley at all.

But neither had Charlotte mentioned Robert. There were silences on both sides, a careful avoidance of names which each thought might land her in difficulties. Charlotte asked no more questions because she knew now that they would not be answered, and that a run of unanswered questions might echo in her own ears afterwards – mocking echoes enlarging and distorting a quite ordinary, neighbourly anxiety. (So, not even anxiety, there was no reason for it, but just wonder at what had become of him, why he had gone to London and why Mrs. Bateman never talked about him.) And by asking no questions she also avoided the distasteful possibility of being thought unduly inquisitive or unduly concerned.

Mrs. Bateman had been, to begin with, less restrained, less daunted by what might be imputed to her in the way of motives. But her questions about Harley Coker had produced such unsatisfactory replies that she too seemed to have decided there were subjects better left alone. Candid curiosity hadn't been rebuked but it had gone unnoticed, because Charlotte was not in the least self-conscious about poor Harley.

She was quite ready to talk about him but there was really nothing to say; she couldn't for pity's sake betray his confidences, tell Mrs. Bateman about his weekly hopes of being left a legacy or his patient search for buried treasure in the garden of Bank House. She wasn't aware that the frequency of his visits had been noted and reported as an interesting variation of his formerly undeviating afternoon walk along the esplanade and back again; the notion of Harley as a man by whom people could set their watches had never occurred to her.

The people who set their watches by Harley, or had done until recently, included the permanent residents in the Pennine Guest House on the other corner of Beach Street. Old Mrs. Carter had lived there for years and Mrs. Bateman knew her well. She wasn't a sharp-tongued gossip but she spent much of her time in her bed-sitting room and occupied herself by observing the esplanade and the Green. It was her little world and she had become an authority on its inhabitants and their customs. Mrs. Bateman rather disapproved of Mrs. Carter's laziness, her ingenious excuses for not taking exercise, not going to church, not doing anything but sit by her window eating sweets, but she knew that Mrs. Carter had had a hard life before retiring to the Pennine Guest House and she dimly understood that almost total inertia might be a reaction from excessive drudgery in the past. It was this fat, placid, reliable observer who had told her about Harley Coker's changed habits.

"The house that belonged to Mrs. Gamalion. I can't see it from my window unless I lean out, but that must be the house he visits. When I first noticed him turning off the esplanade and coming across the Green I thought it was the corner house, the one just across Beach Street, but I can see that one from the bathroom window and he doesn't go in there. No, it's the one beyond – Mrs. Gamalion's house with the great high hedge. Though it looks as though it's been trimmed, as well as one can see from the bathroom."

A sortie to the bathroom window indicated keen interest, for Mrs. Carter usually limited herself to the view she could see without moving. That explained why she had missed seeing Robert last autumn when he did so much work in Charlotte's garden; she would not have seen him approaching because he went in by the back gate. Mrs. Bateman knew that Mrs. Carter was quite harmless, so she at once told her who lived in Mrs. Gamalion's house now and explained that Harley Coker and Mrs. Moley were old friends, they had met in Italy years before Mrs. Moley came to Nything. She would have felt silly herself if she had concealed the fact that she knew Mrs. Moley; sooner or later Mrs. Carter would have discovered it by seeing them walking on the esplanade together. Indeed she had already observed Charlotte, a newcomer in her window-world but one who appeared quite often on the esplanade, especially early in the mornings or towards sunset.

"So that's who it is," she said, when Mrs. Bateman had described Charlotte. "I've often wondered about her and now I know. Mrs. Moley."

She sounded pleased. Another name to add to the long list of people she knew by sight, whose comings and goings were her only amusement; for after all she knew half Nything by sight but hardly anyone to talk to. She did not know Robert or Charlotte or Harley Coker . . . there was a great difference between knowing people by sight and actually *knowing* them.

When you knew people only by sight it didn't matter, Mrs. Bateman thought confusedly. Whatever Harley was up to, whatever Charlotte thought of him, didn't matter to Mrs. Carter. Perhaps it didn't matter, wasn't important, at all. Perhaps Harley wasn't up to anything when he repeatedly abandoned his afternoon walk and came across the Green to call on Charlotte. Perhaps she could find out by asking Charlotte herself. Very tactfully, of course.

Once a month, or thereabouts, was the right interval for Mrs. Carter. Mrs. Bateman had several people whom she visited regularly, but not too regularly in case it became obvious to them that they were names on a list of the lonely and friendless. She couldn't remember how Mrs. Carter had first come to be on the list, for she seemed perfectly contented with her view and she was quite capable of going out and getting to know more people if she wanted to. Or perhaps not, now. Anyway, she need not be visited again for at least another month. It would soon be summer, there would be holiday-makers to fill up the view and give her plenty to watch.

Of course they did not interest her as much as the residents because she did not know their daily routine and could not tell if they were behaving differently. Still, she could be left to look out of her window for at least a month.

It would soon be summer. Mrs. Bateman had been saying so for a long time but now other people were saying it too. The weather had settled down, the Green looked greener and the estuary at high tide looked calm and blue, almost like the real sea. At the sheltered place beyond the pier the deck chairs had been set out, and there were children with buckets and spades on the shore and even a few hardy bathers.

"It's summer already," Charlotte said, talking to the Wakelins on the esplanade.

"Not yet," said Bart. "On the way to it, I'd say. Quite warm for the time of year."

The Wakelins, under doctor's orders, took a walk every day, weather permitting, and with practice they had become capable of reaching the esplanade. But today they looked terribly hot, still dressed in thick coats and what they described as their spring scarves, which were only slightly shorter and less fleecy than their long winter mufflers. Lily suddenly stopped and unwound hers, dodging behind Charlotte so that Bart should not notice.

"That's better," she said. "But could you just arrange it a bit?"

Charlotte understood what was needed, she draped the spring scarf round Lily's shoulders so that it looked as much as possible as if it were still tightly wound round her throat.

"Thank you, Charlotte. Isn't it lovely that winter is over?"

"Can't be too careful, Lily." Bart had looked back suspiciously, but the loosened scarf passed muster and he turned away again, walking slowly ahead of them along the esplanade, gazing at the sea and the cloudless sky and the circling gulls. Behind his back Lily permitted herself a confession.

"I wonder about it each year, you know . . . in autumn, I mean. I wonder whether Bart and I will still be here in the spring."

"But there's no reason —"

"Of course not. It's silly of me – isn't it?"

She smiled and tossed her head, shaking off her fears.

"But the winter's over now, everything is all right again and we shall be able to have our picnic. We have it at the beginning of summer, as a kind of celebration . . . you must come with us this year."

"I'd love to," said Charlotte. She did not need to ask where the picnic would take place. Lily gave a little skip of excitement.

"Bart thinks we might look over the house! He's going to write and get leave – though it seems ridiculous to have to ask, when we lived there and it's standing empty. But men are so fussy, aren't they?"

CHAPTER XVIII

NO DATE could be fixed for the celebratory picnic because it depended entirely on the weather, they needed a really warm day with the sun shining brightly and the barometer set fair – the kind of day you could absolutely count on. A week of cloudy weather followed Lily's first announcement of it, and then the sun shone again but an east wind tempered its warmth. The days slipped by and Charlotte ceased to expect a summons; it would be June or later, she thought, before the great event took place.

"It won't be this weekend, anyway," said Mrs. Bateman, appearing at the back gate on her way home from her Friday shopping. "The glass is tumbling down and the wind has changed. It's blowing up for rain." She tut-tutted at Charlotte's laden clothesline and asked if she hadn't seen the forecast. Not that one really needed a forecast when the wind changed suddenly like that.

On Saturday morning Charlotte woke early, to hear the rain beating on the window and the window rattling in the wind. There was another sound too, a slow plop-plop of water; she recognized it at once and sprang up to lay old towels along the window-sill where the rain was driving in and dripping on the floor. Mrs. Gamalion had kept a cache of worn-out towels and sheets in a box on the landing labelled "rain stoppers" and after initial bafflement Charlotte had realized what they were meant for, not to make the rain stop but to keep it at bay. She hurried round the house putting rain stoppers in every front window and mopping up the water that had already penetrated. It was a dismal start to the day.

It was a dismal day altogether. The wind blew and the windows rattled and when she lit a fire it smoked. The sight of the curtains and counterpanes on the sagging clothesline was a reminder of her own foolishness; she ought to have heeded Mrs. Bateman's warning and brought them in last night.

But it was too late now, they were soaking wet and there was nowhere to hang them indoors. Heavy rainstorms followed one another, sweeping in from the sea, blurring the windows and producing a damp patch above the front door; the house felt almost as damp inside as out. The gale lasted all day, and somehow it was more depressing than a gale at the proper season, in autumn or winter. The pink tulips in the garden, bent and bedraggled, were the saddest sight of all.

"Come and have tea and cheer us up, if you don't mind an awfully wet walk," Lily wrote. The invitation was brought by one of the Bunces, a large family who lived in Church Street and were very useful to Lily and Bart – this particular Bunce came home for his midday meal and could deliver notes on his way back to work. Charlotte hardly felt equal to cheering people up but she had no objection to a wet walk; wind and rain were less depressing out of doors than in. The mere fact of her coming had a good effect on Wakelin morale. They had invited Mrs. Bateman as well, but she had only to cross the road whereas Charlotte had struggled all the way from the Green, pleasing evidence that she enjoyed their company.

She enjoyed it, in fact, less than usual. It was her fault, not theirs; she was feeling dejected and in the wrong frame of mind for listening to their reminiscences, and the presence of Mrs. Bateman was an irksome reminder of her refusal to listen to the voice of reason yesterday.

"Did you get your curtains dry?" Mrs. Bateman asked, and Charlotte was obliged to confess they were still hanging on the line, had been left out all night and were now wetter than ever. She deserved the tut-tutting, she didn't resent it, but it made her the more aware of her shortcomings. The curtains weren't important but they hung in her mind more damply and depressingly than they hung on the line, a symbol of foolishness and obstinacy.

It had been a wet walk coming and it was a wet walk going home. The wind had slackened but it was still blowing off the sea and driving the rain in her face, cold rain that seemed to have the salty taste of tears. She went the shortest way, turning into the cul-de-sac that brought her to the door in the wall of the back garden. The clothes-line with its dripping burden screened the house from view and it wasn't till she had walked up the path and dodged between the wet curtains that she saw the figure waiting under the backdoor porch, sitting hunched up on what looked like a small suitcase. A girl with a suitcase sheltering from the rain. . . . Charlotte just had time to wonder who it was when the figure stood up and turned towards her.

"It's me, Mother."

"Alison!"

"I came to the front door and you were out so I came round here to be out of the rain."

"Alison!" Charlotte repeated incredulously.

"Couldn't we go indoors?"

"Oh yes – wait while I find the key – you must be soaked. Have you – have you been here long?"

"Not very long. I came by train, the same train as last time, and walked from the station."

"You should have taken a taxi," said Charlotte, She found the key in her bag and opened the door. Among all the other perplexities this minor one stood out – that Alison had walked from the station in the rain.

"I rather wanted a walk, after sitting in the train so long," said Alison, almost as though she was aware of having acted oddly. "And anyway, you were out. I mean, even if I'd come in a taxi I would still have had to wait."

"But I couldn't help being out! I didn't know you were coming."

"Oh, I didn't mind waiting. It was my own fault, I ought to have let you know."

"Is there anything wrong?"

She knew something must be wrong, the only question was what. Not illness, because Alison was *here*, but something calamitous and urgent. Her imagination at work on disasters – a fire at The Laurels, a débâcle at the Ministry – Charlotte missed the beginning of the explanation. When she caught up with it Alison was saying:

"Because it seemed so long since – since I'd seen you."

"You just came to see me?"

"Well, yes," Alison said nervously. "I haven't got Monday off so I shall have to go back tomorrow evening."

Her nervousness had been evident from the start but Charlotte had been too flustered to notice it. She noticed it now, and noticed in the same moment that her daughter was extremely wet. She wasn't wearing a mackintosh and her suit and head-scarf were sodden with rain. It was a long walk from the railway station.

"Alison, you're wet through! You must change at once, and have a hot bath. Oh dear, nothing is ready – those are the bedroom curtains out on the line."

"I thought they were. You've been spring-cleaning."

"Not really. Everything's dreadfully untidy."

"It doesn't matter a bit."

Alison pulled off her scarf and added it to the clutter on the kitchen table, which was looking much as it did in Mrs. Gamalion's day. It didn't matter a bit. She wasn't politely ignoring the clutter, she wasn't deliberately refraining from criticism; she simply didn't mind. Charlotte could feel her relaxing, as if the journey and the walk and the wait in the porch had been exhausting obstacles success fully overcame.

"A hot bath would be wonderful. And I'll help you to make up the bed afterwards. That's all I need, just somewhere to sleep, so don't rush about doing more spring-cleaning. Goodness, I'm half asleep already! I shall sleep like a log tonight."

A hot bath, supper, early bed. Alison yawned and yawned, and would sleep soundly all night. It was Charlotte who lay awake listening to the dying gale and the waves breaking against the sea wall, acknowledging her own selfishness and preparing herself for the return to Marston. Tomorrow, with all day for it and Alison refreshed and rested, they would have another serious talk. But it need not be so prolonged this time, and it would not end in disagreement.

She had run away from Marston, but she had never intended to cut herself off from Alison. She had not foreseen that Alison would mind her rebellion so much, would go on minding and turn into a deprived daughter. That exciting moment when the idea first occurred to her; the sense of freedom and happiness and the concurrent enjoyment of the past ('Italy over again!'); the pleasure of making friends with people who knew nothing of the

Marston legend; all this had been at the expense of Alison. One should not run away – for once the Marston voices echoed her own conclusion. It had been wonderful, the escape from oppression, but in the last weeks she had been less happy, less and less able to forget that she was after all a mother. (Like Mrs. Coker; but how unlike her in the airy disregard of maternal ties.) She must go back.

Charlotte was sleepy at last. Other thoughts strayed through her mind whimpering for attention, but her mind was made up. It had been made up by the sight of Alison, wet and tired and *nervous* – which had shown more clearly than any argument the desperate importance of her mission.

The house and its treasures (Italy over again), the house with all its imperfections, Nything with its mild climate and the Green and the ships in the channel, even Nything on a wet day – Charlotte was looking at them with a nostalgic last-time vision that embalmed them in beauty. It was premature, she wasn't leaving them today; she knew Alison had not arrived with any such cut-and-dried plan this time and would be content with a promise, a settled date in the near future. But it must be settled, and it must be soon, and already it was rushing towards her – the day when she came out of her house for the last time and locked the door and drove to the station and caught a train that would take her back to Marston.

"I noticed the house next door is up for sale," Alison remarked.

"Yes, several people have been to look over it."

"I wonder who'll buy it."

Mr. Lazenby would buy it. He was a builder who had called more than once, wanting to buy Charlotte's house as well. He wanted the whole site, either to convert the 'twin houses into flats' or to pull them down and build nice modern flats in their place. Depended on whether he could get permission; things were difficult, with all the shortages and government regulations, but he definitely wanted the whole site. He would give her a good price, he had said, and she had smiled and explained that she meant to stay there, and Mr. Lazenby had gone away and come back again, urging her to reconsider it. She had only to let him know and he would buy the house tomorrow.

"I didn't know you'd been to the early service," Alison said. "I didn't hear a sound. You must have crept out like a mouse."

"This house is quite solid," said Charlotte, thinking of the thin walls that had been put in when The Laurels was made into flats. It would be like that here when Mr. Lazenby had finished with it.

"It's solider than I thought. I didn't even hear you getting breakfast. I slept marvellously – it must be the sea air! – Let's go out for a walk."

"It's still raining."

"You can lend me that old mackintosh, the one hanging by the back door. We needn't go far but I'd like a walk. I shall be sitting still in the train for hours."

Charlotte said Alison must wear her *good* mackintosh, the other let the rain in a bit and she mustn't get wet through again – she mustn't travel in wet clothes. They argued about it amiably and Alison agreed to wear the good mackintosh. She was determined to go out.

"Just a short walk on the esplanade and then we can sit in one of those glass shelters and look at the sea."

It was an echo of last time; Alison was again seeking neutral ground for the serious talk. But it didn't matter now. Charlotte did not need the collective support of the Old Faithfuls and was glad to escape any reproachful squawks that might be imagined as coming from Mrs. Gamalion.

She wore the leaky mackintosh and to please Alison took an umbrella. Everything was the same but different, rain instead of blazing sunshine, and instead of the deserted November scene a surprising number of people about. They were of course mostly sitting in the shelters, reading Sunday newspapers or disconsolately gazing at the sea, summer visitors regretting having taken their holidays so early. Charlotte and Alison had to go some distance before they found an unoccupied seat.

"Not towards the pier, it's more crowded that end," Alison said. So they walked briskly towards Moss Bank, overtaking a few other walkers and leaving them behind, until they reached the deserted end of the esplanade and an empty shelter, where they sat down facing the sea. The wind had dropped, it was a grey wet morning but warmer than yesterday and the incoming tide moved quietly, its waves breaking in gentle ripples on the muddy sand. Charlotte marked a thin board of yellow wood lying on the beach, left there by the last high tide and soon to be set floating again. She watched the waves running up the sand and told herself she would wait till they reached the board. It was a respite, but it was also a time limit; she wouldn't wait any longer than that. She mustn't weakly postpone things by letting Alison embark on the serious talk.

Alison was watching the board too. "Has there been a ship-wreck?" she asked, pointing to it. Charlotte said no, it was just a strip off an old box. It seemed strange to be instructing Alison, strange too that her capable daughter should think ships were built of such fragile materials. The waves were nearer now, their foam-edged ripples lapping at the end of the board. Then it *moves*, Charlotte thought.

A seventh wave came surging in and the board was suddenly afloat. "There it goes," said Alison. She had been watching it all the time but now she turned and looked at Charlotte, who was preparing to announce her readiness to return to Marston. But Alison spoke first.

"I'm sorry I was so horrid last time. That's what I came to say really. To tell you . . . I mean, to *say* it – that I'm sorry – and to tell you –"

"Oh no, Alison! Don't think –"

"And to tell you that you're perfectly right."

"Right?" Charlotte echoed faintly.

"I see it now," said Alison. "But I wouldn't have seen it if you hadn't just gone off and *made* us reorganize our lives. Of course I was angry at the time because it seemed such a – a –" A bitter insult to The Laurels, to the memory of Mrs. Field, to Alison's own belief in conventional family life; her gesture explained this without involving them in details. "Because I was angry I wouldn't let myself see it at first. Evelyn was much more sensible."

"Evvie!" Charlotte cried. Alison did not even correct her.

"Oh yes, she realized almost at once that it was a better arrangement. Just as you did, when you pointed out that other girls left home and you were only doing the same thing in reverse. Giving us our independence."

"And you don't want me back!"

How lucky, Charlotte thought afterwards, that Alison had heard in that shrill protest only the relief she was expecting to hear. How lucky too that Alison had spoken first, saving her from what would have been an embarrassing mistake. Saving them both, for it would have been awkward for Alison too if she had nobly declared her intention of returning to Marston. All that belated maternal solicitude, all that self-reproachful anxiety, had been utterly unnecessary. She wasn't wanted at Marston. Alison and Evvie – as she had once hoped – had discovered that they were happier without her.

It had been a wonderful day. Of course, of course it had been wonderful. How else could she describe a day that had seen her reconciled with Alison? (And not only forgiven but warmly praised for being right, her rebellion accepted and sanctified by all the ghostly Marston advisers hovering behind Alison, who was their heir and mouthpiece.) It had been a wonderful, though exhausting, day. Too bewildering, too topsy-turvy, and of course far too short. When Alison turned her attention to the house she had scarcely begun to list the improvements needed to make it habitable before it was time to set off for the station.

Kissing her goodbye on the platform, listening to her last instructions, waving cheerfully as the train drew out, Charlotte still held on to the idea of a day altogether wonderful. She even began to invent a conversation with Mrs. Bateman, telling her all about it, or at least all that could be revealed. Not about her decision to leave Nything, her mistaken belief that she ought to sacrifice her freedom because Alison needed her; that couldn't be related because in retrospect it was all too – absurd. Without it, however, the imaginary conversation dwindled into trite exchanges – "How exciting for you!" "Yes, it was wonderful!" – which even in their author's ears sounded hollow and misleading.

For it hadn't been wonderful after all.

Oh yes, she was thankful to be friends again with Alison. But as well as that – weighing her down as she plodded home in the rain – was the feeling of disillusionment and failure. How noble she had felt that morning, keyed up to make the great sacrifice and convinced that her daughter's happiness depended on her returning to Marston. How noble, how important and essential! And how she had dramatised the situation, indulging in 'last time' gazings, gauging the fateful moment by the incoming tide. After such heroic preliminaries it wasn't wonderful – it wasn't anything but deflating – to find that you weren't wanted, that your daughter was perfectly happy without you.

Charlotte turned the corner and emerged on the Green. She opened the gate and walked up the path, stepping over the puddle Robert hadn't had time to deal with. She had come the long way round but she was back at last.

Perhaps Mrs. Gamalion had felt like this, returning to her home after that disastrous expedition – returning from Italy that last time. Much impoverished, disillusioned, ill-used . . . and here was the house waiting to welcome and sustain her.

CHAPTER XIX

THAT had been a wet day too. Charlotte remembered how the rain had drummed on the station roof at Florence that morning as they waited for the train. Mrs. Gamalion was wearing her best straw hat in honour of the occasion and they were both dressed in summer clothes. They told each other it was just a thunder-shower, and Mrs. Gamalion expressed her satisfaction at having brought, as an afterthought, an umbrella and scolded Charlotte for not having done the same.

"But it won't last," she added. "You'll see, Charlotte – it will be a beautiful day by the time we get there!"

She was excited and happy. They were going to see La Residenza. At last, at long last, Miss Glyn-Gibson had succeeded in her negotiations and the house was theirs. They were on their way to meet her and be shown over it.

Watching Mrs. Gamalion and listening to her chatter Charlotte guessed that her extreme exuberance was partly due to relief. The negotiations had been protracted, it was a whole year since Miss Glyn-Gibson had tantalized them with the description of the house, that ideal residence whose whereabouts could not be revealed, and there had been a good deal of dissatisfaction among the founder-members of the Scheme as the months went by and nothing was achieved. Some of them might have backed out if it hadn't been for Mrs. Gamalion, whose staunch faith and ready acceptance of the reasons for the delay had soothed and silenced the waverers. So it must be a great relief to her that her confidence had been justified.

Yes, relief was the note that sounded loudest. Charlotte heard it again as the train drew out, bearing them southwards, and Mrs. Gamalion cried "At last!" and began to explain all over again why it had taken so long to buy La Residenza. As if she was running through all the tedious reasons for the last time before thankfully jettisoning them.

First, of course, it had turned out to cost more than they had reckoned on. Then, when the extra money had been raised, the owners had changed their minds about selling. They had taken umbrage, broken off negotiations, been thoroughly captious and difficult. It was not until this spring that Miss Glyn-Gibson had finally managed to mollify them and persuade them to sell.

"An old titled family – but very poor nowadays – of course she had to go carefully as Italians are so proud and she had to pretend it was just for herself as they wouldn't have liked it to be a guest-house," Mrs. Gamalion explained. "That's why she couldn't take any of us to look at it."

"I still think she ought to have taken you or Margery Mollison. After all, you've provided the money."

"But I've just told you she *couldn't*, because of the owners having to think it was just her! And because of other people finding out too – news gets round so quickly and she said there would have been any amount of people after it if they'd known it was going to be for sale."

"I suppose so."

"Oh yes! And I know she knows exactly what will suit us as she's so awfully clever and business-like. Except that it's a pity it isn't nearer Florence but she says it's wonderful country – not isolated but on the slope of a hill with terraces of olive trees all the way down to the main road. A really valuable orchard! All *ours*!" Mrs. Gamalion shrieked happily, "There's a long drive leading up from the road – huge gateposts just by the bus-stop, so we'll know where to get off."

"But Miss Glyn-Gibson is meeting us at the station – she'll be on the bus with us."

"Of course she will! Only she told me all about it in her letter as I'd asked for full particulars as I didn't know she was coming to meet us."

"I hope it isn't a very long drive," Charlotte said. "Your visitors won't like having to toil up a steep hill."

"Oh you silly girl – Miss Glyn-Gibson wouldn't buy a house on top of a mountain! No, no, it's just a little way up from the road. Can't you remember the description she showed us last year – about the lovely view from the terrace and the marble steps going up from the drive, a short cut for people coming on foot? Oh, just think, Charlotte – think of walking up a marble staircase to your very own house! And we'll have chairs on the terrace," Mrs. Gamalion added, as a kind of concession to the idea that visitors might arrive tired and panting. "Just *imagine* sitting there in front of the house and looking down at the olive trees and knowing it's all ours and we can stay there always! Oh how I wish Margery Mollison could be with us today!"

Charlotte wished so too. She felt herself an inadequate substitute for Mrs. Mollison, who as another founder-member would have shared Mrs. Gamalion's pleasure and as an experienced Old Faithful would have kept her excitement within bounds, checking her raptures by some brisk though kindly criticism, reminding her in advance, so to speak, that there were certain to be some snags. Even at La Residenza they would not be living in paradise.

But Mrs. Mollison had gone back to England, she could not afford to prolong her holiday and moreover she had been summoned to help her sister-in-law through some domestic crisis.

Sisters-in-law and other encumbrances had been uncommonly troublesome that year, and of the party Mrs. Gamalion had gathered in Florence only Charlotte now remained. She too ought to have gone home a week ago, but Mrs. Gamalion had persuaded her to stay on so that she could visit La Residenza. It was too bad that Miss Glyn-Gibson hadn't been able to settle things sooner so that they could all have seen it – all the founder-members who would be coming to live there when the house was ready – but Mrs. Gamalion intended to have a grand meeting at her club when she got back, to arrange about furniture and other details. Furnishing La Residenza would be quite easy because each member would bring some from the house or flat she was giving up.

If Charlotte had ever been to Nything she might have boggled at the thought of transporting Mrs. Gamalion's household goods to Italy; all those hoarded relics of the past, which even then could hardly have survived the stresses of the journey. But she imagined them as solid and useful contributions, though it did dimly cross her mind that La Residenza would look rather a hotch-potch of incongruous chairs and clashing carpets. What matter, when everyone was going to be so happy,

"Oh, Charlotte, you *must* join us! You must persuade your trustees to give you some of your capital and then you can belong to the Scheme. We'll have room for one or two more. And I know you'd simply *love* it!"

"Perhaps I could join later on," Charlotte said, though she knew very well it was impossible. Her trustees, her advisers, her mother, even Alison, would be of one mind about the folly of leaving Marston, the even greater folly of living abroad. It would be useless even to mention it.

"But I hope I can come and be a paying-guest next year," she added, wondering at the same time whether she would be able to escape from Marston next year. Her mother's letter, replying to her own announced that that she was staying another week, had arrived that morning; it did not augur well for future holidays.

The train was a slow one. It stopped at Arezzo and everywhere else. The thunderstorm rolled away among the hills and the sun came out briefly, cheered on by Mrs. Gamalion, but soon the sky clouded over and the rain began again, not torrential rain now but a steady drizzle. "It's been a wretched summer," Mrs. Gamalion said crossly; and indeed it had been a wet one. Charlotte watched the country sliding past, the strips of maize between the vines, a team of white oxen pacing along a stony lane, black-clad women sheltering under the wide eaves of a solitary building, with the hills rising steeply beyond the patchwork of little fields. It all looked much greener than usual because of the wet summer.

Not like last year when the sun had turned everything to dusty gold and brown, when even the Italian sky had looked blanched and faded by the heat. But Charlotte wasn't sorry that this one had been different, too wet for many expeditions; that their picnic up at Fiesole had had to be abandoned almost before it had begun, had ended with a long wait in the cathedral and a damp walk down the old road to San Domenico in misty rain. Of course Harley was not with them this year. Charlotte had foreseen, long before Mrs. Gamalion told her, that his mother's health would not permit of his leaving her. She had known it would be so, but she was thankful to be spared the Roman amphitheatre and the brilliant sun-drenched landscape, which would have recalled too poignantly her last visit. She did not want to think about that summer again.

"Charlotte, wake up! We're nearly there!"

It was Mrs. Gamalion herself who had been asleep for the past half hour, but now she was awake and brimming with restored energy, patting and preening herself like the bird of whom she had once reminded Charlotte, dabbing fresh powder on her face, putting on her gloves, excitedly pointing out a church as the train drew in to the little town, scrambling over the feet of the other passengers when it became evident that the platform was on the other side. They were Italians, sympathetic to a traveller whose journey could be sensed as momentous, but Charlotte thought they looked faintly surprised that it should end here and not in Rome. The platform to which she now descended, following Mrs. Gamalion who had bounded out as the train stopped, looked an unlikely setting for anything dramatic. It was rather dirty, unswept and unwelcoming. It was also, except for the ticket-collector by the exit, entirely empty.

"She must have mistaken the day," Mrs. Gamalion said at last.

It seemed as good a reason as any for the absence of Miss Glyn-Gibson. Absent she certainly was; they had searched the station, questioned the ticket-collector, given her another five minutes in case she was late, and extended it twice. They could do no more; for it wasn't at all clear, re-reading Miss Glyn-Gibson's letter, whether she was staying in the town or travelling from somewhere else to meet them there. She had written from Rome.

"But she can't be coming from *Rome*," Mrs. Gamalion declared. "She'd be here *now* if she'd come from Rome on the right day, anyway! Oh dear, it's too stupid of her not to read my letter properly – I wrote to her in Rome by return and she must have had it! But she doesn't *say* Tuesday, does she?"

Charlotte unfolded the crumpled letter again. "No, she doesn't. She just says 'that day will suit me beautifully and I shall be on the platform to meet you.'"

"I told her the time the train arrived and everything. But that explains it, Charlotte! She's mistaken the day – and we couldn't know because she doesn't say which day she's coming. She hasn't read my letter properly."

She read it as Thursday, Charlotte thought, Mrs. Gamalion's handwriting was far from legible, especially when she dashed off letters in a hurry – that explained it all right. She felt extremely relieved – like Mrs. Gamalion earlier in the day – by the discovery that Miss Glyn-Gibson had not actually committed herself to being there on Tuesday, just 'that day' – which must be Thursday. So there was no need to worry about her non-appearance.

"How lucky she told me exactly how to get to La Residenza," Mrs. Gamalion exclaimed. "The bus starts from the piazza – I asked the ticket-collector and he says there'll be a bus in half an hour and there's a restaurant in the piazza so we'll just have time to get something to eat. Come on, Charlotte!"

There was no need to worry, it was absurd to feel apprehensive when Mrs. Gamalion was so jubilant and gay. Everything was all right, the town was attractive, the restaurant was clean and the service remarkably speedy, smiling Italians directed them to the right bus-stop and the bus itself started nearly on time – only ten minutes late which as Mrs. Gamalion said was *nothing*. And the rain had almost stopped, already there was a small patch of blue sky visible and it was going to be a fine afternoon.

Mrs. Gamalion leant forward, pointing out the patch of blue sky, pointing out the hilly skyline ahead and the view to the south as the bus left the town. It was all new, and exciting, and beautiful; at each bend of the road she found something to exclaim at and praise. And Charlotte listened and agreed, trying hard to sound as happy as her benefactress, while wisps of doubt – like the wisps of cloud that were now cowering the blue sky – hung in the background of her conscious thoughts where reason could not disperse them.

The bus had been packed at the start but now it was nearly empty and rattling along the road at its best pace. The driver was singing, the two old women on the back seat were apparently asleep, lulled by the strains of Verdi or possibly deaf, for it wasn't the kind of bus with a separate cab for the driver and he sang with full-throated passion, sometimes letting go of the wheel to fling out his arms in a dramatic gesture when the aria demanded it. He was lost in a dream, the tenor facing the footlights in a crowded opera-house, his dull everyday occupation quite forgotten. If Mrs. Gamalion had not spotted the gateposts he would have carried her on to the next village.

But she saw them in time. Her loud cries drowned even the tenor; Verdi stopped short and after an application of squeaking brakes the bus stopped too. Mrs. Gamalion gaily reproached the driver for carrying them beyond their destination, and he with equal zest defended himself and promised on his honour that he would look out for them on his return journey, would even wait there if the English ladies should be delayed. They could trust him absolutely.

He waved his hand. Mrs. Gamalion waved her umbrella, furled now as it wasn't actually raining. The bus drove away. Charlotte and Mrs. Gamalion walked back towards the gateposts, which were tall and conspicuous just as Miss Glyn-Gibson had described them in her letter. From a distance they looked impressive, but less so at a near view which revealed them as much decayed and rather crooked. Moreover there was no gate.

"I daresay they had to sell it as I believe they were awfully hard-up – hardly two pennies to rub together!"

"Lire," said Charlotte.

"Oh, don't be silly, you know what I mean!"

They walked on up a long, rutted drive which led steeply uphill. Decayed gateposts at the bottom on either side, ruined terraces of olives, earth spilling out where the stone embankments had crumbled, the valuable orchard a tangle of gnarled black branches among high grass; wild olives now, and barren. The house could not be seen from the drive, it stood on a plateau above them, hidden by a high wall and three cypresses. But already the approach had told Charlotte what it would be like.

The door in the high wall hung open, tilted on its hinges which had pulled away from the jamb. Inside the door a narrow flight of steps went up between flanking walls to the upper terrace. The terrace where the chairs were to be set out for arriving guests.

"Look, Charlotte – the marble staircase!"

Still jauntily, Mrs. Gamalion added that it needed repairing. "But it won't be expensive – those steps just want pushing back into place."

Charlotte went first, turning back to give Mrs. Gamalion a helping hand; some winter deluge had left the marble slabs lying crookedly and at the top there were no steps at all, only a scooped-out hollow of bare earth. They surmounted it, Mrs. Gamalion scrambling and stabbing with her umbrella, Charlotte facing her and tugging. They stood on the upper terrace and looked at the house.

Pock-marred walls where the stucco had crumbled, a broken balustrade in front, blank windows with one or two shutters still in place but hardly any glass, and a great crack at one corner of the building. Their eyes travelled up and both together saw the holes in the roof, the rotting rafters visible where the tiles had fallen off; and looking down again they perceived the heaps of shards at the base of the wall, which were the remains of the tiles.

Mrs. Gamalion gave a very faint shriek.

Charlotte, knowing it wasn't so, suggested that they might have come to the wrong house.

"No, this is it – it said so on the gatepost and the man on the bus said so too. But it *isn't* – it's just a ruin."

It had been a house once. But now – like the gold-mine, Charlotte thought – it wasn't really there.

And now, in a sense, Marston wasn't there either. The prison had become, as far as Charlotte was concerned, a ruin – its walls had fallen, she was free.

It took some getting used to after all these years. La Residenza had been no more than a dream (with a horrid awakening), but The Laurels had been solid and permanent. So in fact it continued to be; a solid, well-built house where Alison and Evvie were living in a flat that had been too small for three people but was just right for the pair of them. It was only in her mind that the curious emptiness existed where a dominating image had crumbled into dust.

As she expressed it to Mrs. Bateman, she had really left Marston for good and it was very strange to think she would never need to go back there.

Mrs. Bateman was mildly scandalized. "But you'll be going back to stay with them! You don't mean – ?"

"That we've quarrelled? Oh, dear no – quite the contrary. Alison didn't altogether approve of my staying here at first, you know, and now she does. That is why she came – to tell me everything was all right."

"I'm so glad. But I don't understand about your not going back – surely they'll ask you to visit them?"

"Yes, but that's what I shall be. A visitor. That's what will seem so strange."

Mrs. Bateman did the sum and got it right. "You won't *need* to go back, because you won't be needed?"

"Always before . . ." Charlotte began. But how could she explain Marston and The Laurels, the strength and tenacity of legends, the oppressive weight of being Mrs. Field's daughter, Gabriel's widow, Alison's mother – an inferior but essential factor in three people's lives?

Mrs. Bateman explained it quite simply. "You just feel hurt because Alison doesn't need you any longer."

"Perhaps I do," Charlotte agreed. "Well, not precisely hurt, but rather lost. Out of a job," she added lightly.

"But you'll get over it. I did. Indeed there's a lot to be thankful for – when your children have grown up and gone away and you can be independent." Mrs. Bateman laughed and then stopped herself, "Not that it lasts. You think you've got years and you find you haven't. And things happen, things keep cropping up to remind you . . . other people fall ill, or turn into old crocks like Lily and Bart, and you wake up at two in the morning dreaming you've been taken to hospital."

"That must be tiresome." She knew how much Mrs. Bateman resented growing old.

"Very tiresome. But you needn't worry about that, Charlotte – not for a long time. You're still young."

The tiresomeness of the hospital dream made her sound quite envious of one who would not, for a long time, be haunted by it. As on a previous occasion, Charlotte protested that she wasn't 'still young', and Mrs. Bateman's envy suddenly burst out in an explosion of anger. Charlotte had not known she could speak so sharply.

"You're no older than Robert! What's that, compared with me? You're independent – your life isn't half over – you can do all sorts of things, you might even – Well, I don't know you well enough. But you and Robert! Only it's different for him. Don't talk of not being young, Just enjoy it while you can. But that's just what you *are* doing if she's right," Mrs. Bateman finished incoherently.

Charlotte spent the next ten minutes soothing her down.

CHAPTER XX

Mrs. Bateman, Charlotte thought, was not quite herself these days. It was difficult to define the change but she was aware of vexation or uneasiness underlying the resolutely cheerful voice and there were moments of silence when cheerfulness quite failed Mrs. Bateman, awkward pauses when she seemed to have forgotten what she was talking about. It was as if whatever had caused that explosion was still smouldering away under the surface and might break out again if she wasn't careful. If they weren't both careful; for Charlotte could not help feeling that she had in some way annoyed Mrs. Bateman, and might so do again. The vexation, the uneasiness, could be imagined as reproachful glances in her direction . . . except that it seemed altogether too fanciful. All one could really say was that Mrs. Bateman was sometimes oddly unlike herself.

But she was herself today, thank goodness, as smiling and set fair as the weather. "They've chosen perfectly," she declared. "They'll be able to sit on the grass. With rugs, of course."

It was the day of the grand Wakelin picnic. Everyone had been alerted yesterday, and messages had been sent round that morning to say it was 'on'. Mrs. Bateman had come to fetch Charlotte and now they were waiting for the Wakelins' car. They waited on the Green near the Pier Hotel, which was supplying the food for the picnic. "It's too fine to sit indoors in that stuffy sun lounge," said Mrs. Bateman. "We shall see the car coming and then we'll go across and join them."

Presently they saw Harley Coker coming, striding quite fast along the esplanade towards the pier. "He looks in a hurry," Charlotte remarked, and Mrs. Bateman said, "He's coming to the picnic. Didn't you know?" It was the voice of Mrs. Bateman-not-herself, unaccountably suspicious, but when Charlotte shook her head all was well again; indeed Mrs. Bateman broke into a kind of apology as if she regretted her lapse.

"Of course you couldn't know – I expect he was only asked yesterday. I didn't mean – I only meant –"

"I didn't even realize he was a friend of the Wakelins," Charlotte said firmly.

"I don't think he is. Not really. But people get asked to the picnic – the more the merrier, within limits, of course. Here he comes."

He had seen them and was advancing across the Green. He was wearing a panama hat, artistically wide-brimmed, and a creased linen jacket which looked a little tight; both of course were relics of a sunnier, younger past, and Charlotte felt a pang of pity as he doffed the hat with a gesture that had once looked charming and now seemed faintly ridiculous.

Poor Harley with his paying-guests and grim Miss Rimmer, still imagining himself the centre of an admiring group of cultured English ladies abroad. A picnic graced by his presence took on the character of an expedition and its destination could be pictured as infinitely more distant, beautiful and rewarding than Warley Hall among its flat fields and neglected gardens. How many miles to Babylon?

Warley was nearer, however one measured it, yet Warley itself seemed remote today, partly because a nice drive was included as an overture. The procession of four cars followed a network of lanes, far out at the back of Nything, before swinging round to approach Warley from a different direction.

It was like a state procession, slow and dignified and hierarchic. The most important guest, old Mrs. Nelson, sat with Lily in the back of the Wakelin car, and the others were graded according to some order of precedence worked out by Bart beforehand. Charlotte went with the vicar and his wife and sister-in-law, and after an initial burst of conversation they settled down to enjoy the nice drive in companionable silence. They watched the fields and the sky, the hedgerows in the flush of summer green, the wood far away to the right that gradually extended itself and became the point towards which they were heading. They drove quite a long way through the wood, before Charlotte suddenly realized that they were at Warley, coming in by the back road past the long brick wall of the kitchen garden. Bart halted the procession, got out and walked across to the cottage opposite the entrance. He came back brandishing a key.

So at last Charlotte saw the interior of the house from which the young Ellans had trooped out to be photographed on the lawn in high summer, the beginning of everything. The beginning and the end, she felt; for the last of the Old Faithfuls had no clue to guide her through the house and the shuttered rooms echoed only to Lily's voice praising the ceilings, to Bart's voice condemning the draughts. Mrs. Gamalion and her contemporaries had gone.

She would have liked to linger behind, to walk round once more by herself. But it was time for lunch and Bart was rounding up his guests and consulting his seating-plan. There were rugs spread out on the lawn as Mrs. Bateman had predicted, and three folding canvas chairs for the Wakelins themselves and their most venerable guest. Old Mrs. Nelson was not only venerable, but something of a local celebrity. She had lived for many years in the largest house on the Green, too grand to know anyone and deservedly unpopular, but now she resided permanently at the Pier Hotel, with a private sitting-room and a paid companion, and in extreme old age had grown slightly more affable. She had condescended to know the Wakelins and a few other Nything residents of long standing, including Harley Coker. Perhaps that was why he had been invited, someone suitable for her to talk to. He was led away to sit beside her.

"I didn't come for that," he protested afterwards, rejoining Charlotte where she stood at the edge of the lawn. "But you should be pleased, Harley. Mrs. Nelson is the guest of honour and you were selected to entertain her. It's a tribute to your social charm!"

"It's hard work entertaining Mrs. Nelson."

"Then the Wakelins must be all the more grateful to you. I'm sure you were a success."

"Even if I've earned their gratitude it isn't, as I said, what I came for. I'd hoped for better than that. What perversity of Wakelin planning condemned us to separate motor cars? – and I'd certainly hoped to have the pleasure of sitting beside you at this alfresco repast. Here – the day half over and we've hardly spoken."

"It's the Wakelins' day, not ours."

"And now we have a chance to escape them. We can talk while they're having their siesta."

A siesta after lunch and then a tour of the garden, Bart had announced, and in this programme – the siesta part of it – Charlotte had seen her opportunity for another look at the house, a private search for the past that had eluded her that morning. The key was still in the door, Bart and Lily and old Mrs. Nelson were dozing in their chairs. She could walk away without being missed. But now she had Harley in his most gallant and tiresome mood, elated by his success with Mrs. Nelson and seeing himself as a man who could bestow happiness by his presence. She could not laugh at him. it would have been too unkind, and she could not shake him off either. He would have to come with her.

Of course Harley saw it differently, as an escape from the Wakelins instigated by himself. Charlotte was coming with him, not he with her, and he marched her off along a path which was not the direct way to the house. But it curled through the trees beyond the lawn and would bring them back to the right path. Presently it did. They arrived at a small clearing, where a lead statue stood in a shallow basin that had once been a pool. Three other paths radiated from the circle of gravel surrounding the basin and one led straight to the house. Charlotte could see it already, looming up behind the trees.

"No!" said Harley.

He had walked round the gravel circle and now stood facing her, dramatically barring the path. He flung out his arm in a gesture that offered an infinity of alternatives (but in fact, she thought ungratefully, only two) to the way she desired to go.

"No, Charlotte, I refuse. Not that stifling house again! Haven't we done our duty by it already – paid it the tribute of detailed observation and more than it deserves of praise?"

"But Harley –"

"Those ceilings, by the way, are much later than the Wakelins pretend; I believe they were inserted in the eighteen-fifties to improve the look of the rooms."

"I'm not going back to look at the ceilings, I'm interested because the Ellans lived there – Mrs. Gamalion's family."

"And a dull lot they were, I assure you. My mother knew the Ellans and she used to say they were as dull as cold mutton. All but Mrs. Gamalion!"

"Still, she was one of them. She used to talk about them and about this house. That's why –"

"But they're dead and gone. My dear Charlotte, it's quite pointless – the house has nothing to reveal, there's nothing left but gloom and dust and cobwebs. I am the last person to suggest that we are not influenced by the past that has brought us to this moment; that has brought us, quite literally, together. My mother," Harley continued solemnly, "was the greatest influence of my life and it would be the grossest treachery to deny it. But I can say – I must say – and without in any way belittling her memory – that she doesn't, in that affective and influential past, stand entirely alone. Here in this garden, here by the battered fountain that so aptly recalls Italy – I salute Mrs. Gamalion!"

An uneasiness, a sudden and incredible alarm, struck Charlotte dumb. It isn't a fountain, she thought pedantically, but in her mind's eye there was the vision of a real fountain, Neptune and his tritons and the glittering rainbow-hued spray.

"It's to Mrs. Gamalion that we owe everything," Harley continued with confidence. "But for her, we should never have met! Just think of it – just consider what we owe her. She brought us together in the past; but how can one describe it as past when it's still so unutterably vivid and so splendidly present? And it's *that*, one apprehends, precisely because our old commander continued to exercise her wholly benevolent influence. She kept the past alive – she ensured our future!"

"No," said Charlotte. But her voice was faint, a mere whisper, and Harley simply ignored it.

"She ensured our future! She brought you back from the realm of the unattainably remote where I had so mistakenly – so reluctantly, need I add? – imagined you as fixed forever. She was and is the commander of our destinies!"

Charlotte looked up. It wasn't a real fountain, the statue was broken and the pool was empty. She knew she must speak quickly.

"No," she said again. "No, Harley – the past isn't still alive for us. Remembering it isn't the same thing. Not even Mrs. Gamalion could command me to feel now what I felt then. It's only memories now – not feelings."

Long ago she had waited by a fountain for Harley Coker. Twenty years ago. Had he really imagined she would wait patiently twenty years for him? She shook her head, rejecting whatever protests or pleas he was beginning to utter, and turned and walked away.

The maze was a good place to hide in.

Beyond the high beech hedges Bart and Lily were showing people the garden, their voices could be heard in the distance as murmurs, they must be approaching the rose garden, but she knew they would not enter the maze. Lily disliked it, it had been left untouched by the great Wakelin restorations, even in summer it was damp and melancholy. No one would come in, she could stay until they had been round the rose garden and then slip out and follow them and be there when they assembled in the drive. She wouldn't get lost in the maze this time, she had stayed in the outermost of its paths, only a short way from the overgrown entrance. She was as safe from discovery here as if she had gone further, for the beech hedges were in full leaf, dense and impenetrable. No one would find her.

She had fled from Harley but he would not follow her; in retrospect flight seemed quite unnecessary, a romantic gesture as exaggerated as his own. For she realised now that his invocation of the past had been prompted by gallantry, that he remembered it only hazily and had perhaps quite forgotten – memory being conveniently forbearing to oneself – the Roman theatre at Fiesole. The past was no more than a picturesque backcloth to the present; Harley wasn't thinking of fountains but of a comfortable future, with a wife who would somehow restore Bank House to its former state and take the place – so far as it was possible – of his irreplaceable mother. It was absurd to turn and run from a practical, middle-aged proposal, she could only hope that by being absurd she had demonstrated her unsuitability for the part. Mrs. Coker would never have behaved like that.

But it wasn't only from Harley that she had fled. There were other embarrassments she did not want to face at present – and other people. There was Mrs. Bateman, mysteriously vexed by her behaviour, giving her reproachful looks . . . other people giving looks too, not reproachful but in this context worse, speculative and curious. (And grim Miss Rimmer, whose 'look' was frankly hostile.) It seemed as if all her acquaintance – everybody but herself – had seen what was coming.

No, she was exaggerating again; one was never so conspicuous as one felt. Yet she was still reluctant to leave the maze, the soft grass that silenced her footsteps, the high green walls that hid her from view. She was being absurd and she knew it. Here they came, Bart and Lily and their guests, she could hear their voices growing louder and distinguish individual remarks, they were close at hand in the rose garden, which had been kept to the end because Bart and Lily had made it (though quite ruined now, he was saying). After this they would all drive off to the place further down the coast where Bart had arranged for tea. It was time to rejoin them.

The buzz of talk diminished as the tour of the rose garden ended. Charlotte thought everyone must be at the far side of it now, following Bart along the pergola that led back to the big lawn. She walked towards the gap in the hedge. But as she reached it two voices rang out, startling her by their nearness.

"Would you like an arm?"

"No. I'm not tired – only trying to get my bearings. Haven't been here since the Ellans left. Extraordinary how different it looks."

Charlotte stood still. She had recognized the voice of Mrs. Bateman, offering an arm, and the other speaker could only be old Mrs. Nelson; no one else could claim to have known the Ellans.

"I suppose it does," said Mrs. Bateman. "Of course the Wakelins made this rose garden."

"Yes, I heard him say so. But I can't remember what was here before. It's all different," Mrs. Nelson complained, "and that's always a mistake, isn't it?"

Her sharp voice changed, it was almost a wail. People said she had mellowed, but some of them went further and said she was getting a little childish. Charlotte, seeing neither of them, perhaps heard the more clearly that note of childish lament, and the controlled impatience in Mrs. Bateman's reply.

"Oh, differences aren't always a mistake, but perhaps it just seems so, looking back."

"Always a mistake. The more one looks back the more clearly one sees it – that's all."

There was a pause. Charlotte felt ashamed of being an eavesdropper and she wished she had come out when she first heard their voices. But it would be embarrassing to appear now, and besides it might startle Mrs. Nelson.

She hesitated, finding new reasons for avoiding the embarrassment, telling herself that eavesdropping did not matter because the conversation was trivial, hoping they would soon move away. With these delaying thoughts she filled the pause and lulled her conscience, so that when Mrs. Nelson spoke again it seemed even more difficult to talk to the gap and reveal herself.

They would know she had been there all the time. They would know it because Mrs. Nelson had at last got her bearings. "That was the maze," she exclaimed triumphantly. "This was the box garden – summer bedding, y'know, and clipped box edgings, and a path going across to the maze. The entrance was just about here, but I can't see it."

"It's all overgrown. The Wakelins didn't care for the maze, they couldn't cope with cutting all those hedges. They let it go."

"Another mistake," Mrs. Nelson said with disdain. "The maze was famous. Such fun we used to have when we were young, sending people in there and losing them. Stupid people we couldn't be bothered with. The Ellans were an amusing lot."

A dull lot, Harley had declared. But old Mrs. Nelson had known them better than Harley. Mrs. Bateman said she had not known them at all, and Mrs. Nelson said "I don't suppose you did" in a way which recalled her former snobbishness and unpopularity. Then suddenly her voice quavered back into elderly regret and she forgot that she was speaking to an outsider.

"Much nicer parties than this, the Ellans used to give. People came from miles round, Lady Ansdell and the Thistletons and all their young folk – our own friends, y'know, though of course everyone came to the parties, young and old together."

"It must have been amusing," Mrs. Bateman said kindly. "Do you think we should make a move now? The Wakelins may be looking for us."

"Young and old together, no one left out . . . the older people could be as gay as the young ones and we were very fond of them. Not like today," the quavering voice said wistfully. "Oh dear, I wish I could remember all the names. Lady Ansdell and – and –"

"The Thistletons, you mentioned."

"I was thinking of someone else. Something reminded me of him just now."

"We ought to be moving." Mrs. Bateman sounded anxious to go.

"Canon Cowper! How could I have forgotten. A very close friend of the Ellans, I can see him now, always so cheerful. Poor Canon Cowper – he had a stick, y'know, but he was perfectly independent. Did you ever meet him?"

"He was long before my time," Mrs. Bateman said tartly. "We really must go now, Mrs. Nelson. We're keeping the Wakelins waiting."

And they really went. Charlotte could only just hear Mrs. Nelson's last words.

"The maze reminded me . . . it was one of his parlour tricks, leading people to the centre. He knew it by heart of course – never got lost . . ."

Her voice died away.

But there was another voice now. Mrs. Gamalion's, even fainter than Mrs. Nelson's, speaking about long ago times and the people she had known when she was young, Lady Ansdell, Canon Cowper, names that had never meant much to the young Charlotte in Italy. "Poor Canon Cowper . . ." and memory had obstinately refused to reveal more than that he was lovable and good and somehow different from other people. Charlotte knew why, now. Mrs. Nelson had unlocked the memory and let him out, an old man with a stick, leading the way through the maze and joking about it.

"The blind leading the blind," Mrs. Gamalion had cried, repeating the Ellan description of Canon Cowper's parlour trick.

Charlotte knew too why Mrs. Bateman had refused to discuss Canon Cowper, why she turned away from his window in the church and welcomed a change of subject. Standing in the maze she knew it with certainty – as if she had been lost in a maze of the mind and had at last found her way to its centre and learned the pattern of its winding paths.

Canon Cowper had been blind.

Robert was living under the threat of blindness, and did not want it known. He had forbidden his mother to tell her – to tell anyone – and that was why Mrs. Bateman was so reserved about his illness; and why he had had to resign his living; and probably why he had gone away, to undergo treatment or to learn how to be blind, and to escape commiserations and the inevitable comparisons with Canon Cowper. And of course that was why Mrs. Bateman could not bear to talk about poor Canon Cowper.

"Poor Robert," Charlotte thought tentatively.

Then for no reason at all she changed it to – "Poor Mrs. Bateman."

CHAPTER XXI

IT WAS summer, not autumn, but it was late evening and the light was beginning to fade; a breeze was blowing off the estuary and the scene looked rather forlorn. On a warm evening there would have been more people about but tonight the cold breeze and cloudy sky had discouraged the summer visitors, those who had ventured out were returning and Charlotte at her bedroom window watched them coming back across the Green, hurrying back to the shelter of the town, until the Green and the esplanade were almost deserted. The tide was coming in and the wind was freshening, she was separated from it by a pane of glass but she could see the white-flecked waves out in the estuary, and far away to the right a gleam of yellow sunset light through a gap in the clouds. It was still daylight, the lamps on the esplanade were not yet lit but she could see everything quite plainly. Then Mrs. Bateman appeared, a short distance away, coming from the entrance to the public gardens and crossing the Green towards the esplanade, Charlotte saw her at once. She waited at the window a moment longer, hoping Mrs. Bateman might be on her way to visit her. But the solitary figure did not turn; she had walked down from Church Street, as she often did, to get a breath of fresh air and to watch the sunset; there was no promise of a good sunset tonight but that did not matter.

It was for Charlotte to take the initiative. She could not shelter behind a pane of glass, she must go out into the windy evening.

Robert had scarcely mentioned Mrs. Bateman. He hadn't said: "Mother will be delighted," nor had he so much as hinted at maternal doubts. Obviously he had not thought about Mrs. Bateman's reactions at all. He wasn't marrying Charlotte to please or annoy his mother.

But it must have been Mrs. Bateman's report, however inaccurate, perfunctory, or one-sided, that had brought Robert back to Nything. Charlotte had thought so – it was almost all she had thought – straightaway, simply because she could think of no one else who might have written to explain to him that she wasn't going to marry Harley, who might have guessed that he would like to know it.

The only other person who could have written would have been herself. A short note about almost anything except Harley – she had composed several such notes, telling Robert how well the roses were doing, asking advice about the lawn, but she had not posted them. They were just excuses for getting in touch with him and their flimsiness, their inherent falsehood, made her ashamed. She might be mistaken about Robert. Looking back, there seemed nothing to justify the certainty she had felt in the maze, about Robert as about herself. (But she wasn't mistaken about herself.) She had not written to him; so it must have been Mrs. Bateman.

And what had Mrs. Bateman said to bring him back to Nything? Nothing encouraging, it appeared; no assurance that he would be welcome if he chose to present himself at the house on the

Green. She could have told him only two things about Charlotte, that she wasn't going to marry Harley and that she had guessed or somehow learned that he was probably going blind.

"I nearly told you myself," Robert said. "You seemed the one person I could have talked to about it."

"I wish you had told me."

"But then I was afraid you would pity me and that it might – You see, when I thought of telling you I'd hardly begun to wonder whether you would marry me. And when I did wonder, telling you about my eyes seemed near to blackmail. The appeal to pity!"

"Yes, I understand now."

"But you don't pity me, do you?"

She shook her head, knowing he did not want to be pitied. "Even when I first guessed it I didn't *really* think 'poor Robert'."

He laughed, "Did you resist the temptation? Begin to think it and then stop?"

"I tried it and it didn't seem right. I was in the maze at Warley, overhearing about Canon Cowper's parlour trick, and I suddenly realized why it was a parlour trick. Mrs. Gamalion used to speak of him as poor Canon Cowper although I'd forgotten why. And then I remembered."

"It's beyond me," said Robert. "You were in the maze and so am I. Start again."

"Mrs. Gamalion used to say poor Canon Cowper. I half began to think 'poor Robert'. But it didn't suit you – I couldn't think of you like that. So I desisted at once."

"Thank you, Charlotte. Though I still didn't understand why suddenly remembering that Canon Cowper was blind should have made you guess about me."

Charlotte explained. "Your mother couldn't bear people talking about Canon Cowper. She was there, and when Mrs. Nelson began about him she tried to stop her. That was how I guessed."

"Poor mother," said Robert, echoing what Charlotte had thought in the maze.

Nothing else was said about Mrs. Bateman. She was no more important at that moment than Mrs. Gamalion, in whose drawing-room they were sitting, surrounded by treasures whose day was over. All the past that mattered was the past they were now recalling, their meetings right from the beginning, talks and incidents they remembered with extraordinary clarity; indeed a shared past in which everything was now beautifully clear. It had become clear to both of them as soon as Robert entered the house. The surprise of his arrival, of opening the door to some ordinary visitor and finding Robert there, had given Charlotte a dizzy moment of incredulity, but nothing after that had seemed unbelievable or strange.

"I thought I might not see you again," said Robert. Charlotte remembered how carefully he had looked at everything last time, at herself and the garden and even at the Book.

He had known then, he told her, that his eyesight was getting much worse. They were sending him to a London eye hospital but it was doubtful whether much could be done for him. Still, he wasn't yet totally blind and that was something to be thankful for, wasn't it?

She agreed that it was. Robert was wearing new and much darker spectacles and she reminded him of the old ones, of the first time he came to tea, the ivy . . . how stupid she had been not to guess when he talked about wishful thinking.

"You weren't meant to guess," he told her. But Charlotte still thought she had been stupid.

She was being stupid now, protesting when Robert said he must return to London tomorrow. She knew he had not come straight from hospital – they had let him out a month ago and he had been staying with Mary – but she had not understood that he was to have more treatment. In fact he was supposed to have gone back to hospital today, but he had persuaded the specialist to give him two days' reprieve.

"But you shouldn't be here," she cried, understanding at last. "Oh Robert, you must go back at once."

"Tomorrow. I suppose I'd better, though I don't think it's going to make much difference. Perhaps I shan't be quite blind, or not for some years."

Charlotte was still lamenting his long journey.

"You shouldn't have come all this way!"

"I came to see you," he said. "Not to ask you to marry me – not yet. I'd hoped you might, later, if there was a reasonable chance of saving my sight. Only I wanted to *see* you. And then, when I did – when you opened the door and said my name – I simply forgot about being blind and a burden and so on."

"And I forgot about pretending I hadn't missed you terribly. I was so glad to see you I just forgot."

"A good thing we're both so forgetful," Robert said happily.

"You must always walk towards the sunset," Mrs. Bateman had insisted, and from the window Charlotte had seen her setting off along the esplanade, facing the wind and the sea and the gleams of brightness showing through the tattered clouds. By the time Charlotte herself reached the esplanade Mrs. Bateman was out of sight, and in the gathering dusk she went in pursuit, pressing forward against the wind that tried to deflect her and the blowing sand that stung her cheeks.

She hurried past four empty shelters but at the fifth one she slowed and stopped.

Mrs. Bateman had come to watch the sunset and there she was, huddled in the corner of the seat on the seaward side, exposed to the wind but ignoring it. Defying it, perhaps – proving to herself that neither old age nor an inclement evening could stop her doing the things she liked to do, had done for the past thirty years. She was wearing her thick coat and a scarf over her head, she was the same anonymous figure that had sat there on an autumn evening last year. But it wasn't yet as dark as it had been that evening; when Charlotte entered the shelter she knew Mrs. Bateman had recognised her. "I followed you," she said. "I saw you from my bedroom window, so I thought I'd come out too and watch the sunset."

"It wasn't a good sunset this evening."

"I've seen better myself."

"They're better in the winter when they're over the sea. The sun is too far round now, it's setting over Moss Bank. You don't get the reflections."

"We should have seen the reflections if there'd been any. Only there weren't, this evening."

"No, we shouldn't," Mrs. Bateman argued. "It isn't the right time of year for sunsets – Moss Bank gets in the way."

"Then why did you come?"

"Oh – because I needed a breath of fresh air. And because" – her companion groped for reasons – "because there's always a chance it may turn out a good one after all, and it would be a pity to miss it. Not that they *are* good, with Moss Bank in the way, as I said – but one can't help that."

"Moss Bank isn't a mountain."

"A mountain? Of course not." Mrs. Bateman sounded shaken. "All that coast to the north is perfectly flat," she added more confidently.

"Yes – but you're making mountains out of molehills. Moss Bank isn't a mountain and if you mean Harley he isn't one either. Truly he isn't."

It was almost too dark now for them to see each other's faces but Charlotte could imagine her companion's frowning comprehension. Out of the darkness Mrs. Bateman said slowly.

"I suppose I did mean Harley."

"I was afraid you did."

"I can't help it, Charlotte. I can't help wondering whether you really know your own mind. I'd hoped at the beginning, you know – but then there was Harley, and I thought – we all thought –"

"But you were wrong."

"I can't help it, I still think –"

"Please don't," said Charlotte. "You were quite mistaken about Harley."

But she was mistaken herself. She thought she was being judged unreliable, blamed for being fickle and heartless. But for Mrs. Bateman the blame and the guilt lay elsewhere.

"No, listen, Charlotte! I must say it now. I'm so afraid it's partly my fault."

"But what – ?"

"You and Robert. When you came back with Robert yesterday evening, and today when we were seeing him off at the station, I couldn't help feeling I had somehow brought it about. Made it happen. Thoughts can influence people, can't they? And my thoughts . . . so selfish, I know, but I dreaded having to look after him, take care of him if – if it came to the worst. I was very disappointed when I thought you were going to marry Harley – and now I'm so afraid my disappointment and selfish longing have influenced you to marry Robert."

"Oh dear," said Charlotte. She couldn't think of anything else to say. After a minute she pulled herself together and added, "I'm not so easily influenced as that."

"But it does happen," Mrs. Bateman persisted. "And you're so impulsive – suddenly deciding to live here just because Mrs. Gamalion left you her house. Do you remember telling me about it that night when we first met?"

"I'm not being impulsive now and I'm not being influenced. Robert and I," Charlotte said very firmly, "didn't need anyone to make up our minds for us. We suit each other perfectly – in a way, we knew it from the start."

It was the nearest she could get to explaining what no one else would understand, the pattern that had been so clear for her and Robert when they traced it out. Inadequate as it was, the explanation must do; she wasn't angry with Mrs. Bateman but it was impossible to confide in her now.

Mrs. Bateman wasn't convinced, of course. She still half believed (it was a kind of egotism, Charlotte thought) that by the exercise of will-power she had brought about a marriage and rid herself of a burden. She felt guilty about it, but less guilty now that she had confessed and been reassured.

"If you're sure of that," she exclaimed, clutching at the explanation in haste. "Oh, Charlotte, I'm so glad. *Really* glad now!"

Like triumphal illuminations the lamps came on, a string of lights all the way along the esplanade, revealing Mrs. Bateman in confident mood and the white-capped waves surging towards the sea wall. High tide now, Nything on Sea at its best; no, the wind was too strong and anyway Nything wasn't at its best nocturnally, it needed pale northern sunlight and a calm autumn afternoon.

"They're late again," Mrs. Bateman said, referring to the esplanade lamps. She looked at her watch and stood up. "We're late too.

Just look at the time!" As they left the shelter she asked casually, "What are you going to do about your house?"

"I shall sell it," said Charlotte. She knew that whatever happened Robert would not want to settle down in Nything as Canon Cowper's heir or understudy.

"Sell it? Oh, but hadn't you better wait and see . . . I should miss you if you went away."

Charlotte shook her head. Mrs. Bateman couldn't have her cake and eat it. "Robert a burden!" she thought indignantly, hardly caring that she would be missed.

They turned away from the esplanade and began to walk across the Green, hurried on by the wind at their backs.

"Alison will be surprised," Mrs. Bateman remarked tentatively. "Have you written to her?"

"Just a postcard to invite myself to stay. I'll tell her when I get there."

A postcard from Nything to The Laurels, the last of a long line. How many shoals of postcards Mrs. Gamalion must have despatched; it had pleased Charlotte to send one more in their wake.

"Oh – you're going to see her?"

"And to see Robert of course. I can visit him in the hospital while I'm staying with Alison. Marston is only just outside London."

"I turn off here," Mrs. Bateman said quickly, "Good night, Charlotte."

Hospitals meant illness and were associated with growing old and feeble and being unable to look after oneself. Even their hygienic smell must be repugnant to Mrs. Bateman.

"Good night," said Charlotte.

Mrs. Gamalion on the ruined terrace; The Laurels in Mrs. Field's heyday; Rivermead with Gabriel's flagpole; Florence and the Old Faithfuls; people and houses and places diminished by distance and time, small pictures recalling the past like the Tuscan views on the wall. They were still vivid for Charlotte as she stood there among the treasures, they had not faded like Colonel Hetherington's watercolours but she knew they would. Already they had shrunk. The bright landscapes were less spacious, the people who had dominated her youth were something less than life-size now. She was looking back and she was further away.

This house itself, Mrs. Gamalion's legacy, would soon slide into the past and become a memory. The improvements Alison had planned would never be carried out, the house itself would be demolished or unrecognisably transformed into flats. Halfway upstairs as this thought struck her, Charlotte paused to observe the shape of the mahogany banisters, the curve of the bottom steps (awkward but by now familiar), the narrow hall and the peculiar niche by the front door. None of these things would survive, there would be nothing left of Mrs. Gamalion's house except in memory, perhaps. Robert had begun its destruction when he opened the front door that had been sealed up for fifteen years. But Mrs. Gamalion would not have objected to that, she had loved sunlight and it was only adverse conditions – the war, the blackout, the incapacities of old age – that had made her seal up the door. She wouldn't have objected, she would have been pleased, Charlotte thought.

"Why, you silly girl – what was the good of leaving Marston if you were just going to shut yourself up here? I meant you to *enjoy* yourself! I want you to live!"

"So I shall," Charlotte said to Mrs. Gamalion, and the stair creaked gently under her foot as she went on her way.

THE END

FURROWED MIDDLEBROW

*titles available in paperback only

**pseudonym of Noel Streatfeild

92005430R00125